JEREMIAH REVEL

The Blackguards of Charlatan

D. Joseph Ziders

PAGE PUBLISHING, INC.
Conneaut Lake, PA

First originally published by Page Publishing 2020

ISBN 978-1-6624-0501-3 (pbk)
ISBN 978-1-6624-0503-7 (digital)

Printed in the United States of America

The Antihero

Jeremiah Revel isn't one who is overly concerned with sugar in his coffee. With a careless smile and eyes that can stare beyond your painted face, he can both love and hate you all in the same moment. He swears in casual conversation; all the while studying your face like it holds some cryptic code that must be deciphered. His eyes embody his soul, and he is never afraid to stare—taking in each moment with great care while holding it in reference for some future cheap joke. He speaks softly while reveling in your laughter; as if laughter sets him free. Simultaneously or circumstantially, he can become a rogue jester or be the sympathetic king; he loves the misfit and hates the thief, yet shares in their sorrow. It is as if he can discern between the good and the ugly inside of people and arbitrate between the two an impartial judgment of character. His kindness has never been a mask for some hidden agenda. At thirty years old, he is experienced, intelligent, and resolute. Having a tall, athletic build is from his father; his eyes, from his mother. In them you will find her compassion. However, they also hold a ferocity that occasionally renders him socially unapproachable to those who do not know him.

Jeremiah Revel is the hero for those seeking the antihero—a maverick. He is his own contradiction. He practices the belief that there is wisdom in silence but speaks with authority when needed. He prefers to sip bourbon with the downtrodden than to drink wine with assholes. He prefers acquaintances over friends. And the few friends he has are a motley crew of characters and con artists who live questionable lifestyles at best. But they are the only ones he can trust; he knows exactly who they are and what they are about.

Our hero begins as a police officer. But *The City* needs a straight cop like recovering alcoholics need whiskey. It is a far cry from when his father was on the force. Politics and honesty are like water and oil. Over time, this bitter reality becomes a burden not worth bearing to an honest soul. But like things that are tangible, the soul, too, can cast a shadow. Knowing the delicate balance between what is right or wrong can sometimes become vague. And in time, even a hero can become jaded.

The City

The City is vile. The once proud factories of the famed Steel Belt now stand as dilapidated edifices in the wake of a failing economy. They once symbolized progress. Now, they are tokens of poverty. And when buildings no longer have residency, the destructive nature of neglect ensues. It's as if the walls and foundation are sustained by feeding on the energy of the inhabitants; when they leave, the structure surrenders itself and dies. Thus we surmise that the accomplishments of men will subside to ruins while the systems of nature feed on their own decay and are everlasting.

Aside from the brick tenements located on the east side of *The City*, the faded paint of advertisements of long since departed shops and five-and-dimes erode while the twisted barber poles stand as the only relics of a comforting antiquity. The boarded windows have become the canvas for graffiti and territorial markings. On the south side *(Skid Row)*, the vagrants sip cheap whiskey from brown paper bags in the light of flickering streetlamps while the messengers feed them hope; at this point, bread will probably suffice.

In the *Museum District*, the writers and poets attempt to objectify and vocalize the world as it destroys itself before their very eyes; it's as if they must capture the evanescence of a moment—a single frame of existence frozen in the cosmos—before it passes into an oblivion of nothingness. And by doing so, they may be able to understand the beautiful secrets hidden within their own fleeting existence.

The west side: It's where *City Hall* holds her post. Some say that these inhabitants are more vile of a creature than those in *Skid Row*; selfish bigots who are more concerned with their social status and greed than those they are sworn to serve. Greed is a disease; a disease that poisons men's souls and turns them into monsters. However, can you really blame them? All those in *City Hall* know they are just puppets who are tied to the hands of hate-mongers and goons who prey on the hapless—choreographed by the vast and highly organized criminal underworld—*The Harvest Union*.

The Puppet Master

No one knows for sure the true identity of the supreme leader of *The Harvest Union*. There is only a name: Happy Hal. Happy is somewhat of a celebrity in *The City*. He will always donate massive amounts of gifts, clothing, and food to the homeless shelters around the holidays and keep the shelves of the soup kitchens in both *Skid Row* and the *East Side Tenements* full year-round with canned goods and meat from the *Northern Port Markets*. It is a hell of a marketing campaign for his propaganda machine. After all, those downtrodden drug addicts need food too; so they can have the energy to go out and pillage for more of Happy's cheap drugs. Happy then will not have to launder all his money after all and use the donations as a tax break for his Happy Children Charity Foundation. Meanwhile, he looks like a godsend to those truly in need; a perfect ploy.

Happy Hal is untouchable, and everyone knows it. He owns *The City*, and in the public eye, he is a mysterious and handsome philanthropist of whom no one has actually ever seen. Even the authorities are content (they are bought); order is maintained in the hierarchy of the criminal ranks, from the idiot goon to the professional assassin. They all answer to Happy; they all fear Happy. He is a mastermind of manipulation—the da Vinci of deception. He knows that fear is more useful than despair, but when used together as one device, all hope can be crushed and the desperate will obey.

The great masquerade that is Happy Hal further builds upon the powerful enigma that surrounds the man himself; if indeed he actually does exist. Occasional and colorful barroom talk will suggest that he is merely a made-up figurehead—fabricated by the lords of the criminal underworld to strike fear and discord into those foolish enough to believe in such nonsense. Many have made frivolous attempts to prove or disprove this very notion. However, one interesting tidbit of information comes via a newspaper investigative report.

Some time ago, one nosy reporter from *The City Tribunal* decided it would be a good idea to go to the *Hall of Records* at *City Hall* and sift through the property transactions in the deed book records. It was an attempt to locate when and where Happy might have purchased property and under what name. The article concluded this:

> There is no evidence of any abnormal transactions or reciprocating patterns of note other than the mysterious absence of pages 376–391 in Deed Book 6810. However, it is worth noting that transactions in that particular book are typically reserved for properties located in the *Northern Regal Estates* area of *The City*—just south of The Northern Ports. (C. H. Billingsly)

They say that soon after, C. H. Billingsly had to leave his post at *The City Tribunal* and skip town due to personal reasons. It is believed, however, that he had come across some highly sensitive information and thought that blackmail was a good idea—all speculation, of course. No one really knows what befell Mr. Billingsly, nor do they pay much attention. Shady happenings of that nature are commonplace in *The City*.

Happy Hal has built himself quite an operation. As they say, however, all empires will eventually begin to crumble. And the very fabric that serves as the tapestry of lies and extortion will soon be torn asunder. This is the beginning of our story. Who will be the hero? Will he be the one we'll learn to hate? Or will he become the villain of which we'll have no other recourse but to love?

2

Home Sweet Home

September 13, 7:21 a.m.

As a common occurrence this time of year, the brilliant hues of amber, orange, and red envelope the small single-room apartment. And for a brief moment, one forgets their troubles and relishes in the cadence of nature's perfect symphony of light that—before our eyes—has suddenly set fire to the twilight. The coffee maker beeps. The aroma of fresh coffee fills the room. The coffee is poured. Jeremiah Revel stands in front of the window and stares. The eastside skyline always looks brilliant in the morning. But doesn't everything look good from far away? He places the pin on the vinyl. He closes his eyes and listens. The warmth of the sun aglow on his face. Today, Brahms Symphony no. 4 in E minor. For a moment, the world is a masterpiece, and we are nothing.

As usual, Jeremiah Revel sets his alarm clock to go off a little before sunrise. He intentionally pursued an eastward-facing tenement apartment for this particular reason. It is small, but incredibly cheap and a place to lay his head at night. It is on the top floor and abuts only a janitor's closet.

Once upon entering through the thick oakwood door of apartment 306, floor 20, one will find a disheveled little abode. Directly to the right, a cot-like twin-size bed dons a gray wool blanket accompanied by a stained-white pillow. To the left, a microwave-refrigerator combo. He has not been in the fridge for a while and should

8

probably throw away its contents. Who wants another microwave-able burrito anyway?

Beyond the fridge, there is a single porcelain bathroom-style sink with old-fashioned (and probably original) hardware; it always drips, and one would not dare drink its water without using chlorine dioxide purification tablets. There is barely enough room to walk in between the sink and the bed. Above the sink, there's a mirrored medicine cabinet containing a rusting can of *Barbasoul's Original Shaving Balm*, disposable razors, and a dented tin first aid kit that is probably thirty years old.

Past the sink, to the left, is a small room big enough for a toilet and a shower; there's no door. To the rear of the apartment, abutting the window, is the workstation area. There, a locked gray metal filing cabinet sits with the coffee maker atop. An old maple-wood desk is to the right, containing six drawers. It was left by the previous tenant. It is a little worse for wear, but was probably top of the line in its day. It functions perfectly for his needs.

On top of the desk sits Jeremiah Revel's computer workstation, accompanied by a functioning antique rotary landline phone. Behind that, a small cheaply made but sturdy wooden utility table sits with an antiquated *Minter Brothers Model 7 hi-fi* record player upon it. Beside it, a wooden crate full of vinyl records neatly organized; both of which are his prized possessions.

It Will Kill

September 13, 8:28 a.m.

He brushes his teeth with *Dr. Kavitee's* brand mint-flavored toothpaste. The shower water is actually warm for a change. Ah, that familiar sulfurous smell.

I'll shave tomorrow.

He gets dressed: black socks; burgundy dress shoes; black dress pants; Dad's leather belt; and finally, his favorite mono-hued deep-blue tie over a black shirt. The long, black peacoat fits as if it were custom-made. The gray fedora hat with a black hatband is reminiscent of Hollywood's golden age. Way to be subtle, Jeremiah.

Jeremiah checks his messages on the VideoPhone while sipping the last bit of lukewarm coffee. Ads, ads, ads.

I didn't know that hemorrhoids are such an epidemic to necessitate daily solicitation of butt cream.

Finally the fourth is from Speedy "Jerry" Gonzo.

"What's up, Private Dick? I tried you on the rotary, but you were probably in the shower jackin' off or somethin'. Anyway, we got a new client. This one's big—mucho dinero, hombre. Give me a call back."

What an asshole. Jeremiah laughs to himself. *I told him never to discuss business on the VideoPhone.*

He is not going to call him back. The message is merely just a heads-up confirming that they actually have a reason to go to the office today. He grabs a *Blue Notebook* from the bottom-right drawer of his desk and his gun from underneath the pillow on his bed. It is an unassuming *Model 1911 Colt 45*. It is old but well serviced. It was his father's. *It will kill.*

The Office

September 13, 8:57 a.m.

The walk is only three city blocks. It's a beautiful fall morning but cold enough for steam to evaporate from the sewer manholes.

I hope that Warren is working his corner today. Warren (owner of *Try My Sausage*, which is Jeremiah's favorite breakfast street vendor) is at his normal spot; and the sausage, egg, cheese, and fried bacon breakfast sandwich is pure evil.

"Warren, you're going to be the death of me."

Jeremiah leaves him the remainder of his sawbuck as a generous tip. Warren is a good, hardworking man, and they have become close acquaintances. He has always wanted to ask him how he lost all his fingers on his right hand, sans the thumb and index finger, but never bothers to bring it up. Warren never speaks of it anyway.

The office is on the border of the east and north side of *The City*; it's a run-down area, but one cannot argue with the one-dollar price tag. *The City* has sold a majority of vacant lots and old factory buildings for a dollar with a ten-year commitment of tenure. So they will be able to collect property taxes, and the buyer will benefit from several tax write-offs, while also building credit and equity at the same time. It is a good idea on paper, but the *Urban Resurgence Plan* is taking a little longer than they expected.

The office is a typical art deco-style building for its time of construction. It has a red brick facade with industrial windows. Due to the ordinance banning shattered, barricaded, and boarded windows from occupied structures, they had to replace them all after the purchase of the building was complete.

The building is three stories tall. All the electrical work was dangerous and outdated for their purposes. Luke decided to rewire the entire building; thirty amps here, fifteen amps there. They only enter through the side door. It is down an alleyway that leads to the rear loading dock's garage door. There is a cargo elevator there; the alleyway does not entertain much traffic except for deliveries, the occasional vagabond, and a stray cat that they name Dog. Upon entering, one will find an antique, black chalkboard with their company decree on it. It reads as follows:

Laws and Regulations of Rabbit Hole Private Eye Inc.

1. *People don't change. They just form better lies.*
2. *Lettuce is not fruit.*
4. *You can shine a turd and call it silver, but at the end of the day, it's just a really shiny piece of shit.*
5. *No one talks about rule number 3.*

It's simple and unbreakable.

The first floor is where all the grease work is done. Their endless cache tools is located there. It is a man's man type of place, as they say. There is a welding station, a car lift, a sewing station (for disguises), compressors, and for some reason, a loom. That was Speedy's idea. No one has seen him use it, but they have a theory that he comes in at night when no one is around and makes ponchos that he sells at the *Chinatown* black market on Sundays. It is all hearsay of course.

Up the open steel industrial-style and semirusted staircase is the second floor. This is where all the electrical and communications equipment is located. There, a maze of wires, blinking lights, and push buttons are organized in seemingly random arrays of unknown purpose; it is Luke's handiwork. He claims it is an "elementary" setup, but no one else can figure it out, nor do they care to.

The third floor, through a locked and heavy steel door, is the armory. It is unassuming. There will be more talk of that later. Bypassing the armory is a staircase to the roof. It is where the crew likes to unwind and relax. There is a olive-drab colored bathtub there. To this day, they still have no idea how it got it up there, as it does not fit through the doorframe; that is why they decided to never drink tequila after work again. In the corner is a greenhouse with tomatoes, jalapeños, bell peppers, and lettuce growing. They are out of season, but Luke has it set up with climate control and other amenities that enables them to grow year-round. To the rear of the greenhouse is Jeremiah's pride and joy—a single yellow calla lily flower. It was his mother's favorite flower.

A Wolfpack of Awakening

September 13, 9:21 a.m.

"Where is Luke?" asks Jeremiah upon arriving at the office.

"He had an episode," responds Speedy. "He's in the bathtub."

"Again?" asks Jeremiah, as he mumbles incoherently to himself. He goes to the roof after grabbing a few items. He finds Luke in a fetal position in the tub. "Get up. We have work to do." Luke does not respond. He gives Luke his *Teddy Bear*, which Jeremiah keeps hidden for such occasions. He then lights a one hundred count of *Wolfpack Firecrackers* and throws it into the tub. Luke scrambles quickly while flailing his arms and rolls out of the tub as they go off. The *Teddy Bear* flies through the air. Jeremiah catches it.

"You're sick, you know that?" says Luke after the last crack echoes through morning air.

Jeremiah's smirk is devious. He gives the *Teddy Bear* back to Luke and says, "Let's get to work."

The Meeting

September 13, 9:30 a.m. sharp

They do not discuss business until the atomic clock on the wall clicks to exactly 9:30 a.m.

"All right, talk to us, Gonzo."

"First of all, you said that next time you do that to Luke, you were going to let me know," says Speedy.

"I guess I forgot," responds Jeremiah with that same devious smirk on his face.

"Anyway, go on."

"Okay, remember that dumb-ass reporter who wrote that article about Happy Hal's so-called 'property transactions'?" Speedy makes air quotes. "Well, he's finally dead. I mean, apparently after having to wait six years, his wife was finally able to have him legally declared dead and collected on his two-million-dollar life insurance policy." Speedy goes on. "I guess she wants us to investigate the 'mysterious circumstances' surrounding his disappearance." He makes air quotes for the third time. "She's putting thirty [thousand] down, plus expenses. This one seems pretty shady, muchacho, but we really need the moola, you know?" As usual, Luke stands silent. He does not like to speak unless absolutely necessary.

Extremely annoyed, Jeremiah says with frustration in his voice, "Remember what I said about making the stupid air quotes during the meetings?"

"*Lo siento, hombre.* It's a habit, man, chill," says Gonzo. He's not sorry. No one is certain why he speaks as if he's Mexican sometimes. He is the whitest Pollock they know. However, he is a master of disguises, accents, and characters. And they never know which version of each of his personalities they're talking to. Jeremiah once saw him convince a drunk lawyer that he was a Frenchman named Juan Pablo.

"Get to the point," says Jeremiah.

"Well, she thinks he might still be alive and walking, broseph, but she's not sure. She only said to talk to an old coworker from *The City Tribunal* named Gavin North. I know, pretty gay name, right? There is something about a yellow envelope that this Billingsly guy left him before he went off the map."

"Is the money in the account?" asks Jeremiah.

"Yes," responds Luke.

"Let's get to work then."

The Plan

September 13, 2:36 p.m.

"Well, we obviously have to talk to this North guy first. Luke, see what you can pull up in the meantime. Gonzo, you're going to take this one. Who are you going to be?"

"I'm thinking I'm going to be a sophisticated asshole with a cane. Some guy with a really bad habit of chewing on salted peanuts and spitting the shells into a tin can around people who are allergic to peanuts. Then I'll get aggravated when they make the air quotes with their four stupid fingers in unimportant conversations."

"You're not going to wear a monocle, are you?" Jeremiah and Gonzo laugh.

"What is your backstory to talk to this guy, anyway?"

"We'll have to find out who he got his life insurance policy through, and I will be an insurance agent rep poking around due to an ongoing investigation upon the mysterious circumstances of the claim." Speedy makes it a point to not make air quotes.

"Sounds reasonable. We can also threaten litigation. Hopefully this North guy is an idiot and will buy this BS." Jeremiah knows Gonzo will pull it off and has no worries. He always has some sort of shenanigan hidden up his sleeve.

Luke is able to gather info on Billingsly's life insurance policy.

"It is through a defunct company that was purchased by *Undertakker's Life and Health Co.* It was formed by a German immigrant named Franz Ündertakker. You cannot make this shit up. His name really is Ündertakker," says Luke as he adjusts his glasses. He then inks up a fake subpoena just in case, and Speedy is on his way.

North

September 13, 4:21 p.m.

As it turns out, Gavin North is a contract janitor for *The City Tribunal's* auxiliary south office.

"Vhat is zee nature of zis inquiry?" asks North. He is eating a salami sandwich, which reeks of Limburger cheese and green olives that wafts throughout the entire room. He is well fit for his age, quite clean-cut, and attractive for a janitor eating a smelly sandwich.

"My name is Hans Unger, representative of *Ündertakker's Life and Health*," responds Speedy.

"Haben Sie Deutch oder Englisch bevorzugen?" asks Gonzo. "English ist gut. Zis is America, no?"

"I am here to ask you about an old friend of yours: C. H. Billingsly," Gonzo says with both an upward inflection and exaggerated diction.

"Ja, I know und Herr Billingsly. Dass mann ist deadt."

Speedy decides to break character and be honest with North.

"His wife asked me to talk with you. Sie glaubt, dass er noch am Leben ist, und sie sagte, Sie einen Umschlag haben."

"Maria spoke dis?" questions North.

"Yes, but her name is Patricia. She said to mention Maria," Gonzo says in an affirming tone.

"Ja, I have zee envelope. Herr Billingsly vas und güt friend. His vife's name is called Patricia. I trust you, Unger. I know someday you come here und questions." North pulls the envelope from somewhere in his desk drawer and gives it to Gonzo. "Wer bist du?" asks North.

"Me? I'm nobody," responds Speedy. They both share a laugh as Gonzo begins to walk out of the small janitor's office. He is disappointed that he has prepared so hard for such a simple role. He has a feeling that North has more information than he is leading on, but there is a time and place for everything. He has accomplished his goal for now anyway.

"Danke, Herr Ündertakker." Gonzo makes like a tree and leaves.

The Envelope

Jerry really wants to open the envelope to see its contents, but he knows the rules. Rule number 2: *Lettuce is not fruit.* He will wait to get back to the office and they will open it together.

September 13, 5:36 p.m.

Gonzo arrives back at the office. Jeremiah and Luke are waiting for him. The envelope is light, and feels as if there is nothing in it. Jeremiah and Luke both put on protective gloves. Jeremiah slowly bends the clasps of the envelope upward. He reaches in; its only contents are an old black-and-white photo of a building, and an old business card that reads as follows:

Schwebly's Icehouse
27 Park St., South Side 14043
Commercial and Residential Delivery
817-555-6970
On time and fast delivery.

"Hmm," says Jeremiah. "There hasn't been an icehouse in *The City* for over fifty years at least, I'm guessing." Luke is prepping the black-and-white photo for fingerprints, when he suddenly notices that the building in the picture has a street address above the main doors. He gets his magnifying glass out and makes out the number *407*. Meanwhile, Jeremiah looks at the reverse side of the business card, and there is the number 3 that is handwritten in pen. Jeremiah thinks to himself, *Why would Billingsly think that these items were so important to have this North guy secretly hold them for him?*

Luke looks up the address for the icehouse. It is an abandoned old factory building in the heart of *Skid Row*.

"We'll have to go tomorrow. It's getting late, and parading around *Skid Row* at this time of night is just asking for trouble. Jerry, you want to go grab a beer at Paddy's [Pub and Grill]?" He does not ask Luke. Luke will not go anyway, and it will be a waste of a conversation.

"Don't twist my arm," responds Gonzo.

"I'll stay here and feed the rabbits," says Luke. They do not have rabbits, but neither Jeremiah or Speedy question him.

Paddy's

September 13, around 6:45 p.m.

Paddy's Pub and Grill is a hole-in-the-wall at best. It is one of those type of places that does not have a piece of shtick on the wall that is less than twenty years old. The ceiling is stained with cigarette tar and there is not one picture hanging that isn't crooked. They have probably not changed the oil in the fryers for years, and the place will not pass another health inspection without a bribe; all these traits are evidence that they have the best food in town. The beer is cheap, and the beer is cold. It's like heaven.

"Hello, boys," says Pam, as Jeremiah and Speedy take their seats at the corner of the bar. She begins to wipe the counter off in front of them with a gray rag. She is an older woman, but they have never thought much about guessing her age. "How's business? Still trading stocks? Or have you come up with some new bullshit to tell me this week?" asks Pam. They all laugh.

"Business is booming. That's why we frequent this classy establishment," responds Gonzo slyly.

"What will it be? Two cold ones on draft?"

"Yes, and please. Hey, is Al here? I need to talk to him," asks Jeremiah.

"Yeah, but you have to go alone. You know he can't stand Jerry," responds Pam. Jeremiah chugs his beer in two gulps.

Al is the longtime owner of *Paddy's*. He has lived in *The East Side* his whole life. People will say that he has ears the size of an elephant and also the memory of one; if someone is talking in his bar, he is listening, and he remembers. Nowadays, he spends most of the time in the bar's office located through an unassuming door toward the rear of the restaurant area. Jeremiah knocks on the door.

"Come in, young Revel," says a muffled voice on the other side of the door in a slow, low, raspy baritone voice.

The door handle feels greasy. Jeremiah reluctantly turns it, and ever slowly, the door creaks open. There is Al. He is sitting in a very old and cracked brown leather recliner in front of the bar's security monitors. There is a cigarette in the ashtray on the end table beside him—still smoking. Next to that, a rosary. The room has pictures of what Jeremiah assumes are family members and friends of Al's across three of the four walls. The office is also stained with smoke—as much so as in the bar. Jeremiah does not recognize anyone in the photos. In the corner is an old tube TV with a rerun of *The Andy Griffith Show* playing. Al puts the TV on mute.

"Sit," says Al in a subtle Irish accent as he points to the stained peach-colored couch next to the entryway. If that couch could talk, Jeremiah would not want to know its story. He sits. "What do you want, young Revel?" Knowing that Al does not like his time being wasted with small talk when his shows are on, Jeremiah gets straight to the point:

"Do you know anything about *Schwebly's Icehouse* from back in the day on *Park Street*?"

"I knew the old man, Pewee Schwebly," responds Al immediately. Al looks slightly annoyed and sad at the same time. He picks up the rosary before he begins, and starts going through each bead as if he is praying. "Listen carefully, young Revel. I have never, nor will I ever, need to speak of this again." He begins.

"It was before *The War* and before refrigerators were a domestic normality. Ice was delivered. A man could find honest work as a bootlegger." Al smirks. "I had met my girl in a speakeasy on *Fourth*

St. I married her. It was a time when you could meet a girl, get married, and fuck your woman without worrying about the distractions we live with today. Pewee had given me my first real job. I ran the books for him. I was good at what I did. Yeah, we were laundering through the business, and I had to move the cash around, but I earned my paycheck. Is that not the American dream?"

Al stares for a moment into space as if he is lost in some former thought. "Anyway, there was a secret room in the bottom of the basement behind a false concrete wall; it is in the southeast corner. There is a safe down there. A mechanical one. None of that electronic shit. It is a permanent fixture—built into the foundation. Unmovable. I assume this is the information you want, young Revel?"

Without acknowledging Al, Jeremiah asks, "Last question. Do the numbers 3407 mean anything to you?"

"Aye. Reverse and add ten. This is the end of our conversation, Jeremiah."

Without saying another word, Jeremiah gets up and leaves. Al unmutes the TV:

> *I'm gonna go home, have me a little nap, and then*
> *go over to Thelma Lou's and watch a little TV. Yeah,*
> *I believe that's what I'll do.* (Barney Fife)

Schwebly's

September 14, 9:30 a.m. sharp

They decide that they will meet in front of *Renee's Diner*. It is only a block away from the abandoned *Schwebly's* building. Plus, Luke collects promotional matchbooks, and he does not have one from *Renee's*. He takes two. The old brick building (Schwebly's) is in disrepair. It is fenced in and littered with "No Trespassing" signs to discourage squatters, curious trespassers, and troublemakers alike. The fence was probably only erected for liability purposes for the insurance company; it does not seem as though it was built for longevity. The chain on the main gate is rusty; it was more than likely cut several years back, exposing the ungalvanized steel. The lock is nowhere to be found. The gate is swaying in the wind. It is screeching as it lurches. Luke is annoyed by the sound. It has dug a shallow trench into the eroded blacktop parking lot. The white paint of the parking spaces is barely visible, and patches of grass and weeds are growing through the cracks in the pavement. Nature always finds a way.

They try the main entrance to no avail. The doors must have been barricaded from the inside. However, there is a partially opened reinforced-type window. Jeremiah enters first. The smell of decay and rat droppings is overwhelming (They do not want to entertain the possibility of the presence of human feces). Speedy and Luke follow. Jeremiah has a flashlight. Luke and Gonzo have headlamps.

There are several moldy mattresses on the floor and discarded garbage everywhere. The broken punch-in clock reads 7:27 a.m. There are hypodermic needles littered on the floor. More disconcerting are the abandoned ice hooks hanging from the ceiling.

Luke has studied the floor plans. He points which way the stairs to the basement are located. Jerry removes a cat carcass from one of the hanging ice hooks that is slung above a pentagram painted on the floor with the cat's blood.

"Humans are animals," he says.

Jeremiah and Luke stand respectfully and wait as Speedy does the best he can to give the cat a proper burial. Gonzo silently recites a short prayer as he grasps the rabbit foot hanging from his necklace. They move on.

"Why the hell would Billingsly have a business card from this place. Did they even have business cards back then?" questions Gonzo.

"Does it really matter?" responds Luke.

"I agree. There is something going on," says Jeremiah. They speak no more.

The stairs leading to the basement are of the type that you would expect in a building of that time period. There is no natural light; they must carefully negotiate their movements. Luke points them to the southeast corner. The false hidden wall has already been compromised. Someone had haphazardly broken through in crude fashion. Jeremiah, Luke, and Speedy can barely fit through the jagged hole; the safe is where Al said it would be.

The Safe

September 14, 9:52 a.m.

It is army green and robust. There are chips and small dents from what looks like previous attempts to breach it. The number dial looks as if it is brass, but is more than likely hardened steel. It is well-made and heavy like Al suggested. It is made by a German-based company called Ündertakker Brüder 1907. The dial spins flawlessly.

"Okay," says Jeremiah. "Three, four, zero, seven, plus ten backward. That's seventeen, ten, fourteen, thirteen," he says out loud as he turns the dial; no potatoes.

"Try seventeen, ten, forty-four," responds Luke immediately.

"Of course, thirty-four plus ten is forty-four," mumbles Jeremiah. *Click*. The safe squeaks as Jeremiah slowly opens it.

"I feel like we are the Hardie Boys," proclaims Gonzo as he chuckles and rubs his chin.

Inside is a small brass-colored key, a note that is handwritten in flawless cursive, and a one-hundred-dollar war bond from *The War* effort, made out to one P. J. Schwebly. Jeremiah removes the note and focuses his flashlight on it. It reads as follows:

To whom this may concern:

Safety Deposit Box 263 at The People's Trust Company and Bank.

C. H. Billingsly

There is no date specified. They assume the key is for the safety deposit box.

"Time to skedaddle," says Jeremiah. They leave the bond there. Luke and Speedy grab several of the two-gallon kerosene cans that are in the basement. Luke uses matches from one of the matchbooks he got at *Renee's Diner*. They torch the place. It is better that it dies with dignity than rots in shame—alone, abandoned, and destitute. Rule number 5: *No one talks about rule number 3.*

Why Does the devil Fear God?

September 14, 12:17 p.m.

They sit on the roof of the office. Speedy and Jeremiah sip whiskey. Luke is in the bathtub drinking apple juice. Gonzo tokes his cigar. In the distance, sirens can still be heard. There is a thick dark-gray smoke cloud billowing into the air to the south. Jeremiah has a blank stare on his face; it's as if he is deep in thought. Suddenly, he starts speaking without specifically addressing neither Luke nor Jerry.

"Remember what I said? About how we can spend our whole lives playing the part of the devil's advocate. But that only raises more questions and never really solves anything." He then turns to the right and addresses Speedy. "Why does the devil fear God, Jerry?" His eyes are serious, and Gonzo knows it. It catches him off guard.

"I don't know, Jer," responds Speedy softly. He awkwardly tokes his cigar out of rhythm.

"Never mind." Gonzo and Luke know that Jeremiah Revel may as well have an answer, but it is not important to discuss it at this time.

Jeremiah then pulls his wallet out and carefully produces a crinkled small piece of paper. "My father gave this to me when he was killed. It was a handwritten poem. He said it was his father's, and that it is now mine." There are faded bloodstains still visible on it. He reads aloud:

Dad

> *I was not born this way.*
> *They tried to teach me how to hate,*
> *But love was on my side, and*
> *Momma said it was all right*
> *To feel.*
> *How can I feel a smile?*
> *How can I touch a laugh?*

I guess I am the joke;
The finest I ever wrote.
Then my father said,
"Stand up," and I stood.
He said, "The weight of the world is upon you."
I said, "This is true."
"When you're not sure,
What's wrong or right,
You can only be the hero,
Of your own life."

Jeremiah stares into the horizon and sips his whiskey; as if reliving some moment of his past. *"They Never caught that fourth guy,"* he unintentionally mumbles out loud.

5

The Monologue of Late December

It was Christmastime. It began to snow. We built a fire. We let its warmth consume our souls, as the crackling of the enflamed timber divided the silence of our condition. We became jealous of the fire; as it was more useful to us than us to each other. And if given fuel, it would burn forever. Outside, the wind voiced her purpose in a cadence of unsequenced howling drones as she was torn and twisted by the very structures that she strove to infiltrate. She was the tempest of the twilight. And newly born of the systems of heaven, frozen crystals formed as flakes and embarked on their maiden descent. Without bias, they congressed into a great white expanse. And with gentle decadence, they attached themselves to whatever they pleased, wrapping the naked earth in a veil of white pearl. And within the warmth of their asylum, the elders hummed dirges to their past as the grandchildren sang along. They'd say, "Bang your drum slow, lone drummer boy. Don't play too fast. And sing your song low, lone drummer boy, just like Christmases past." To the children, they were songs of amusement. They knew nothing of the evanescence of time; that it was delicate and fleeting. So the elders would sit, detached and lonely, while listening to the silence of the burning embers. In the chaos of life, silence deafens the most. It's as if it begs to be heard; silence is the monologue of late December.

The Tree

It was the early evening on Christmas Eve. A certain boy of seven years old and his parents meandered down *Fifth Avenue* to *Main* en route to *The City Square* to partake in the Christmas Eve festivities. It was an accustomed route that held no unique purpose other than convenience; they had traversed it many times before to run errands to the *Fifth and Main Market* or to go to the *Main Street Barbershop*. However, that night, there was an excitement in the air. It was a crisp winter evening and quite cold—well below freezing. There was a tranquil ambience in the winter twilight; the breeze was nil and the snow fell delicately and rather uniformly. Their exhaled breath left their body in a thick white fog. As they walked, the boy wandered like a curious puppy, observing and inspecting the landmarks of their route.

"How big do you think it is, Papa? Six hundred foot tall?"

Laughing to himself, his father responded, "I suppose so. Maybe. We'll see when we get there. Deal?"

"Deal, Papa."

When *Main Street* came closer into view, the boy fixated his eyes on the horizon until he could make out the decorated reefs hung upon the trunks of the streetlamps. Instantly and subconsciously, his pace hastened, and his movements became direct. They were heading to *The City Square* to see the *Christmas Tree*.

In *The City Square*, the people reveled in a giant pine tree that sacrificed its longevity for the splendor of the moment. However, this tree held no grievances; for when decorated in lights and garland, and placed in the center of the square as a grand spectacle, it became something more than a tree. It was a symbol of the joy and kinship between people who struggle through the common endeavors of life and so celebrate in the spirit of a common resolve. This tree embodied that spirit. Accompanying this spectacle, the carolers sang songs of holy reference that were as old as time itself. And in archaic tongue, the preacher vocalized a greater meaning through scripture while strengthening his words with rhythmic hammering hand movements; as if his words had a pulse. And upon arriving at the cadence of a certain anecdote, he would culminate the address with open palms toward the heavens. Amen.

As they approached the city square, the preacher was in mid-sermon, standing behind a thick handmade oakwood pulpit with a cross extruding from the center of its facade. Directly behind the preacher stood the unlit tree. A well-respected man of thirty-eight years, the preacher was the archetype of his profession. He was tall, with broad shoulders and high cheekbones. His dark hair was highlighted with the first signs of graying. When he spoke, his voice held a rumbling euphonic timbre, and his dark eyes would pan the audience as he argued the nexus between the spiritual and physical world.

"I can't see, Papa."

"Here, son, get up on my shoulders." He lifted the boy to his shoulders, then exchanged a quick smile with his wife and held her hand. The preacher was about to give the final anecdote of the sermon.

The preacher spoke: "When I was a young lad, I would often go in the woods to reflect, pray, and meditate. I would write down thoughts as they came in a *Blue Notebook*. When God took my father home to be with my mother, I found this old notebook among my father's belongings. This is a paraphrased excerpt from one of the entries that I believe will allegorize my point today." He cleared his throat.

"I remember the forest that began at the edge of my grandfather's land. I remember how, in this particular forest, the timberlands of pine, oak, cherry, and silver maple congressed in motley assemblies of bark and leaf. They would dance with the wind and spread their seed, while the ancient ferns and mosses stood rampart at the base. In my revelation, these great species of pine, oak, cherry, and silver maple embodied two great dispositions; two independent desires for life. The first is of light.

"The great timbers reach toward the heavens. The limbs praising God's sun, worshiping its warmth." The preacher raised his arms toward the heavens, as if to surrender to his own words. "There, they photosynthesize and metamorphose the rays of His sun into life's process. The second desire of these great species is that of water.

"From the time of conception, the roots subdue the soil and harvest its nutrients in a vast network of strength and will. Here, these two independent desires of light and water become symbiotic, a perfect balance of worship and will with each desire being both opposite and necessary. Amen." The preacher paused momentarily to gather his thoughts and then continued.

"In life, we can be several different things at the same time. However, it is all part of a greater whole; the marriage of spirit and flesh, worship and will, bound to each other to maintain a balance."

The crowd began to echo the preacher. "Amen." They could tell he was approaching the climax of his sermon.

"However, I then saw a tree that had succumbed to the saw of a logger. And I asked myself, what can we learn from a tree that no longer lives? What is *this* tree's legacy?" He gestured to indicate he was speaking of the Christmas tree to his rear. "And then an epiphany materialized from the deep chasms of my own understanding. *A tree that is dead can teach us more than one that is living.*" The preacher's inflection grew more intense. "I saw the rings on the tree where the saw had passed. And I saw how the tree had begun as a small sapling and how each season of growth had produced another ring. And after every season of growth, the trunk became stronger and stronger. Ladies, men, children, everything you do in life, every decision you make, makes a difference. For every season of growth, a stronger base is begotten. But we can only live one ring at a time. Amen." The sermon concluded with a final prayer. Then the order was given to light the tree.

Chaos

The first shot was heard seconds after the tree was lit. It ripped through the preacher's right shoulder and exited with little resistance through the body from the rear of it. Upon impact, the bullet had severed most of the arm off from the clavicle. The preacher, who at the time was slightly turned to the left to observe the lit tree, was spun around to the right and fell headfirst into it. Several other rounds had hit the pulpit and lodged themselves in the thick oak facade, saving the preacher from further injury. By the time the first screams from the crowd were heard, the carolers began to fall. The sound of full metal jacket hitting flesh and the sight of an unfortunate soul holding their own entrails sent terror through the spectators. The chaos that ensued for the next thirty seconds was pandemic. It was a war zone.

Four gunman wearing metallic hockey masks and dark navy-blue peacoats opened fire into the crowd. They were all wearing black leather gloves and military-style boots. Three had .45-caliber tommy guns, and the fourth maneuvered his .30-06 Browning Automatic Rifle atop a bipod in a panning motion from a fixated position within a cube van. Unbeknownst to the crowd, the cube van had quietly backed up to the left rear edge of *The City Square* sometime during the tree lighting ceremony. The assassins had exited both quietly and quickly; they had used the bowed heads and closed eyes of the praying congregation to assume their positions without being noticed. The weapons hung from a sling and stayed relatively hidden behind their arms until the signal (the lighting of the tree) transpired. They were highly organized and had obviously planned this melee for some time.

The three *tommy gunners* stood juxtapositional, as if in firing squad formation. They were roughly twenty feet apart and to the left of the van. From their masks came a thick white fog of breath, as their adrenaline and intense circumstance invoked heavy breathing. Their arms were rigid and taut as they struggled to control the kick of the large .45-caliber round throwing lead everywhere. However, it was evident that all four men were experienced and comfortable with their respective weapons. Tonight, the four gunmen held no specific agenda other than to kill. Chaos was their symphony, and death was their masterpiece.

In times of hopeless fear, we are either imprisoned by its paralyzing venom, or we subjugate the cause of that fear through confrontation. Both are tactics of survival. Without hesitation, Isaiah chose to fight. With his family located to the aft and left of the embattled crowd, they avoided the first barrage of bullets only by circumstance. Moments after the first shot was fired, Isaiah instantly and instinctively tackled his wife and child to the frozen concrete ground. Despite the nature of its purpose, this concrete tundra was somehow their loving asylum; as if they tried to become part of its fabric by pushing themselves into its cold bosom.

"Stay down!" yelled Isaiah. The savage inflection that resonated from the vocal structures within Jeremiah's father was terrifying; yet it was also comforting at the same time.

His father had become a stranger to him. He no longer recognized the man who had raised him. He was no longer Isaiah; he was hardly still a man. He was more of a vicious creature trapped in a human anatomy, hell-bent on survival, and protecting what is his. Humanity had dissolved within him, and natural instinct subsisted both chemically and physiologically. He pulled a *Model 1911 Colt 45* semiautomatic pistol from his shoulder holster, which was located beneath his coat, and said, "Don't get up until the shooting stops."

Isaiah moved both quickly and methodically. He flanked the first and closest shooter from the rear without being noticed. He fired from close range into the back of the assassin's head. His metallic mask flew forward from his face and landed on the ground in front of him. Instantly, his breath withdrew from his lungs in a gale, his tommy gun fell silent, and his body went limp. He fell to his knees and hunched over to his left. He was dead before he hit the ground. Without a wasted moment, Isaiah turned his attention to the second closest gunman and assumed a kneeling position. He fired three rounds; all of which hit the second gunman in his left torso. The gunman contorted his body and flew to his right. He was gravely wounded and screamed out in pain, as he was not yet in shock. The third tommy gunner, who was closest to the cube van, had noticed in his peripheral the commotion to his left. The assassin's attention instantly turned to Isaiah. By then, Isaiah had left his kneeling position and was attempting to flank the third assassin. Both men fired at the same time.

Without having a chance to get a good aim, Isaiah fired from his hip. He emptied his gun toward the third gunman. Bullets were ripping through the air inches from him, hissing in his ear like demons suggesting death. Almost instantaneously after his last round was fired, Isaiah felt as if someone had taken a red-hot iron rod and hit him in the left thigh and the right rib as hard as they could. His feet were removed from beneath him, and he fell flat on his face. He had been hit. The pain was numbing. The breath had been knocked from his lungs. Adrenaline became his resolve. With having almost no breath, and not knowing if he had neutralized the third assassin, Isaiah willed himself to barrel-roll back to the second downed gunman. He attempted to retrieve the wounded man's tommy gun. The man was still screaming from severe pain, and the weapon's sling was wrapped in a loop around the man's arm; he could not free it. So Isaiah maneuvered the weapon as best as he could toward the third tommy gunner, using the wounded man as a shield. When Isaiah finally got his bearings, he saw that the third assassin was lying motionless on the ground beside the cube van in a pool of steaming blood. Without the ability to move effectively, Isaiah decided that firing into the side of the cube van would be the most useful tactic.

He fired the gun in short bursts, hoping the bullets would pass through the thin walls of the cube and hit the assassin inside. With each pull of the trigger, he was growing weaker. It was becoming harder to control the weapon. After the fourth burst into the cube van, Isaiah had noticed that the vehicle was moving. He continued to fire as it sped off, before bouncing off a light pole and disappearing into the darkness. He could no longer control the weapon anyhow. The world fell silent.

Goodbye

Isaiah tried to get up. He was very weak. He perched himself against a nearby blue postal service mailbox. He sat with his back against it, facing toward the decorated tree. Adrenaline was subsiding within him, and excruciating pain was taking over. The snow began to fall more aggressively. The large flakes were gathering atop his head. The sulfurous smell of gunpowder saturated the air and burned his nostrils. Blood was beginning to pool in his throat. The wound to his leg had begun to bleed profusely; it steamed as the warm blood hit the frozen atmosphere. Isaiah sat and stared. He panned the *City*

Square as if he were within a separate plane of existence. And in this seemingly eternal moment, a deafening silence persisted among the crowd. As if one could hear the drag of the snowflakes dividing the atmosphere. Within this fleeting moment, time and space had lost its measure to Isaiah and reality was intangible.

"Isaiah!" yelled his wife, as she and Jeremiah ran to his side. "Are you okay?" she asked.

"Tourniquet," responded Isaiah, as he awoke from his state of partial comatose. "I think they got my femoral."

"Someone help us!" yelled Annabelle.

"Papa, are, are you okay?" asked Jeremiah with a soft inquisitive voice. The numbed crowd was beginning to wake from its own oblivion. Erratic screams and a different form of chaos enveloped the crowd as some searched for loved ones and others struggled for life. Some had already passed.

"I love you, Annabelle. More than you can imagine."

"I love you too. You're going to be fine," she said.

"Jeremiah, come here." Jeremiah moved closer to his father. "I love you, son, and I'm proud of you." Isaiah's voice was growing fainter. "Listen to this. Whenever things get confusing in life and the line between right and wrong is obscure, ask yourself this. Why does the devil fear God?"

"I don't know what you mean, Papa," said Jeremiah.

"The answer will come to you someday, son. Be patient. Annabelle, don't grieve too badly for me."

"You're going to be fine." She interrupted.

"This is what men do, and what better way to die than to die for love and sacrifice. People don't believe in anything anymore." Isaiah was fading quickly. "Here, take this. My father wrote it and gave it to me. Now it is yours." It was a short handwritten poem. He looked toward the sky and closed his eyes to let the snow fall on his face. Large flakes were getting caught in his eyelashes. He mumbled something incomprehensible and let out a final breath. It left his body in a white fog as if his spirit was exiting his body. Annabelle wanted to capture this white fog and force it back into her husband's lungs, but it evanesced into the winter twilight.

6

Heather

If I were a painter, I would paint her in my picture so I could know the details of her beautiful design. However, I am just a poet, an inventor of perception, recklessly deciphering the enigma that is love. I surmise a painting would do her no justice anyhow. For it is only a reflection of light upon a canvas, and even the brightest hue would insult her tangible beauty.

Before he knows it, he is holding her—a protective embrace. His hands are half her body. And as his fingertips run through her hair, he is convinced that she grew it long for this purpose—for him alone to enjoy. She looks at him. Her blue eyes are a vacuum. Every breath she draws makes love to her soul and exits her body knowing her deepest secrets. He pulls her even closer into himself. Without refrain, a thousand words burn in the sweetest places of his embattled soul and assemble at the tip of his tongue; with refrain, he will never speak of them. Nor is it necessary. He is the candle. She is the flame. He melts himself to keep her lit. Yes, love is a kinder form of pain.

No one will ever know him the way she does. Looking back, all his past dating endeavors seem frivolous; pointless conversations characterized by blank stares and a nervous laugh when they do not know what he is talking about. She is different. Her smile is persuasive and addictive.

They make love. He knows every inch of her body and every whisper of her soul. The cadence of every breath on his neck is like a warm summer breeze in the death of winter. He loves her more than he can ever love himself. She is his only peace. A beacon of hope and beauty in the dark world that surrounds him. How can something so lovely be so frightening? He does not want to know the answer.

Jeremiah wakes up first in the morning. He sips coffee as he stands leaning against the doorframe of her bedroom. As the light wraps itself around her delicate frame, she looks like angel to him; he asks himself why he deserves something so perfect. Heather wakes up.

"Hey, babe." She could tell right away that something is bothering him. "What's wrong?"

"Nothing. I was just thinking of my father a lot lately. I have to head to the office this morning. There is fresh coffee made."

"Okay, babe, I love you," says Heather.

"Ah-errr, I love you too," he mumbles.

She laughs at him. She knows he gets nervous around the L word. She ponders for a moment and decides she is going to wait to tell him she's pregnant.

Conduits

September 16, 9:30 a.m. sharp

Jeremiah starts talking first. "Obviously, we know we're on to something pretty big here. There are some shady happenings afoot. We're not going to just walk in there and retrieve whatever's in that safety deposit box without raising red flags. And it's Happy's dirty money sitting in that bank, so I was thinking it's time we might be able to pull off *Operation Bait and Switch*."

"Don't be toying with my emotions, hombre," says Gonzo excitedly.

"I am not kidding, Jerry, and don't call me Shirley." Luke giggles.

Jeremiah continues, "We finally have the funding to do it right. Luke, go get the folder." Luke hurries and unlocks a metal filing cabinet located against the back wall. He retrieves a legal-sized manila folder stuffed with documents.

Jeremiah takes out the floor plans and blueprints of *The People's Trust Company and Bank*. "Okay, so the only wrinkle we have in this caper is the addition of the safety deposit box. We are going to want to get whatever is in there without the bank knowing. It has to happen fast and subtle."

Pointing to the blueprints, Gonzo says, "We can probably take a couple of the clerks in here; as if we're rounding them up to lock them in. We can have them face this way, and I'll secretly grab whatever is in the box. They'll never know, gentlemen. Where do you think I get the name Speedy from?" Gonzo says in a prideful way. "Back in my pickpocket days—"

Jeremiah interrupts him. "I thought you got the name Speedy from that one girl you hooked up with from Paddy's." Jeremiah slowly produces a wide grin yet makes no eye contact with either of them. Luke giggles. Jeremiah continues, as he points at Jerry.

"Okay, so you're on the box, Gonzo."

"Luke, you can start building a scale model of the bank."

"Gonzo, you're also in charge of surveillance and disguises. They cannot know who we were before, who we will be after, or ever. We also need to understand everything we can about the schedules and tendencies of the guards that work in both the bank and the armored truck."

Jeremiah stresses his words: "I mean everything—first names, last names, family member names. I want to know their favorite colors." Jeremiah slams his fist on the table. "If we're going to do this, we're going to do it right. Go through the itinerary, and try and find faults with the plan. I am going to set up a meeting with Mrs. Billingsly and attempt to fish for more information. It's about time we talk with her again. Got it?" Jeremiah pans his eyes back and forth, as if staring into Luke and Jerry's souls through the conduits of their eyes.

They know that look. They know that when Jeremiah Revel separates himself like this, he sees beyond what others see. Even if he does not have the words to define it. He sees it.

Mrs. Billingsly

September 16, 11:15 a.m.

Jeremiah arrives back at his apartment building. The elevator creaks and moans as it jerks its way to the twentieth floor. As usual, he makes it to the top with no stops; there has been an exodus of tenants and evictions in the past year. Upon entering his apartment, he hangs his fedora and peacoat on the coatrack located next to the filing cabinet. He looks in the mirror. He can see the stress in his own face. He shaves and washes up. He sits at his desk and opens the *Blue Notebook*. It contains a loose-leaf handwritten page of Jerry's notes; the notes he took from the original phone conversation he had with Mrs. Billingsly that led to her hiring them. It reads as follows:

9/12

Billingsly, Patricia. Got our number from man at Paddy's. Missing husband. Six years. $2 mil insurance policy. Talk to Gavin North, Tribune. Tell him Maria sent you. Yellow folder. She would not give address, only 817-555-1172. No VidPhone. $30k + exp.

9/13

FYI. I think that North is actually part of the Undertakker family.

Jeremiah will use the rotary. As ritual, he unscrews the head-piece and microphone to check for bugs. The entire reason they use the rotary for delicate communications at *Rabbit Hole* is because they are almost impossible to tap, other than at their source (i.e., the ear-piece and microphone). Otherwise, one will have to go to the under-ground sewers to access the lockboxes, then sift through hundreds of unlabeled wires, by trial and error, to get the right connection to tap. That's if the beaver-sized rats don't attack you by then—fresh meat. Luke claims he can do it, but it never comes up as a needed endeavor. Jeremiah finds nothing abnormal in the earpiece nor microphone.

Jeremiah dials. There is something comforting about the sound of the rotary spinning. It suddenly reminds him of a particular mem-ory when he was calling the comic book company to ask about a decoder ring he had sent in for. He had worked all summer and saved up all the money that he earned for push mowing Mr. and Mrs. Banks' lawn. It was almost September by then. Jeremiah's mom was concocting Grandma's favorite goulash recipe when she overheard the unfortunate soul on the other end of the line telling Jeremiah that they were out of stock. Jeremiah Revel had never heard his mother swear before.

Isaiah was in the den trying to replace a vacuum tube in their TV. It had burned out the night before. He had heard the commotion and knew something was amiss. He came into the kitchen and gave Jeremiah a quick and clever smile. Isaiah was hoping that Annabelle was distracted while he carefully leaned toward Jeremiah's left ear. Jeremiah can still hear his father's voice: *She is really cute when she's angry.*

They chuckled together.

Of course, Annabelle heard them; they both looked up at her remorsefully. Even at his young age, Jeremiah could see how his mother could be angry and beautiful in the same moment. Isaiah tapped Jeremiah's shoulder twice, said good luck, then retreated back to the den with a smirk on his face. It is so strange the simple moments that people recollect and hold close to their heart.

"Hello?" The soft voice on the other side of the line breaks Jeremiah's daydream.

"Yes, this is an agent from *Rabbit Hole Private Eye Inc.* Is this Patricia Billingsly?"

"Yes. I assume that I can trust you. No one else alive has this number. It was my parents' from a long time ago. When they passed, I kept it open," replies the voice on the other end, providing unnecessary details of the origin of the phone number.

"Mrs. Billingsly, you and I can trust my phone, but I can't trust yours. Can we meet in person?"

"I suppose so, but—"

Jeremiah cuts her off. "At 2:00 p.m. today. *Undertakker's* office."

"I see," she says.

Jeremiah hangs up immediately. "Well done, Gonzo," he says to himself.

Ündertakker's (North's) Office

September 16, 1:47 p.m.

Speedy says that the office is located near a boiler room. Gonzo had charmed his way through the main building but mentioned that there is also an entrance down an alleyway leading to North's office. Jeremiah chooses the alleyway. There are four wet concrete steps leading to the subsurface where there is a sky-blue-colored door with random surface rust spots. It has a small aftermarket peephole and a crooked sign that reads in red letters, "Keep Out."

Jeremiah knocks on the door. The knocks seem as if they echo into a large cavern with a low cacophonic tremble. Footsteps can be heard approaching. Jeremiah removes his fedora. Several bolt locks can be heard sliding; they can use some lubrication. It does not seem this door is used very often. It is now ajar a couple of inches; the safety chain is still attached.

"Vat do you vant?" the voice asks; he sounds annoyed.

"I am here to meet Maria. Patricia sent me."

"Vat? Here? Vhen?"

"Two o'clock," responds Jeremiah. Just then, footsteps that resemble the sound of high heels can be heard echoing throughout the alleyway.

A very attractive middle-aged woman is walking toward them. Her clothing and posture are regal; she has a large and lavish jet-black purse hanging at her side. Jeremiah does not recognize the brand. North undoes the safety chain and pans both directions of the alleyway with his eyes before opening the door. Jeremiah offers her his hand for the stairs, but North overrules him. Jeremiah thinks to himself, *I don't think she got dolled up for me.*

"Hello, Sebastian," she says affectionately.

North's cheeks are beet red. "Hallo, meine Rose." They do not look at each other like they are just old acquaintances.

"Ehem. Shall we go in?" asks Jeremiah.

In the office, North turns on a device that is round—about the size of a softball. "In Deutschland, *War ich und* inventor physicist, *hier bin ich ein* inventor janitor." He laughs, then elaborates in broken English that no electronic device can possibly transmit signals in the confines of this room while it is activated. He then hands Jeremiah a pencil and piece of paper. Jeremiah sits across from Patricia. Sebastian has his hand on her shoulder.

"Mrs. Billingsly—"

"Please, call me Patricia."

"Patricia, I am going to sit here and let you talk. Whatever you feel is necessary to tell me, I will listen. I do not wish to waste neither your, nor my time. And Mr. *Undertakker*, we already know who you are [that was a semi-lie]. So if you have anything useful, I am all ears. I am not being paid to delve into the affectionate matters of my clients. Mrs., eh, Patricia. You first."

"Well, Charles and I had grown apart toward the end. We were happy once. But after the children moved out, he became obsessed with trying to get that story that would make his career. I told him to not do that stupid story." Sebastian hands her a tissue. "I loved my husband, but our marriage was failing. The only reason I seek your help is to get closure for my two boys. I want a body. I want something to bury. I have all the money in the world now to retire and bless my children." There is a cross around her neck. She rubs it gently with her thumb and index finger as she stares into nothing for a moment.

"Do you think he is still alive?" asks Jeremiah, remembering what Speedy said.

"I don't know. I just want it over."

"What do you mean?" asks Jeremiah.

"I just want peace for my boys and their families. I've offered to move them far away, but they are stubborn like their father. They still believe that there can be good in this *City*. There will never be…" She trails off before exhaling thoughtfully.

"Can you tell me of the last time you saw Charles?" A moment passes before she continues.

"It was over six years ago. August the seventh. He frantically rushed into the house one night, saying that he had to leave for the sake of me and the family. He said there was information that he ditched at one of the banks and hid the key somewhere. He was so frantic. He kept looking out the window. He handed me an envelope. He said to hide it in the lockbox upstairs. When everything is safe, give it to Sebastian to hold. He packed a suitcase and tried to leave. But as soon as he walked out the door, two men dragged him off. I could not make them out. It was raining hard and very dark. But they were big men."

Patricia goes on. "Charles' suitcase was left behind, sitting in the front lawn in the pouring rain. So I grabbed it, locked the door, and took it upstairs with me to where the lockbox was up in our bedroom closet. I was in a daze and decided to refold his cloths. When I opened the suitcase, I found a mask that looked important. Then I heard the downstairs door being kicked open. So I threw it in my purse along with the yellow folder. I was so scared." She starts crying. "I slipped out the upstairs window and climbed down the lattice. It snapped, but luckily the bushes below broke my fall."

"I'm sorry," says Jeremiah as Sebastian comforts her.

"I ran to a neighbors. Our house was burning soon after. I lost all my possessions except for that stupid folder and this. It's been haunting me for six years," she says with disgust. What she pulls from her purse and hands to Jeremiah will forever change the course of his life.

Am I Evil?

Jeremiah holds the mask while staring in disbelief. His hands become cold as ice. In the infinite possibilities of time and space, sometimes one becomes the other—equal, opposite, and immeasurable. And only in the bizarre realm of the human experience is where this law applies. Jeremiah clenches his teeth. His eyes become a distant, dark void.

In life, there are times when darkness subdues the soul, and we ignore it; it is what we are taught to do. It is what separates us from the animals, they say. We are brainwashed from childhood to ignore the primal instinct that has let our species survive for thousands of years. Suddenly, we think too much and feel too little. The balance is broken; not only our hearts, but also our minds. The two become polarized. And all that's left is anger and emptiness.

However, they say that anger is more useful than despair. That is true, but only if that anger is born of love—not of passion, not of lust, not of vengeance; only in the love that exists in the form of which there are no words in the human language that can possibly define it. Then and only then can we truly begin to understand why good men are capable of evil.

He flips the *Metallic Hockey Mask* over. There is brown leather padding on the rear with three matching leather straps intended to hold it upon one's head. Attached to where the three straps meet in the rear, there is a name crudely etched into a tin plate that was sewn into it. It reads as follows:

"R. James 'Happy' Henry."

"Hal is a nickname for Henry," Jeremiah mumbles under his breath, without looking away from the mask.

"Oh, he said someone found it in a garbage can the day after the Christmas Eve Massacre. I don't know how Charles came across it," elaborates Patricia quickly.

"Thank you, Patricia, Sebastian. I have what I need. I will be in touch. I cannot discuss any details of our investigation at this time, but we have found some substantial evidence thus far that corroborates your statement." He leaves without shaking their hands. They are not insulted. They seem more interested in each other's company by now anyway.

The Pizza Delivery Guy

September 16, 5:56 p.m.

Jeremiah walks aimlessly for several hours. The world surrounding him seems trivial and useless. His only solace is knowing that he is going to see Heather tonight. They are going to have their pizza and movie night. Of course, it is her idea. Jeremiah doesn't really care for the movies they watch. But once in a while, he gets to pick one; he can never decide (on purpose). She always falls asleep—wrapped in his arms—halfway into the movie anyway. And he needs her sleeping in his arms tonight.

After stopping at the office to leave the mask and grab a couple of things, he arrives at her apartment building. The doorman knows Jeremiah by now and lets him in right away. Jeremiah does not trust the doorman's eyes but thanks him. He takes the elevator to the tenth floor. Fancy: they have elevator music. The doors open and Jeremiah turns to the right. Her door is straight ahead, just before the L turn. He sees the pizza delivery guy talking with Heather at her door. It is a short man; his cloths are in disrepair and stained with restaurant grease. He is portly and has a generous comb-over. He hands her the medium cheese and pepperoni pizza and says in a tone that Jeremiah doesn't care for, "That will be thirteen seventy-five, pretty lady."

She smiles awkwardly and hands him a twenty. He then turns and quickly walks away. She yells, "Give me my change, you scumbag!" The delivery guy turns his head and laughs at her.

Jeremiah bears witness to this egregious offense; he catches him by surprise when he grabs him by the throat with his left hand. He pins him against the wall; with his right hand, Jeremiah pulls his .45 from his shoulder holster and forces it into the mouth of this piece of shit. The delivery guy is stunned.

"Give me all your money, asshole." Jeremiah pulls the hammer back; he stares intently into the man's eyes. He wants to see this guy's brains on the wall. The delivery guy gives him a wad of cash—at least $300. "Why does the devil fear God?" he asks sadistically.

"I don't know. No, no, no, no, no, no," he mumbles as Jeremiah pushes the gun farther into his mouth. He pisses himself.

"Jeremiah Isaiah Revel, you will not take that man's money!" Heather yells.

He looks at her. Her eyes speak. She is standing just outside her door with her hands on her hips. When she is angry, she scares the shit out of him. Jeremiah listens. He unravels the money wad that the delivery guy gave him and throws the cash onto the ground. It scatters everywhere. He puts his gun away. He bends down and retrieves a twenty. He pokes the delivery guy on the side of the head, then points at Heather while never looking away from him.

Quietly, he says, "She saved your life, and thank you for the free pizza."

Movie Night

"What is wrong with you?" she yells at him as he closes her apartment door behind him. "You were going to kill him!"

"There was nothing in the chamber." Jeremiah assures her (there was).

"I don't even know you."

Jeremiah looks through the peephole. The delivery man is entering the elevator. He turns to Heather. "Here's your twenty." He holds his hand out with a one-dollar bill in it.

She starts smirking and quickly yells at him again. "Give me my money back. Don't make me get rough."

"Please and thank you, ma'am. I like it rough. You know you're cute when you're angry?" Jeremiah is laughing.

Heather rolls her eyes and says, "Oh god, what movie did you get that from?"

He slips the twenty into her cleavage and says, "I don't know, but this is much better than a movie. Keep the change." She can't stay mad at him.

After eating the pizza, they watch some stupid chick flick. Jeremiah made homemade popcorn. Heather is on the right side of him, with her legs lying across his. His right arm is supporting her.

Suddenly, she says, "You scared me, Jeremiah."

"I know. I'm sorry," he responds.

"You never talk to me. I don't even know what you do."

"I told you. It is better that you don't know so you will never have to lie."

"Can't you have a real conversation with me?" responds Heather.

Jeremiah thinks for a moment and says, "You know when I'm away from you, the world has no purpose. Then when I'm around you and I hear you laugh, everything else becomes trivial. So I guess you are my world, *Nerd*."

"You're such a dick," she says as she smiles and begins to nod off. Her head is on his chest. She always likes to listen to his heartbeat for some reason. Her hair smells wonderful. They both fall asleep on the couch.

Jeremiah wakes up sometime around 3:00 a.m. They are both still on the couch. He jostles her to try and get her to wake up.

"What time is it?" she says softly and barely awake.

"I'm going to carry you to bed if you don't get up." She does not respond. He lifts her up.

"I love you," she says. He carries her to bed. They both go to sleep. Life is good.

The Museum

September 17, 7:57 a.m.

Jeremiah tells Heather that he has business to take care of as he puts on his peacoat and is about to leave.

"I was going to make you breakfast," she says while making a pouty face.

He does not like waiting when he has something on his mind but obliges anyway. She is just too damn cute. She cooks him eggs, toast, and the wonderful part of the pig that is known as bacon. And when she makes him coffee, it always tastes amazing for some reason. He does not know where she gets it from. The aroma alone reminds him of her—in her little white shorts and blue tank top with no bra on. It should be a crime against humanity to look that sexy while cooking bacon. Her hair is a mess, but it is perfect.

"Thank you, love," he says as he kisses her. Her breath smells like breakfast sausage. He needs to catch the eight fifty (bus).

Public transportation in *The City* is a spectacle. There is always some vagabond who, the night before, had checked into *The Night Rider Motel*. Amenities include their own plastic two-seat bed, newspaper blankets, a panoramic view of *The City*, and a fully functioning two-liter pop bottle toilet; all yours for the price of two dollars a night. The bus drivers gave up a long time ago trying to kick them off. They usually share their liquor with them anyway. It helps pass the time and makes the night a little more interesting. Then you have your talker. It's the person who insists on trying to initiate a conversation with you despite your best efforts to ignore them. They are worse than the vagabonds; at least they keep to themselves. Then there is everyone else. Nobodies who are faceless; they go unnoticed in the archives of time. They merely exist in this moment. They ride the bus to work, do their job, and go home. Then they show up in the obituaries and become a name etched in stone; there will be a date that defines their beginning, and one for their demise. Everything in between will become lost within the memories of those who have passed before them, and those who will pass after. And eventually, the memory of them will die. Maybe if they are lucky, the only thing they have left to offer this world is a witty epitaph or a census statistic; some find comfort by living in the shadow of their own dreams because it is safe. But what's the point of living life without being a little nervous sometimes?

Jeremiah gets off the bus a couple of stops short of his destination. He is in *The Museum District*. It is near *The City Square*. He doesn't know why he decided to get off the bus early; he is lying to himself. He knows. There is a small exhibit in *The City Museum* dedicated to local heroes. It's a beautiful building. It has four Romanesque pillars preceding the entryway. There are two tiers of stairs leading up to them. Most of the roof is adorned with a beautiful aqua-green patina. As he walks up the steps, he wishes there was less bird shit on them. This part of *The City* is always windy. He has to hold his hat on with his right hand.

When he gets to the main platform that is just before the covered, stone-arched entrance, it starts to rain. *That is befitting,* Jeremiah says to himself. Luckily he is not made of sugar.

"Jack, are we open yet?" asks one of the security guards to the other.

The other guard checks his watch. "Close enough."

Jeremiah checks in his gun with them before he walks through the metal detector. They appreciate it when you let them know you are armed ahead of time. They give him a ticket labeled number 7 to retrieve his gun when he exits. He has not been here in years.

The main lobby is floored with marble. There is an exhibit map standing like an eyesore located just after the security checkpoint. Most of the letters are crooked. A few have fallen off. Jeremiah studies it and moves his index finger across the list as he reads the map. The *Local Hero's* exhibit is still in the same location it has been since he was a child. It is just down the annex to the right. His father's blue police hat—7 3/4"—is on a Caucasian mannequin's head. His matching navy-blue police coat hangs on its torso.

Jeremiah reminisces of how regal his father looked when he would stop home for lunch. Annabelle made Isaiah's lunch every day. Looking back, it's funny how he never understood until he was an adult why she would take so much time delicately and carefully crafting the masterpiece that would be Isaiah's sandwich. She wanted it to look perfect. Jeremiah always ate his lunch beforehand. It was Annabelle and Isaiah's alone time. He could still hear his father's low voice, and his mother's laugh coming from the kitchen.

Among other personal items that Annabelle loaned *The Museum* is Isaiah's police belt (with an empty holster), his badge (number 405), and a portrait of him from when he graduated the police academy. There is also an etched plaque. It tells of his heroism and ends with the following words:

> *In the face of evil, there is a light that shines and illuminates the darkest corners of places it does not belong. But it shines because it must.*
> *To whom much is given, much is required. (Luke 12:48)*
> *In loving memory of Isaiah Armor Revel*
>
> *—Annabelle Revel*

Annabelle always said that humans pervert the Word of God.

It's odd that she chose that parable, Jeremiah thinks to himself. It has always irked him that there was nothing of hers in the display. Without her, there would be no hero; so he pulls out a silver broach that he always keeps in his breast pocket. It was Annabelle's. It was given to her from her grandmother. In the middle is a brilliant scarlet-red rose. When she and Isaiah first got married, they did not have much. The broach was her prized possession. She almost pawned it when they were short on food. Isaiah would not let her.

He places it in the breast pocket of his dad's police coat and rebuttons it. Someday he will come back and retrieve it, but it belongs here for now.

"Mom, I can't believe it's been seventeen years. I miss you and Dad so much," Jeremiah says in a solemn whisper.

They say that she died of a broken heart.

The Fourth Wheel

Before exiting *The Museum*, Jeremiah gives a quick glance at three metallic hockey masks that hang in the exhibit and moves on. He hands the security guard his ticket and retrieves his gun.

It's ironic that I am not allowed to bring it into the museum when that's where it belongs in the first place, Jeremiah thinks to himself.

He walks south for several blocks. The gradual change from *The Museum District* to *Skid Row* is unraveling before his eyes. There are very few pay phones left in *The City*, but there is one in front of *Fox's Pawnshop*. Speedy will recognize the number. He will know that it is Jeremiah calling; it is one of seven phones throughout *The City* they use from time to time.

He dials Speedy's rotary phone. It is ringing.

"Dave's Repair Shop, how may I help you?"

"Yes, I was calling to see if the oil change and tire rotation was done on my car? The last name is Koch," says Jeremiah.

Gonzo recognizes his voice. He immediately responds, "We are still working on it. It should be done this afternoon, probably around 2:00 p.m."

"That late, huh? Okay, I'll be there then." Jeremiah hangs up.

September 17, 2:00 p.m.

Jeremiah meets Gonzo at the office. Luke is there too; it was not planned, but Luke often shows up at random times to check on the equipment. Jeremiah walks over and opens a drawer at one of the workbenches. He pulls out the mask and throws it on the meeting table. It is sitting faceup.

"Did you get that from Billingsly?" asks Jerry.

"I know what that is," says Luke.

"What is it, Luke? Do you know what the fuck it is?" asks Jeremiah angrily.

"It's from *The Christmas Eve Massacre*," replies Luke softly. Then, while looking down and without making eye contact, Luke softly says, "It looks like the other three that are hanging in *The Museum*."

"It looks bulletproof," adds Gonzo. Jeremiah pulls his gun out. He points it at the mask and fires. The bullet ricochets, bouncing off several objects around the office before finally coming to a rest. It sounds like a spinning coin that is slowly settling. "Your scaring me," says Jerry. The shot surprised both him and Luke. But Luke is more focused on the mask. He is leaning over it. He looks up. His eyes look huge through his thick glasses.

"It is definitely bulletproof," says Luke.

"Look on the back. I think that Happy Hal was part of the group that killed those people and my father." Jeremiah trails off. Luke pulls out his magnifying glass; he and Speedy study the mask for a minute. All are silent.

Suddenly, Gonzo says, "We are going to need a fourth wheel. A driver."

"I've been doing the math. We need a another." Luke interrupts quietly.

Jeremiah trusts their judgment. "Who can we get? Do you think Stefenski would be interested? He is the best in the business."

"Who, Sonny? No way, man. He found God. He's on the straight and narrow now, hombre. He's a family man," says Speedy.

Jeremiah points at the chalkboard and smirks. In almost perfect unison, they all say out loud, *"Rule number 1, people don't change. They just form better lies."*

"Give him a personal visit, Jerry. You know the drill. Also, I am going to wear the mask during the job, and I want the security cameras running inside the main lobby but not in the safety deposit box vault. I want this Happy Hal asshole to know who he is dealing with. Jerry, design the mask into my disguise."

"That's what I'm fucking talking about!" yells Speedy excitedly as he slams his hand on the table.

"I'm going to go feed the rabbits," says Luke.

September 17, 6:21 p.m.

Gonzo buzzes Sonny's apartment from the ground floor.

"It's Jerry. Let me in."

A few moments later, a voice on the other end asks, "Jerry who?"

He makes sure he buzzed the right room. He knows he has the right one. "Let me in, Sonny."

"What's the password?"

Jerry exhales dramatically and says into the microphone, "Two Ds are better than one."

The lock on the door makes a clicking noise. Gonzo enters. It is a fairly nice tenement apartment building located on the northeast side of *The City*. Sonny lives on the sixth floor. Speedy takes the stairs.

"I could use the exercise."

He knocks on the door of apartment 607. Sonny opens it.

"What's up, Sonny?" asks Gonzo.

"Come in."

Sonny is tall—at least 6'3". He has graying dark hair. He is a driving savant. He knows *The City* like the back of his hand—every road, alleyway, and safe house. Speedy has only seen him a handful of times in the past couple of years. Sonny wanted out so he could start a real life. They would not seek his services unless it was important. Sonny knows this.

Jerry and Sonny are brothers—not by blood, but by circumstance. They both had very troubled childhoods. They were both physically and mentally abused as they passed through various broken foster homes. Eventually, they ended up in juvie. That is where they met. Sonny was in for stealing cars at twelve years old. He was the youngest person in *The City* to ever lead the police on a car chase. Jerry was in for chronic pickpocketing. The judge would have been lenient, but his own public defendant turned against him after he stole his wallet during the hearing. Their bond was instant. Sonny was the first person Jerry didn't hate. They would always be trying to pull shenanigans together. They would often sneak out at night and steal cigarettes and beer from gas stations. Then they would sell the items to the other kids in juvie for an inflated price. Business was good.

Eventually, they both ended up in the foster home of the Stefenski's. This only happened after the system tried to separate them. At first, Jerry was at the Stefenski's and Sonny was elsewhere; but Mrs. Stefenski would find Sonny sleeping on the floor next to Jerry's bed almost every morning (he would sneak out and walk the two miles to the Stefenski's). She had such a soft heart for the boys and the only way to keep them together was to adopt them. Mr. Stefenski was a good man and taught the boys many life lessons. But when Mrs. Stefenski wasn't around, he would teach them how to properly count cards, hot wire cars, and manipulate the books among other things. It was their bonding time. Suddenly, they were a normal family.

Mrs. Stefenski insisted that the boys learn how to sew and tailor. Sonny did not care for it, but Jerry loved it. He used it as a form of therapy and a creative outlet. It kept him out of trouble. Mr. Stefenski had passed away suddenly from a heart attack a couple years later. Mrs. Stefenski soon followed. The best years of their lives were suddenly memories. It has been some time since they visited them in the graveyard.

"What do you want?" asks Sonny as he is feeding his daughter at the kitchen table. The food is smeared all over her face, but she is adorable nonetheless.

"We need a driver. Not just anyone. You. This one is big. Five thousand plus one-fifth and expenses paid for. Is it safe to talk?" asks Gonzo.

Sonny looks around and says, "Not if you're talking."

"I would not be here if we did not need you. This is not a business transaction. This is me talking to my little brother. This one is bigger than us. Mom would be proud."

"Mom always said to not be like Dad." They both smile at each other.

"This is different. Do you want your little girl to grow up in the world we lived in? We have a chance to really make a difference. We only have to hold up a bank."

After Sonny finishes feeding her, he pulls her out of her high chair and hands Lillian to Jerry. "Look into her eyes, and tell her that what you're saying is true."

Gonzo realizes that his niece was a newborn the last time he held her. He looks into Lillian's eyes for a moment. He then looks toward Sonny and says, "I think Jeremiah knows who Happy is."

Suddenly, there is a knock on the door. Sonny moves quickly and picks up a bat that he keeps next to it. He nervously looks through the peephole; his posture immediately relaxes, and he opens the door. Jeremiah is standing there; he is wearing all black except for the gray fedora. His face is statuesque and cold, but his eyes resolute.

"Are you in or out?"

"I need—"

"Are you in or out?" He cuts him off as he asks more sternly.

"I'm in."

"Then we have a fourth wheel." Jeremiah turns and walks away without saying another word.

Just for Fun

Gonzo leaves Stefenski's apartment sometime later. He can't tell him too much, but enough to give him an idea of the operation. He will be at the meeting on the nineteenth anyway, where he will be filled in. Speedy decides to go to Paddy's and have some drinks. It is Saturday night after all, and it's only a few blocks away. Plus, he thinks that Telisha is behind the bar tonight.

Just as Speedy suspects, Jeremiah is sitting at the end of the bar—alone in his usual spot. There are only a few other patrons (the regulars) in the bar. Business will pick up later. Gonzo sits next to Jeremiah.

"You all right, Jer?" he asks.

Jeremiah breaks his daydream and looks at Gonzo. "Let's tie one on tonight—no business—just for fun." He smirks slyly.

"All right, my man. Telisha! One beer and two shots please. Keep them comin'."

Speedy has been enamored with Telisha since the first time he saw her. She is a beautiful woman. Her ebony skin is soft and smooth. As she walks toward them, her hips sway back and forth and hypnotize Gonzo. She carries herself with both class and unparalleled raw sexiness.

It is not common to find a black woman in this part of *The City* working at an Irish pub, but she is Al's daughter. Her mother was a tenant at one of the apartments he owned and ran. She was pregnant with Telisha when she first rented the place. She had very little and worked two jobs just to pay the rent. Al had a soft heart for her and could not possibly kick a pregnant woman to the street when she couldn't pay. He would come over several times a week with groceries and to fix the place up. When she found out she was having a girl, he built her a crib and organized a diaper party. He had it at the bar and invited all the regulars. Imagine the group of hooligans in attendance at that party. Al's ex-wife even threw her a baby shower.

When her mother passed away due to complications with the birth, Al was heartbroken. Some think he was in love with her. He adopted the baby girl and named her Telisha, after her mother. She even has his last name—O'Sullivan. Telisha grew up in the bar. She is like a daughter to all the regulars. They love her like she is their own. They always tip her extremely well; they like to think that they paid her way through veterinary school; they called it *The Paddy's*

Scholarship Fund. She is saving up to open her own volunteer pet clinic. Al could probably loan her the money, but she refuses.

"Good evening, Jeremiah, Jerry," she says his name with a sneer.

"Hello, beautiful," says Gonzo.

"What do you want, white boy?" she asks.

Speedy replies, "I'm not white, I'm Polish!" They all burst out laughing.

"You always make me laugh, Jerry. Too bad you're not a real man like your friend Jeremiah here," she says in a seductive voice. "So you still got that girlfriend?"

"Yes, I do, sweetie. Sorry."

"That's too bad," responds Telisha.

"What am I, chopped liver?" questions Gonzo. They never have to pay for half of their drinks when she is working. They usually stay after the bar closes and have some after-hour drinks with her. She is one of the only mutual friends they have outside of work and they can both trust her.

Mrs. Olejniczak

September 18, 11:23 a.m.

Jeremiah awakes to water dripping on his forehead. He is staring at the ceiling.

"How did I get home?"

His head is pounding. The ceiling only leaks during really heavy rainfall. He is still wearing his clothes from last night. Jeremiah sits up in his bed, and pulls a bucket out from underneath it to catch the dripping water. He pulls a jug of spring water from his fridge and attempts to hydrate. Slowly he comes to his senses and remembers walking home with Gonzo. Gonzo had bought a burger for a homeless guy. They then went their separate ways because they do not want to know where each other lives. He makes coffee. Outside his window, there is a torrent.

I better go check on Mrs. Olejniczak, Jeremiah says to himself as the lights flicker.

Mrs. Olejniczak is a widowed Polish immigrant who lives down the hall. She is elderly, and Jeremiah checks in on her occasionally, especially during storms. On most Sundays, he will go there and make them brunch; they talk about anything and everything. Jeremiah looks forward to it. She is a fascinating women. On top of that, she also has a fine selection of scotch that she shares with him. He definitely needs a little *Hair of the Dog* this morning. He takes a quick shower, and throws on his comfy clothes from the trunk underneath the bed. Jeremiah knocks on her door exactly three times, holds, then once more. She knows it is him.

"Come in, Jeremiah."

It is hard for her to move around, so she gave him a key a long time ago. He opens the door.

She is sitting at the same place as usual—a reclining chair in front of an old black-and-white tube TV. She is a lifetime chain-smoker and, sure enough, is smoking when he walks in. He grabs the full ashtray on the end table and goes to the connected kitchen to empty it. There are a couple of dirty dishes in the sink. He washes, dries, and puts them away. As he is finishing wiping down the counter, he asks, "Do you want some scotch?"

"Bring out the top shelf stuff this week," replies Mrs. Olejniczak in a raspy but inviting voice. Jeremiah is excited. It is the finest scotch he has ever had. He fills two glasses with ice from the refrigerator, then grabs the scotch and a couple of candles.

He lights the candles just in case of a power outage. There is a flash and a deafening boom. The whole apartment seems to tremble. The lights flicker.

"That one was close," she says.

"Why the good stuff? What's the special occasion?" asks Jeremiah as he pours the scotch in each of their glasses.

She takes a sip, and then a slow drag from her cigarette. "It was a day just like today, storming and pouring rain—you could hear the rainwater pelting the window—when my Oscar told me this story. He never spoke of his experiences in the war except for this one time. He was sitting where you are. We were drinking from this same bottle of scotch." She points to the bottle sitting on the table. "Now, by no means was my Oscar perfect. He would hit me on rare occasions. He had so much anger sometimes. But he always took care of me and treated me like a queen when he would take me out. He worked his hands to the bone to get our family what we needed. But he never spoke of the war." She takes another sip of scotch; it's even larger than the last. Jeremiah joins her as he leans back in his chair. He grabs one of her cigarettes and smokes it as she continues on.

"He told me this story. Oscar and nine others were assigned to hold an old farmhouse that would serve as an outpost. They were ordered to hold it at all costs; it was supposed to be an easy gig. The war was about over. Things were quiet for about a week. Oscar and a guy by the name of Schenk were peeling potatoes in the kitchen of the farmhouse when they heard a barrage of gunshots that were too close for comfort."

The Firefight

"Those aren't ours," says Oscar.

"They sound like Mausers," replies Schenk.

Oscar runs to the living room at the front of the farmhouse. He looks out the window; the two *M1919* machine-gun nests on each side of the field are being attacked. A bullet crashes through the window he is looking out and hisses by his head. He ducks for a moment with his back against the wall. Oscar is in a daze. This is his first combat experience. Just then, Second Lieutenant Maxwell runs down the stairs from the second floor.

He looks out the same window for a brief moment and yells, "To your posts! Everyone, now, that is an order!"

Just then, a bullet rips through his neck. He drops to his knees, then to all fours. Blood is hemorrhaging from his neck like a dark red waterfall. Lieutenant Maxwell tries to get up, but falls facedown and motionless. Oscar has never seen so much blood. He snaps to, however, and follows orders. The guys need him.

Oscar's job is to resupply the machine guns. He grabs his M1 Garand and slings it over his back. He then grabs two .30 caliber ammo boxes (containing tracer rounds)—one in each hand. The enemy's bullets are slapping the wooded facade of the farmhouse. They pop and snap and sound louder than he had thought they would. Small wood splinters and glass seem to be flying everywhere. Some hit him in the face. He meets Schenk at the front door. Despite the chaos, Schenk is poised and has his rifle ready.

"One, two, three!" yells Schenk as he opens the door.

Oscar is out first. He cannot believe he is still alive. He can hear Schenk's M1 Garand behind him providing suppressing fire. He tries to keep his head low, using the stone wall in front of the farmhouse the best he can for cover. A bullet tears through the side pocket of his pants, somehow missing him.

Oscar makes it to the first M1919 nest where Muller is the gunner. He puts the ammo box behind him. Jackson, who is feeding the ammo, looks back at him and yells, "We need another barrel too!"

There are mortar rounds starting to fall on their positions.

"I'll be right back!" yells Oscar.

He begins to make his way to the second nest, when a mortar makes a direct hit into it. It is a hodgepodge of dirt, fire, smoke, and flesh that explodes into the sky; the mediums used by the devil to paint their portraits of death. Oscar's ears are ringing. Everything is in slow motion.

He looks back and sees Schenk lying in front of the front door on the ground, holding his own entrails. He is screaming. He looks back to the first nest. Jackson is dead. The bottom of his jaw is missing except for his tongue and a couple of teeth. Muller is also dead. Oscar cannot tell from what, but he can see the absence of life in his eyes. He drags the ammo box toward them while crawling on his stomach; it is only five meters away.

Oscar removes his M1 from his person and throws it into the nest. He tries to stay as low as possible. Muller's lifeless finger is still on the trigger. He removes the limp hand from the weapon. Oscar decides that he does not care anymore. All his friends are dead. He is not going to make it out of this anyway. Orders are to hold at all costs. Just then, a young private with a M1 Garand slides into the nest with him; a small beacon of hope.

Oscar instantly says to him, "More ammo and get me another barrel."

The private runs off without questioning him. There are only five rounds left on the belt. Oscar fires them and loads a new belt. With his palm facing upward, he pulls and releases the cocking handle twice and begins to spray the field with lead. The tracers guide his way. There is a group of roughly forty-five enemy infantrymen charging the outpost.

Should the men who invented such awful machines of war be proud in moments such as this? Or should they be ashamed of their own creations? The M1919 fires with fine precision, catering a buffet of carnage. Maybe it is a testament to the fact that Muller and Jackson had nothing better to do this past week other than fine-tune their weapons. All is a blur.

The enemy is making a more desperate charge into the open field. They have no cover. Most are less than fifty meters away. Oscar is tearing them to pieces—literally. He notices that the young private has returned with a fresh barrel and a box of ammo; he asks him for suppressing fire while he changes it. Suddenly, a potato masher grenade lands in the nest. The private immediately throws it back. Oscar finishes reloading for a second time when he notices that there is nothing left to shoot at. All becomes quiet.

There are faint gargles and screams both close and off in the distance. The aroma of sulfur and death is pungent in the air. The metal of the machine gun can be heard crackling as it cools. There are enemy bodies stacked everywhere. He turns and leans with his back on the sandbags, facing away from the battlefield and toward the farmhouse. The farmhouse is destroyed. He sits silently for what seems like an eternity. He then looks at the private sitting next to him and asks, "What's your name?"

"Henry, Robert James Henry. People call me Happy." They shake hands. The bodies of Jackson and Muller are on each side of them.

Oscar looks around puzzled and asks, "Where did you come from?"

"I'm a runner," says Henry. "I have this correspondence for one Second Lieutenant Maxwell." He pulls a folded piece of paper out of his pocket.

"I guess I am the highest-ranked soldier here," says Oscar. He takes the message and begins to read it. *"Oscar Olejniczak is due to go on leave tomorrow following the arrival of his replacement."*

Private Henry gets up, brushes himself off, and starts walking toward the field. This surprises Oscar. He watches from the nest as Henry pulls out his service pistol. He begins executing the fallen enemy—the ones still alive. One by one, he puts a bullet into their heads. He can hear some of them begging. Henry does not care. It seems as though he is smiling and enjoying it.

A Photograph and A Medal

"They both received the Distinguished Service Cross for their actions," says Mrs. Olejniczak. "There were the only four survivors. Oscar and Private Henry were the only ones physically unscathed. They held off fifty-four enemy infantrymen and several mortar barrages. My Oscar could never get over what he saw that day though. He never told a soul about it, except for me that one time.

"When he got home from *The War*, he was different. But it wasn't until our only child was killed while she was caroling—you know, *The Christmas Eve Massacre*—that Oscar really lost it." She sighs and stares off into space for a moment. "Here," says Mrs. Olejniczak suddenly, as she opens a drawer from the end table next to her. It is an old black-and-white photograph. "Oscar never saw him again after this photo was taken."

Jeremiah studies it for a moment. "Can I borrow this, Mrs. Olejniczak?" asks Jeremiah.

"I don't know why, but sure. I am leaving everything to you anyway when I pass. Oh, and I want you to have this." She pulls out a small box from the same drawer. Jeremiah opens it. It is Oscar's Distinguished Service Cross medal. "I have no use for it. Take it. It only reminds me of his sorrow," she says. Jeremiah does not argue with her. He makes lunch for both of them. They eat. As he is walking out the door, Mrs. Olejniczak says, "Jeremiah, life is too short to live in darkness. We can only learn from the past, not live in it."

September 18, 2:20 p.m.

Jeremiah is back in his apartment. He sits on the side of his bed. He reaches under it and pulls out a half-full bottle of whiskey. He leans back against the wall. He opens the bottle and takes a big swig while studying the photograph. The storm is still raging outside. The rumbles of the thunder shake the whole building. But the violent storm raging outside is nothing compared one raging within Jeremiah Revel.

There are two men in the photo—Oscar Olejniczak and Robert James Henry. They are both in full military formal wear. It was taken just after they were presented their medals. Mrs. Olejniczak said that Oscar had never seen him again after the photo was taken. Henry is shorter than Oscar. Jeremiah sips whiskey and stares at the photo longer. He is studying every shade of alternating gray and black hues that make up the face of Henry. At this moment, these are the only hues in the spectrum of visible light that matter to Jeremiah.

You have destroyed so many lives, he says to the photo and takes another sip. *Why did she wait to tell me this story until now?* Jeremiah asks himself regarding the ironic timing. There is a darkness that is taking over his soul. It is not just anger, but a hatred that he's afraid he cannot contain much longer. He stands up and looks in the mirror. He can see darkness in his own eyes. Sadistically, he says, *They are going to pay.* He lies down on his bed and falls asleep.

When Jeremiah wakes up, the storm has passed, the sky is clear, and the sun is setting. It is shining through the glass of his window in such a way that it acts like a prism. The refracted light adorns the wall of his apartment in a collage of varied hues—all different and unique, but beautiful in their own way. He moves his hand into the light. The individual colors rap themselves around it as if they are a blanket. But in all their illustrious beauty, the colors merely exist, bound to the laws of nature and circumstance. They cannot love; they cannot hate; they cannot feel. They can only be absorbed or reflected and misunderstood as a menagerie of hues of something they are not. Then when there is nothing left, there is only darkness—the absence of light—until the next sunrise.

10

The Itinerary

September 19, 9:29 a.m.

Jeremiah looks at his watch, then up at the atomic clock. Gonzo, Stefenski, and Luke are standing around the meeting table silently. The clock strikes 9:30 a.m.

"Luke, hand out the watches and everyone put them on."

Luke reaches into a small cardboard box sitting on the table, and hands each of them a cheap black digital *Time Saver*-brand watch. They have used them before and know they keep accurate time. The wrist band is also robust and unlikely to break.

"Okay, everyone set the watch to 9:32 a.m." They all fumble with the watch. "Hit the top right button in three, two, one, set." All their watches make a synchronized beeping sound.

"Okay, our goal is Monday, October 4, 9:37 a.m. We will have a dress rehearsal here on Saturday, October 2, at 9:30 a.m. for disguises. Luke, hand out the itineraries, then go get the scale model of the bank." Luke hands each of them a packet of papers. It looks like a movie script. Luke brings the scale model over. It is incredibly detailed.

Of course there is the bank, sans the roof," Luke explains. "This replica toy car represents the armored vehicle. This is the toy model of the van we will be riding in. It will be around the corner over here. I've measured out the distance between the light poles; the times of the red light changes are listed in the itinerary. The model is perfect to provide a timed visual of the operation." Luke pushes his glasses back up on his nose.

Jeremiah speaks: "Now, the goal here for *Operation Bait and Switch* is to make it look like we are robbing the bank. However, as we all know, our goal is the armored truck delivering the weekly cache of goods. Security will be lax. Happy Hal must be getting cocky and doesn't think anyone has the chutzpah to pull a fast one on him. We need to be precise. The itinerary will be your bible. Study it, love it, and know it better than you know yourself. Times are plus or minus eight seconds.

"We will be attacking the financial heart of *The Harvest Union*. Our disguises are key to protect our identities. Listen to Gonzo's every instruction. As far as armed resistance goes in the bank, the only thing we might encounter are some of Happy Hal's cohorts who frequent the bank to check on 'operations'." Jeremiah makes air quotes and looks at Gonzo with a smirk. "Their timing is random. That is why we need to move with both speed and precision. There is no room for mistakes."

"What is the booty?" asks Stefenski.

"Gonzo?" asks Jeremiah.

"Me and Luke think it'll be around $7 million plus or minus 1.5," he replies.

"Holy shit," says Sonny. "How the hell are you going to move that kind of cash?"

"Melt it," replies Luke. Stefenski realizes that they will be taking the armored truck with gold bricks in it.

"Read your itinerary. It is all in there. Stop asking stupid questions," says Gonzo. Sonny leans against the table and starts sifting through it. "Stand up straight for a minute." Gonzo starts taking his measurements. He gets to his groin area and says, "I'm going to need a smaller tape measure."

Jeremiah pulls Luke aside. "What are we going to do about the bank alarms?" he asks quietly.

"They are connected to the phone lines."

"I told you I could do it."

Luke adjusts his glasses on his nose. "Will you need help?"

"Yeah, it would be nice to have someone to keep the rats away."

Luke smiles, but is not actually kidding. "What about the telephones and radios?" asks Luke.

"I think I have a plan," says Jeremiah; he does not elaborate. Jeremiah goes over a couple of other details with the group and states that they will officially meet again in one week. Sonny leaves. Jerry and Luke stay behind.

"What's our budget up to?" he asks Luke.

"About fifteen. I can move funds around between the accounts to balance out the expenses and our fees. We are actually right on schedule."

"Good, I want a buffer of $7,000. Here, take a look at these, guys."

He places the war medal and the picture of Oscar and Happy on the meeting table. "Look here." He points to the guy on the right. "This is Happy Hal from *The War*. Some hero, huh?"

"Are you serious?" asks Speedy.

"Yes." Luke pulls out his magnifying glass and inspects the picture.

"Look on the back," says Jeremiah.

"Oscar Olejniczak and Robert James Henry," reads Luke out loud.

"The medal is Oscar's. He's a family friend. I want the medal sewn onto the coat of my disguise," Jeremiah states.

"No problem," responds Speedy without questioning him.

"Luke, when do you want to tap into the sewer phone lines?"

"The sooner the better," he responds.

"But with all the rain we had yesterday, we should probably wait for the water levels to recede a little bit. How does Wednesday sound?" suggests Jeremiah.

"That should work," replies Luke.

"I'll be back later. Luke, stay here until I get back."

"I'll be here."

The Device

September 19, 3:17 p.m.

Jeremiah knocks on the sky-blue door. Ündertakker unlocks it and opens it fully this time.

"Vhat now?" he asks.

"I need your help," says Jeremiah.

"I know you vould be back," responds Ündertakker.

He follows him to the janitor's office. Ündertakker enters first and turns on the device that sits upon the shelf; Jeremiah watches intently. It does not make a noise as it does its job. Ündertakker sits down at his desk with his arms crossed and his head cocked to the right. His blue eyes are burning holes through Jeremiah.

"Ift you are honest vith me, I vill be honest vith you. Vhat is you your name?"

"I am Jeremiah Revel."

"I know zee name Revel. Your father vas und hero."

"Enough of my father. We need your device. We are going to take down Happy Hal."

Ündertakker laughs out loud in a mocking way. "I know who he is. I know his name. Zis Happy Hal destroyed meine family. We were excellent in business vhen we came here. Zen he took everything."

"There is a lot of that going around," says Jeremiah. "Can we borrow it or no? Time is of the essence, Herr Ündertakker. The only reason we are this close is because of Patricia. She started this, and we are going to finish it."

"I vill give you zee jamming device for Patricia. But you must never come here again. Und zat you kill zis man Happy if you get zee chance."

"Sounds reasonable," responds Jeremiah. "But we are not guns for hire."

Ündertakker unplugs the device and removes it from the shelf. He shows him how to use it properly and explains that they will have to make an AC-DC converter if they want to make it mobile. It is unique in that it can jam both infrared and radio waves for roughly a one-block radius at the same time.

"That will not be a problem," explains Jeremiah.

"Goodbye, Ündertakker."

"Gut luck, Jeremiah."

He carefully places the device in the leather satchel he brought. Ündertakker eyes Jeremiah intently as he leaves. The door slams behind him. He heads straight back to the office.

September 19, 4:23 p.m.

Jeremiah arrives at the office. Speedy is too busy at the sewing machine to notice him enter. Gonzo is wearing his glasses; he rarely wears them in front of the guys because they pick on him. However, they have more important matters at hand. Luke is walking down the stairs from the second floor holding schematics.

"Luke, come take a look at this." Luke meets Jeremiah at the meeting table. He pulls the jammer from the leather satchel and places it on it. "This is the jammer for both infrared and radio waves—every channel and every frequency. We need to make it mobile. Convert it from AC to DC current."

Luke picks it up. He is fascinated and excited at the same time. Jeremiah figured he would like this project. After turning it every which way, Luke responds, "No problem. Where did you get it?"

"I can't tell you."

"I figured," replies Luke.

Jeremiah walks over to where Jerry is working. He looks at his creation and nods with approval. *This is coming along,* Jeremiah thinks to himself. "Luke, what time and where do you want to meet on Wednesday?"

"Follow me," he says.

They go upstairs to the armory. Luke is solely in charge of it. He is the only one that ever goes up there. Jeremiah and the others are not allowed to touch the keypad unless it is an emergency. He often spends hours in there cleaning the equipment, making sure everything is in perfect working order, and that there are no fingerprints on anything. Luke unlocks the heavy reinforced door.

"Wait here," he says. Shortly after, he returns while holding yellow industrial-rated waiters, an orange hard hat with an attached headlamp, yellow elbow-length chemical gloves, and a reflective safety vest. He then holds out a bottle of spray. It is cat piss.

"C'mon, Luke, are you serious?"

"Oh, and this." Luke hands him a tire iron.

"We will meet at 6:00 a.m. on Wednesday morning. Stefenski will drive us. We'll leave by 6:29 a.m."

The Storm Sewers

September 21, 5:59 a.m.

Jeremiah kept a low profile the day before. He had met Heather out for lunch, but could not get his mind off the adventure they are going to partake in today. He is not looking forward to it. As Jeremiah arrives at the office, he sees a white utility van with an unlit orange light on it toward the back of the side alleyway. It is still dark out. He unlocks the side door and walks through. Sonny is standing there in a standard city utility worker's uniform. He and Luke get dressed. All of Luke's tools and equipment are already packed in the truck.

I swear that he never sleeps, says Jeremiah to himself. They leave.

"You're not going to spray that shit on yourselves before I drop you off, right?" asks Gonzo.

"No," responds Luke while smiling as he is spraying the cat piss on himself. He hands it to Jeremiah. He sighs before spraying it on himself as if it were bug spray.

They stop two blocks north of *The People's Trust Company and Bank.* They jump out of the back doors of the van. After a quick scan of the area, Jeremiah uses the crowbar to remove the storm sewer's drain cover as Luke equips himself with his tools.

"You first," says Luke.

Jeremiah starts making his way down the steel ladder. He can smell the dampness. He reaches the bottom. The water is only three or four inches deep. He holds his hands up to support Luke. He has a lot of tools; it's a heavy load. Jeremiah goes back up the ladder and negotiates the manhole cover back into place with Stefenski's help. He hears the van's V8 engine rumble as Sonny drives off.

He lands on the subsurface floor. The water splashes up.

"Shhh. Don't disturb the rats. Up there, we rule. Down here, they rule," says Luke ominously.

Jeremiah clasps the tire iron tightly. The cat piss seems to be working. He can hear little squeaks on either side of him. Luke had told him not to shine the light on them; it would startle them.

The sewer tunnel is tall enough for Jeremiah to almost walk upright. It has an arched roof and is constructed entirely of brick. It is probably original to *The City*. There are occasional patches of concrete where repairs were made. There are several PVC conduit lines running down the wall. There is also very old lighting crudely attached to the ceiling. Who knows if it actually works or where the power switch is. He can hear drip noises that echo down the entire tunnel.

Jeremiah recalls a story he heard from the old-timers about a utility worker who entered the sewers alone to do maintenance and was never seen or heard from again. They only found his helmet and tools. He always thought it was an old wives' tale, but not so much anymore. Jeremiah can't get over the feeling they are being watched. They walk very slowly for fifteen minutes.

Finally, Luke says, "Here it is."

Both of their headlamps focus on it. It is a phone utility lockbox. It reads "306" with a defunct phone company's emblem on it. The rats seem agitated. Luke opens the box. It is a maze of wires. The rats are more agitated. It sounds as if there are thousands of them. Jeremiah tightens his grip on the tire iron.

Luke pulls something from his tool belt and says sternly, "Do not move or touch anything."

He then hooks one part of the device to something in the box and drops the other part into the water. There is a short and distinct buzzing sound that lasts less than a second. Instantly, everything is silent. As he looks down, Jeremiah can see at least a hundred dead rats lying around his feet.

They weren't lying. They are massive in size and mean-looking sons of bitches, he says to himself.

Luke turns to him with a smile on his face and says, "Lightning bomb." There are a few rats left that Jeremiah beats away with the tire iron while Luke works.

"This is very interesting. Someone else has tapped this box before," Luke says. "I can bypass their device. It actually makes it easier to identify which lines to tap." Luke wires a device inside the box that will allow them to reroute the phone signal for the bank's emergency panic buttons, the bank's alarm system, and their phones. Instead of notifying the authorities, the signals will go to a pay phone in *Skid Row*. Luke finishes, tests the device, then looks at his watch and says, "Two minutes. Over there."

They wait under a nearby manhole for a minute. Just then, the cover can be heard being worked open with a pry bar. It is Stefenski. Within forty-five seconds, they have exited the sewer in a back alleyway and are on their way.

"You smell like shit. But good timing. Everything was smooth up here," says Sonny.

Luke pulls out a small device with two buttons on it—one green, one red. "On, and off. The rabbits will be proud," he says while smiling.

"We're in business," says Jeremiah.

A Dress Rehearsal

October 2, 9:30 a.m. sharp

Three of the four are both nervous and excited. Jeremiah is neither. The jig is only two days away. There is a full-length mirror that Gonzo has pulled from somewhere in storage. Several weapons and a pile of gear that Luke has brought down from the armory are sitting on the meeting table. Gonzo is coming from the rear of the office. He is pulling behind him what looks like a hotel luggage cart. The wheels squeak as he approaches. The cart has an assortment of apparel hanging on it—shirts, coats, pants, etc. There are two totes sitting on the base of the cart.

"Luke, you're first, hombre. We'll start from the feet up," says Gonzo.

Luke strips down to his undershirt, socks, and underwear. They are patterned with little yellow ducks.

Speedy hands him a pair of black military surplus boots and a pair of dark tan cargo pants. Luke puts them on, then takes a utility belt from the table and a Glock 19 9mm pistol. The belt holds two dual magazine holders, a small utility pouch, and a holster for the weapon. In the pouch, he puts two flash grenades; all four will carry two. Next is the bulletproof vest—also the same make and style of which they will all be wearing. Gonzo custom-made a white pirate-style shirt. It has poofy wrist cuffs. It fits perfectly.

"I need suspenders," says Luke.

Speedy immediately hands him black suspenders, and says, "I know."

He then removes a custom-made black trench coat from the rack. It has various pockets. Luke puts the remote phone line access actuator in one of them and the signal scrambling device—of which he had converted to DC current using two six-volt lantern batteries—in another hidden pocket that Gonzo has made specifically for it. Finally, he hands him a plastic clown mask. Luke is terrified of clowns. It is befitting.

He will be carrying a flintlock blunderbuss pistol loaded to the max with double odd pellets—at least twenty. It will fire only once, but quite effectively; it is mostly only practical for intimidation purposes. Luke puts on the mask. His disguise is complete. He looks ridiculous.

"What do you want to be called?" asks Jeremiah to Luke.

"I am Pewee the Clown," responds Luke. They all burst out laughing.

"Pewee the Clown it is," says Jeremiah, smiling. Luke walks over to the mirror to check his disguise out. Immediately, he is taken aback and jumps away from his own reflection. He truly is scared of clowns.

Stefenski is next. Gonzo hands him a modified pinstripe gray suit, a pair of designer black shoes, a white dress shirt, and a burgundy-colored tie. He will also be wearing a custom-made long black peacoat and carrying a Glock 19 with extra ammo. To cover his face, Gonzo gives him a black ski mask with no mouth hole and a pair of aviator sunglasses with reflective mirrored lenses to cover his eyes. Lastly, an all-black fedora. Since he is driving, he will not carry another weapon.

"What is your call sign?" asks Luke.

"I am Silver Fox," responds Stefenski.

"Oh god," says Jeremiah sarcastically.

"Speedy, you're next. I'm last," avers Jeremiah in a strong tone.

Gonzo gets dressed. His disguise consists of black alligator shoes, white dress pants, a black dress shirt with a white tie, and a white three-button dress coat. He had made the suit himself, and it has hidden pockets in many places. He will be carrying a Glock 19 with two extra clips and a black twelve-gauge pistol-grip shotgun with a heat shield and a sling. It holds six rounds of double odd nine-pellet shells. Jerry then slings a brown leather satchel over his head where he puts the two flash grenades, a sting grenade, and twenty-five extra rounds of shotgun ammo. The strap is long but fits in such a way that it stays snug to his hip. Hopefully, the satchel is big enough to hold whatever is in the safety deposit box. He puts on a white ski mask with no mouth hole and also dons blue reflective mirrored aviator sunglasses. To top it off, a white fedora with a black hatband.

"Oh, and this." Jerry pulls a blue cashmere scarf off the hanger rack of the hotel dolly and wraps it around his neck. The blue somehow matches the reflective hues of his aviator sunglasses. It is a beautiful scarf.

"I knew you were using that loom," Jeremiah says with a big smile on his face. Luke giggles. Speedy's shoulders slump slightly.

Even though he is picking on him now, what no one in the room knows is that Jeremiah had come in into the office late one night to pick up the mail. He saw Gonzo making the scarf on the loom while listening to Beethoven's Symphony no. 5 in C Minor. His hand and body movements seemed to be in rhythm with the music; as if he were some mad maestro conducting an orchestra. It was a spectacle. Gonzo is a genius on that thing. Jeremiah keeps this memory to himself.

"And what will be your call sign?" asks Luke.

"I don't know, hombre. I think it is bad luck to give yourself a nickname. You guys choose."

"Jack Frost," says Luke quietly.

"Jack Frost? I like it. Always keepin' it cool," responds Jeremiah with a smirk. They all agree that it is a befitting name. Speedy walks over to the mirror.

Jack Frost, he whispers to himself while looking upon his own reflection. Without looking away he then says, "Jeremiah, you're up." Gonzo then turns back to the dolly and starts removing the remaining items.

On the meeting table, Gonzo lays out several items of apparel. Jeremiah begins to get dressed. He first puts on black dress pants and his father's black leather belt. Then he slips on the brand-new pair of burgundy-colored dress shoes with black laces. He will be wearing a white collared dress shirt with a black tie. After putting on the shirt and tie, Speedy hands him a navy-blue six-button peacoat. Jeremiah puts it on. Gonzo had tailored it to a perfect fit. The buttons are flat, large, round, and dark bronze. They have a skull and crossbones etched into them. He has no idea where Jerry might have gotten them, but they are cool. On the left breast area of the peacoat is where Oscar's war medal is sewn on.

Jeremiah then puts on his father's dark leather shoulder holster over the top of the coat that holds his Colt 45; opposite the holster, there is a dual magazine holder for extra ammo. Gonzo then gives him a brown leather satchel of the likes of which he is wearing. Jeremiah places two flash grenades and a sting grenade in it. He slings it over his head. Luke reaches underneath the table and pulls out the gun Jeremiah will be donning. It is a surprise what Luke hands him. It is a M1928 Thompson submachine gun with a nylon sling—a tommy gun. It has a one-hundred-round drum cylinder.

"That's a lot of lead," says Stefenski.

"We thought that if you were going to send a message, you might as well go all out," says Gonzo.

Jeremiah only responds, "I guess it's time for the mask," as he puts the gun's sling over his head.

Chills run down Jeremiah's spine as he puts the mask on. It seems to fit perfectly; as if it belongs on his face. Speedy tightens the straps for him to make a snug fit. He puts on a gray fedora with a black hatband that Gonzo has modified to fit his head while wearing the mask. He walks over to the mirror. Reflecting back at him is something that scares him to death. Jeremiah Revel has become the very thing he hates the most. He has become his own nightmare. He does not know whether the thing staring back at him is the monster or if the monster is the man behind the mask. But one thing is certain; he now knows why the devil fears God.

"Who are you?" asks Luke like an excited child.

After a brief moment, Jeremiah avers in a strong and almost-vicious tone, "I am the faceless man—the dark side of God's perfect plan. I walk in the shadows so others will not have to. I am the Shadow Walker." He speaks while still fixated on the mirror. The blue eyes staring back at him are cold and icy. He wonders if God is ashamed of him—baffled by his own creation.

"All right, Shadow Man it is. That's a wrap, fellas. Be ready for Monday," says Jerry nervously, in an attempt to snap Jeremiah out of his comatose. But Jeremiah just stares into the mirror. Jerry then takes off his sunglasses, puts his hand on Jeremiah's shoulder, and asks, "Are your all right, hombre?"

Jeremiah slowly turns his head toward him. With his head slightly cocked to the right, he just stares into Gonzo's eyes intently—as if Jeremiah was trying to understand his soul—looking for something that he is not sure exists. Jerry looks away in order to avoid eye contact.

"Heather. Her name is Heather. I love her." Softness and human qualities return to Jeremiah's eyes and voice. He has never spoken of her to the guys before.

"You know, you are scary as shit in that mask," replies Speedy.

Jeremiah puts his hand on Gonzo's shoulder and speaks in a tone that is somewhere in between sadistic and funny. He says, "You should see me without it." Luke giggles.

11

The Blackguards of Charlatan

October 4, 9:35 a.m.

Sometimes people like to roll a loaded dice so they always know what they're going to get. But in the end, they are just cheating their way through life—cheating themselves. And the thrill of uncertainty and chance is lost. Then there are those who walk upon that fence of indifference knowing they will eventually fall to one side or the other; Jeremiah Revel—he likes to roll an honest dice and let it choose for him.

They all sit silently within their own focused meditation. Every creak, squeak, and squeal of the van's suspension is amplified; every bump of *The City* road can be felt. The drone of the tires moving across the pavement seems comforting in some way, as it breaks the silence of their moment of uncertainty.

"Two minutes!" yells Stefenski from the driver's seat.

Looking around, Jeremiah thinks to himself, *We look like a bunch of idiots.* He then smiles to himself under his mask.

"One minute." Stefenski's tone is more assertive with a hint of nervous inflection. It is time to speak.

"Is everyone ready?" Neither Luke nor Gonzo respond. "I asked a question," says Jeremiah in a more aggressive tone. They snap back to reality.

Gonzo and Luke both respond, "Yeah."

"Remember, just stay focused and expect the unexpected. But stick to the plan."

"Thirty seconds." Stefenski's voice is more intense. Luke turns on the signal scrambler and the phone access actuator.

"It is time," says Jeremiah.

All four bow their heads and recite a prayer in unison: *"Angel of God, my guardian dear, to whom God's love commits me here. Ever this day be at my side, to light and guard, to rule and guide. Amen."*

"Go!" yells Stefenski.

They carefully step out of the sliding side door of the van, and casually walk through the front doors of the *People's Trust Company and Bank*. Stefenski drives off with the van.

As they walk into the lobby, everyone seems to be going about their daily business—people making deposits, making withdrawals, attempting to negotiate loans, etc. There is some awfully generic elevator music playing. Jeremiah, Gonzo, and Luke are standing three abreast in front of the main entrance, and no one notices them.

"This is awkward," says Jeremiah to Speedy.

"I want to say it," says Luke.

"No, I want to say it." Gonzo interrupts.

"No, me," responds Luke.

"Will the both of you shut up. I will pull this car over right now," avers Jeremiah in an almost comical tone. He then shouts, "LISTEN UP! THIS WILL ONLY TAKE A SECOND!"

Everyone in the bank suddenly turns their attention to the three hooligans. There are roughly twenty customers in the bank and nine employees. There is no security guard on duty. It is the oldest bank in *The City*. The sun is shining through the arched windows on what would otherwise be a beautiful day for these people. A lady screams; an older woman faints and is caught by a patron.

"Everyone here get on the ground with your hands where I can see them. You"—he points to the managers and tellers—"stand there with your hands up."

A teller in a booth farthest from them can be seen making a motion that resembles one frantically pressing the panic button located underneath their booth's counter.

Jeremiah notices that one of the customers is missing the lower portion of his right arm. He nudges Gonzo, points toward the man, and says to Jerry, "Don't be rude."

Speedy notices and says, "Oh, and you, keep your hand where I can see it." Jeremiah, Gonzo, and Luke all have a brief chuckle.

Everyone obeys except for one man. He is well dressed in an expensive black suit. He is clean-shaven with slightly graying dark hair. Jeremiah tightens his grip and focuses his tommy gun toward the approaching man. All three suspect that he is one of Happy's men. The man stops ten feet from them.

"Who are you affiliated with? What is the name of your operation?" Jeremiah is momentarily taken aback by this question. He looks at Jerry; Jerry looks at Luke, who shrugs his shoulders and looks back at Jeremiah with perplexed body language. In all their planning, they forgot to name their group.

"I am the Shadow Walker."

"I am Jack Frost."

"And I am Pewee the Clown—the mayor of *Butthole Hollow*. Do you want to be my first citizen? Pew, pew, pew, pew." Luke begins to dance around as if he were a sparring boxer-clown and is pretending to shoot his blunderbuss at the man. It is quite a disturbing spectacle.

"We are the Blackguards of Charlatan," says Jeremiah.

Gonzo tilts his head toward Jeremiah and whispers, "Nice one."

The man speaks assertively and with a touch of arrogance. "Do you know what you are doing? Do you know whose bank this is? You are already as good as dead. You're like a dog barking up the wrong tree that you will be hung from." He has a slight smile on his face.

Jeremiah knows he's probably armed. "Who are you, and who do you work for?" asks Jeremiah.

"Let's just say, I am responsible for the interests of a very important individual. You can call me Rudolph Depaulino. And you will see me again in the most unpleasant circumstances."

"I'll look forward to it," responds Jeremiah in a mocking tone. Rudolph begins to laugh redundantly loud.

Jeremiah looks down at his watch before looking back up at Rudolph and says, "I'd like to sit here and chat, but I don't have the time."

He then pulls out his .45 and shoots Rudolph in his right kneecap. The man falls to the ground in agonizing pain. It is one of the most painful nonlethal places to be shot. Many of the bankers and customers alike scream and tremble in fear. Their faces are pale white. Jeremiah nods to Gonzo, and he begins rounding up some of the bankers to take them into the vault where the safety deposit boxes are located.

Jeremiah looks at his watch again. *One minute,* he says to himself. He walks up to Rudolph who is lying on the ground, and holding his knee with both hands. Jeremiah looks down at him and stares at the man with piercing blue eyes. He pulls out his .45 again and puts it against Rudolph's head.

"Fuck you!" yells Rudolph.

Jeremiah pulls the hammer back as he reaches into the man's suit coat. He aggressively removes Rudolph's weapon and slides it toward an empty corner of the bank.

"We will destroy everything you care about!" yells Rudolph nervously.

"You already have," responds Jeremiah (he momentarily thinks of Heather). "You're not worth a bullet. Just tell Mr. Henry that I am coming for him." He uncocks the hammer and walks away.

"Hey, Pewee, it is time. Stand guard. Forty-five seconds."

"Yes, sir, Shadow Man." Pewee then yells to the crowd, "Stay calm, and we can all go home and feed the rabbits!"

Jeremiah exits the bank while shaking his head. The armored vehicle has just pulled up. Right on schedule, Stefenski is driving by in a heavy-duty tow truck. Ironically, the emblem on the side reads, "Happy's Towing Service." He stops quickly and hands Jeremiah a baseball bat. Just as the rear doors of the armored vehicle open, the guards see Jeremiah standing there; a baseball bat clenched in one hand, and his tommy gun in the other. They try and close the doors, but Jeremiah jams the bat in between them before they close. He quickly grabs one of his sting grenades, pulls the pin, and throws it. He can hear the two guards grunt in discomfort. So, he also throws a flash grenade in for good measure. Jeremiah pulls the doors open. The two men exit with their hands up. He disarms them. They are just working men. He instructs them to start walking away, and they listen.

Meanwhile, Stefenski has backed up the tow truck to the front of the armored vehicle. There are a couple of cars in the way, so he has to gently maneuver them out of the way with the front bumper of the tow truck. The driver of the armored vehicle has no idea what to do. As the front wheels rise off the ground, Jeremiah is tapping on the driver's window with the barrel of his tommy gun. If the driver does not exit, they will tow it with him in it and deal with him later. Wisely, the man opens the door and exits with his hands up. Like the others, he is instructed to just walk away.

"Silver Fox, how long?"

"Twenty seconds."

Jeremiah hears several gunshots come from the bank and the distinct sound of the blunderbuss going off.

"That's not good," he says to Stefenski nervously.

He wants to run inside, but that is not part of the plan. Suddenly, Jack Frost and Pewee run out of the front doors. They both hop into the back of the armored truck. Jeremiah follows. They can feel the sway of the armored truck as it is being towed. Jeremiah can see a bloodstain quickly growing on Gonzo's white suit in the area of his right lung. He is breathing with difficulty.

"There was another guy in the vault. He had a gun. He is dead now," says Luke.

The bullet passed through his bulletproof vest. Jeremiah instructs Gonzo to stay still in a comfortable position and for Luke to apply pressure to the wound. The ride to the safe house (an abandoned building near the ports) is only a five-minute ride through a maze of back alleyways that are just wide enough to pass through. Stefenski is a genius. Luke empties one of the bags of cash and tries to soak up some of the blood with it. They don't even notice the fifteen .9999 purity, 400-ounce gold bars sitting on the shelves of the armored vehicle. This endeavor was never about the gold; but it will certainly help.

An Ugly Dog

October 4, 10:04 a.m.

Two men open the garage door to the safe house. Stefenski pulls in with the armored vehicle in tow. He gets out and knocks on one of the back doors of the armored vehicle. Jeremiah opens them.

"We have a problem. It's Frost. He's hit." Jeremiah does not know the two men, so he is still using their call signs.

"Damn it. Is it bad?"

"He needs medical attention stat," responds Jeremiah.

"Where the fuck are we going to go? We can't go to the hospital," says Stefenski.

Meanwhile, Luke is helping Gonzo out of the truck. He is wincing in pain. The bloodstain is growing larger by the minute.

"I have a plan. I need a vehicle. You stay here with Pewee. Follow the itinerary. I'll be in contact with you later."

Stefenski hands Jeremiah the key, then walks over to Jerry. He kisses him on the forehead and says, "I love you, brother. You'll be fine."

Gonzo just nods. It was the first time anyone else but his mother had said that to him.

"Are these guys good?"

"Yes," responds Sonny as he throws them a bag of the cash. They all remove their gear. Jeremiah drives to Paddy's. Telisha lives in the apartment above it.

There is a knock on her door. She does not have visitors often. There is another knock that seems more frantic. Telisha looks out the window. She can see Jeremiah supporting Jerry and his blood-soaked white suit coat. She quickly opens the door.

"What happened, Jer?"

"Telisha, we need your help. Jerry has been shot. It went through his vest."

After the astonishment of the moment wears off, she says both frantically and entreatingly, "I am not a doctor. I am a veterinarian." she responds.

"We cannot go to the hospital. Now, are you going to let us in or are you going to let Gonzo bleed to death out here?"

Reluctantly, she says, "I'll see what I can do."

They enter. Jeremiah is almost fully supporting Speedy at this point.

Her apartment is well-kept, as one assumes a lady's would be. It is adorned with modern decor. She leads them to a back room that resembles an in-house vet clinic.

"I don't know what you guys are up to and I don't want to know."

"That is best," responds Jeremiah.

He helps Gonzo onto a short stainless steel table made, at best, for a large dog. Telisha removes his suit coat and cuts off his dress shirt. Jeremiah helps her remove his bulletproof vest, which has a noticeable bullet hole in it. There is no exit wound. The vest sticks to the coagulated blood around his wound. Speedy lurches and grunts in pain. With every move he makes, more blood comes out.

"You need to lie down now."

He listens. It is hard to breath. She thinks his lung is collapsed. Jeremiah watches as she puts an oxygen mask made for a dog over his face, administers an IV into a vein on his left arm, and then injects a drug that will help him cope with the pain. He hates needles. His biological parents were heroin addicts, but it makes him feel good enough to speak.

Gonzo notices that Telisha has a frightened look on her face. He wants to comfort her.

"Am I going to make it? You don't have to answer. I'm just glad that if I go, the last thing I see on this earth is your eyes and your pretty smile."

Telisha smiles and says, "You know you are the ugliest dog I ever treated?"

Gonzo smiles and asks, "Can I have a kiss?"

She bends down and gives him a short, soft kiss on the lips. He smiles again and falls asleep.

Telisha grabs her hemostats and places them into the wound.

"That is good."

"What is good?" asks Jeremiah.

"It is a shallow wound. It did not penetrate his lung, but the impact collapsed it. The vest saved his life." She pulls out the bullet. Luckily, it is still fully intact. "I hope this is long enough," she says as she pushes a tube into Jerry's air pipe. She then takes a syringe and puts a needle into his lung. "He will be fine."

Jeremiah cringes, then puts his hand on her shoulder and says, "Thank you, Telisha. You saved his life."

As she prepares to sew up Gonzo's wound, he walks into her living room and turns on her TV.

Jeremiah intently watches the "Breaking News Bulletin" on channel 4. He doesn't have a feeling of pride as one would normally have watching their crime on TV. He is more interested to find out what information is being made to the public and how well their plan was executed. Channel 4's opening music montage plays as the red banner reads "Breaking News" in white letters.

"Good morning, I am Walter Lexington."

"And I am Norma Price. The time is 11:03 a.m., and this is a special breaking news bulletin."

"We have breaking news out of the northwest side of The City. The People's Trust Company and Bank was robbed by three men in masks, with a possible fourth accomplice, early this morning. It is unclear why the police were never called, but several witnesses report that all of the phones suddenly and mysteriously stopped working while the perpetrators robbed the bank. The robbers did not make out with any cash, however, because of two brave men who stood up to them, possibly saving innocent patrons and employees from harm, while scaring off the villains. Norma."

"Thanks, Walter. Witnesses report that one of the men, a well-known and respected local named Rudolph Depaulino, was wounded and another unnamed man was killed during their heroic actions to thwart the robbery. It is believed that one of the assailants was also wounded, as witnesses report a large bloodstain developing on the robber's chest. Police are scouring local hospitals and clinics in search of the man."

"We will provide you with more information as it becomes available."

"There is no mention of the armored truck. That is interesting," Jeremiah mumbles under his breath. This does not surprise him.

They had actually planned on it. Happy Hal owns *The City Tribunal* and the various news stations throughout *The City*. Somehow his goons are now heroes and saviors of the day because no money was taken; it's a cover up, of course. They would never admit that someone had pulled a fast one on Happy Hal, or they would end up in a barrel at the bottom of a lake.

Jeremiah suddenly notices that Telisha is standing next to him. He quickly walks up and turns off the TV. He makes direct eye contact with her.

Suddenly, she says, "He's all patched up. I reinflated his lung. He's going to be very sore for the next couple of weeks. Can I ask you a question, Jeremiah?"

"You can ask whatever you want, but it doesn't mean you'll get an answer," responds Jeremiah.

"Am I going to get paid to be your guy's personal and secret physician?"

"Oh yeah. Your silent services will be handsomely rewarded," he says with a slight smirk.

Telisha smiles. "You can leave him here overnight. Just help me get him into the spare bedroom." Jeremiah helps Telisha, thanks her, then leaves for the office.

The Contents of the Satchel

October 4, 12:01 p.m.

Jeremiah ditched the car in an alleyway; he left it running with the keys in it. Hopefully, someone will steal it. He walked several blocks, then stopped to get a couple of hot dogs at Warren's *Try My Sausage* street vendor stand. There was a long line, but Warren immediately had them ready for Jeremiah. They were delicious and somehow comforting. Warren knew something was off with Jeremiah and asked if he was okay. Jeremiah just nodded and gave him a five-dollar tip. A block from the office, there is an elderly woman with a wooden cane attempting to cross the street via the crosswalk. She is very slow, and a couple of cars are honking because the light has already turned green. Jeremiah offers her a hand and guides her across the street while giving a death stare to those who had honked. By the time he makes his way back across the street, the light is red. Jeremiah pulls out his locking pocketknife and jams it into the sidewall of the driver's side tire of one of the cars that had honked at the elderly woman; he then just walks away as the driver watches in disbelief.

Luke and Stefenski are at the office when he enters. They have already cleaned up and followed the itinerary perfectly despite the unforeseen circumstance of Gonzo being shot.

"How is he?" asks Sonny.

"Better than expected," responds Jeremiah.

"Good. The rabbits were worried," says Luke.

The satchel with the contents of *Safety Deposit Box 263* is sitting on the meeting table. It is stained with random spots of absorbed and dried blood spatter. Jeremiah unclasps its cover and looks inside as Luke and Stefenski observe with nervous anticipation. He pulls out a handwritten note written in flawless cursive; a small black leather-bound notebook; and a cardboard cylinder. Outside, Jeremiah can hear a cat meowing in the alleyway.

"Luke, go feed Dog." Luke goes to the fridge and pulls out a small fish, as well as bowl of milk. He opens the door and leaves it on the steps leading up to the office.

Jeremiah first reads aloud the note:

> *If you are reading this, you found the safe. Your life is in grave danger. I am probably in a barrel sitting at the bottom of the lake or riding the trains. The enclosed notebook is my journal—most of which is just written nonsense of my daily life and some poems. Tear out the last page to keep, and give the rest of it to my wife if possible. Good luck, stranger, and God bless.*
>
> C. H. Billingsly

"Luke, burn this." He hands the note to Luke. Luke puts it in an old tin coffee can, then lights a match from a *Renee's Diner* matchbook and throws it in. Jeremiah skims through the journal and tears out the last page that shows any evidence of written content. It is a cryptic code of Roman numeral numbers. They are written in pencil and look as if they were written in haste; the handwriting is much sloppier than that of the rest of the diary. On the reverse side is a cryptic poem that reads as follows:

> *Four score, year of our lord,*
> *Four more, we cut the cord,*
> *At the apple tree, we'll arrive,*
> *Will we walk, or will we drive?*
> *Can't we all be regal?*

The Roman numerals read, *"I, II, VII, VIII, XV, XVI, XXV, XXX."*

Luke looks at it for a moment. He then says, "The Roman numerals each represent a word of importance in the poem. Let me see. It would be four and score—eighty, four, apple, tree, drive, and regal—the Regal Estates."

"It is an address," says Stefenski. "Eighty-four Apple Tree Drive, in the Regal Estates. I know exactly where that place is. It is more of a compound than an estate," he says excitedly. In moments such as these, Jeremiah is glad he has the team he has. It would have taken him forever to figure that out, if not never.

"Well done, fellas," Jeremiah says as he pops the lid off the cardboard cylinder. He pulls from it several documents; fifteen to be exact. They are all Quit Claim Deeds with the grantee being Dynamix-Burr Corp. The signature of the executor of the corporation is one R. J. Henry. Most of the properties are in the *Regal Estates* area of *The City*, but there also are several factories in the *Northern Ports* included. All the dates of execution are between fifteen and twenty years old, and the grantors vary. However, one of them catches Jeremiah's eye— *Sebastian W. Undertakker.*

"Didn't that Billingsly guy write about missing pages from the courthouse deed books?" asks Jeremiah.

Luke quickly goes to the filing cabinet and skims through a manila file folder. "It's 376–391 in book 6810," responds Luke as he looks up; his eyes are magnified through his thick glasses.

"I think Billingsly took them for whatever reason."

"Do you want me to burn them?" asks Luke.

Jeremiah responds with a smirk, "No, these are legal documents. We wouldn't want to do anything illegal."

Jeremiah and Stefenski burst out laughing. Luke giggles. It has been a short but long day. They all need a laugh.

"We will return them to the courthouse via the mail."

They all go up to the roof of the office. For once, Luke partakes in a glass of whiskey with Jeremiah and Sonny. They are all silent, staring toward *The City* skyline.

Then, softly from the bathtub Luke says, "The rabbits are sad. Pewee the Clown killed a man today. He blunderbussted him. He had to save Mr. Frost."

Jeremiah would have never dreamt of the day that the kind and softhearted Luke Treadwell would be the first of them to have to take a life.

He looks back at Luke and says, "It's okay that the rabbits are sad. It was not Pewee's choice. Pewee never wanted violence."

Luke begins to cry for a moment, but suddenly stops and says, "You know how they say a bullet sounds the same in every language. Well, so does a handshake. But the rabbits aren't going to shake hands with the devil. So a bullet it is."

12

Dominick Shaw

October 5, 9:37 a.m.

"Sir, here is the security footage."

There is a man sitting at a large maple wood desk with a dark walnut stain. His hair is silver in color, but he has a younger-looking face. His eyes are dark brown and stern.

"We found where they tapped into the underground phone lines. Most of the security footage is compromised and useless, but there is one short clip of them."

"Leave," says Happy as he motions with his hand. He wants to watch this alone. He watches the seventy-eight-inch TV built into the wall with an aggravated disposition.

He clenches his fist as he sees the image of the men, particularly the Shadow Walker. Happy knew this day would come.

"Copycat bastard," he says in an almost prideful tone.

The clip is just ten seconds long and only shows the Blackguards of Charlatan enter the bank before the camera shuts off. He then presses the red button on his intercom to contact his receptionist.

"Melanie, can you give Mr. Dominick Shaw a call? Tell him I have a proposal of the nature that will befit his 'delicate talents.' We need to meet ASAP."

"Yes, Father," responds the voice on the other end.

"Thank you, sweetie." Happy leans back in his brown leather chair with his arms raised and hands clasped behind his head.

"Dad, he just walked in," she responds, roughly fifteen seconds later. (Shaw knew his services would be needed and showed up on his own accord.)

"Send him in."

Happy Hal is not a good man. He has more blood on his hands than even the most exaggerated estimates of those who keep tabs on things of that nature. However, Dominick Shaw is a monster. He has no concept of empathy; he has no rules. He just kills for fun. But that being said, how many people get paid to do what they truly love?

The large oak door opens. Shaw walks in casually but with implicit authority. He is a tall yet stocky man. His hands are abnormally large, even for a man his size. By Happy's estimate, he is in his early forties but never cares to ask. And as customary to every other time they have met, he is wearing an all-gray suit, a white undershirt, and a mauve-colored silk tie. Happy has a can of SPAM waiting for him, sitting at the edge of his desk. Shaw looks uncomfortable as he tries to work himself into the leather desk chair that is observantly too small for his frame. After he settles, Shaw pops open the can of SPAM, and starts eating it with his hands.

"SPAM is a lot like our meetings, Mr. Henry. Every time, it gets better and better for Dominick," says Shaw deeply and slowly in a thick Russian accent.

"I'm sure you understand the precarious nature of this negotiation," responds Happy as he hands him the security footage recording. "Fix it, and find my gold. I want them to suffer."

Shaw finishes chewing the last piece of SPAM, and, after obnoxiously licking his fingers, says, "Of course. What do you think I'm going to do? Read 'em a bedtime story and smother 'em with a pillow?"

He then points his index finger at Happy with his thumb raised, as if mimicking a pistol. Shaw pulls his thumb back with his other hand and makes a noise similar to a gun cocking. And with a pretentious smirk on his face that Happy does not care for, Shaw says, "You know the difference between me and you, Mr. Henry? I have no enemies." He then gets up and leaves without saying another word.

Pathos and Void

October 6, 6:50 a.m.

Telisha is checking in on Jerry. She does not have the proper equipment to monitor a human, so her mind is preoccupied with her patient; she cannot sleep. Gonzo opens his eyes, and sees Telisha sitting in the chair next to his bed with her legs crossed. He stares at her for a moment.

"I must have died and gone to heaven because I see an angel," he says, followed by a smile and a couple of coughs that cause excruciating pain.

"Stop it. I'm not going to restitch your wound. I'm too tired." They are silent for a moment, until Jerry speaks without looking at her.

"You know when you were working on me, I remember staring at your ceiling. I remembered how when I was a child, I would wake up in the morning looking up at the ceiling of my real mom's house. And I'd wonder how they made the ceiling look like popcorn." Gonzo smirks slightly—a smile that holds no happiness.

"I used to pretend I was a bird, and the bumps were great mountain passes. I could fly high wherever I pleased—far away from where I was. I was free for a moment. Then my mom would wake up, get high, and tell me why I should be ashamed of being born." Gonzo gathers himself for a moment. "So when you were working on me, all those feelings came back, and I just wanted to die instead of feeling ashamed. But then I saw your smile. I felt your kiss. I had no pain. I had no fear. I only had your soft lips. Everything else was pathos and void.

"Somos todo marionets en este mundo. Pero eres mi amor. Por lo tanto, debo luchar para vivir," he mumbles to himself as he falls back asleep. Telisha cries, gets up, and kisses him on the cheek. She readjusts his blanket and goes back to bed herself.

Looking Evil in the Eye

October 6, 12:35 p.m.

Jeremiah is at Paddy's having a drink before he goes to visit Gonzo. Al is behind the bar. He is in good spirits.

"I can't believe someone had the chutzpah to try and pull one off against *The Harvest Union*," says Al while making an upward motion as if he were crushing a man's nuts with his hand.

"What's the word?" asks Jeremiah.

Al slowly scans the bar in both directions, leans close to Jeremiah and whispers, "Word is you, ah, or I mean they, did not rob the bank but stole a fortune in gold." Jeremiah looks at Al with an inquisitive look. Al responds, "Aye, I figured it was you is all. I listen. I don't talk unless it is necessary. But answer me this. How did it feel to pop a cap in that son of a bitch's knee?" Jeremiah nods, and Al bursts out in joyful laughter.

Suddenly, they are distracted and both look up at the ceiling. There are footsteps in the apartment above that do not seem right. They are heavy and would not come from Telisha. Al and Jeremiah both look at each other with concern.

"Is that Jerry?" asks Al.

"I don't think so," responds Jeremiah.

Al stands up, and grabs a double-barreled shotgun from underneath the counter.

"Dixie Jane, watch the bar for a minute." They both exit hastily. Quietly, they make their way up the steps in the side alley to Telisha's apartment.

"You wait outside as backup," says Jeremiah to Al.

"Aye," says Al softly as he nods in agreement.

The apartment door is slightly ajar as if someone left it that way on purpose. It creaks as he slowly pushes it open. The sun is shining brilliantly, engulfing the apartment in vibrant hues while exacerbating every shadow. Jeremiah enters with his .45 drawn. Immediately to the left, Jerry and Telisha are sitting at the dining room table. There is an empty can of SPAM resting on it and a man in a gray suit sitting behind it with his legs crossed. He has a Glock with a silencer pressed against Telisha's head. He will never forget the look of terror on her face. Gonzo is passive, as he is still medicated. He is slightly hunched over.

"Hello, Mr. Shadow Walker. You are a hard man to find."

"Why are you here? These people have nothing to do with him."

"I suggest you holster you weapon, Mr. Shadow Walker." He sticks his hand in the empty can of SPAM, then smells his fingers without looking away from Jeremiah. Jeremiah recognizes his eyes. He saw them in the mirror as his own during the dress rehearsal when he first put on the mask. They are absent of human qualities. Even the animals will treat each other with more sympathy when they hunt and kill their prey. Jeremiah is looking into the eyes of evil.

Jeremiah holsters his weapon.

"Mr. Shadow Walker, I do not want to be here today. I was on vacation. Sit, sit. Let's talk business. I am being paid a lot of money to have this conversation."

Jeremiah sits while never looking away from him. "I'd rather you pointed that gun at me."

"Ah, we have a noble fool among us. You see, Mr. Walker, men will die for foolish causes. Men will fight for foolish causes. Men will kill for foolish causes. Mine is more of a monetary influence. Does not a man need to make a living?" the man asks.

"What is your name?" asks Jeremiah sternly.

"I am Dominick Shaw." He pulls the hammer back on his Glock. "Ticktock, says the Glock, as the man on the moon adjusts his clock." Shaw's eyes are evil and dark. They lust for blood, as if it is their only sustenance.

"Let me ask you a question, Mr. Dominick Shaw," says Jeremiah.

Shaw looks at his watch and smiles. "You get one."

"Why does the devil fear God?"

Shaw looks at him perplexed and starts laughing sadistically. "Goodbye, Mr. Shaw," says Jeremiah as Al rushes in. He pulls both triggers of the side-by-side double-barreled shotgun. Shaw's head explodes into a hodgepodge of flesh and blood. His brain matter sticks to the back wall of the kitchen. Telisha screams. There is blood splattered on her face. Jeremiah just sits there staring. He will not say a prayer for that man. Al is shaking as he is still pointing the gun at what is left of Shaw.

"Nice one," says Gonzo.

Jeremiah picks up the empty can of SPAM. "I'm going to call Stefenski. He knows someone who will take care of this mess. Al, go back down to the bar and try and act like nothing happened. Gonzo, take Telisha to the armory for now. Things are getting a little chaotic."

Al takes the two spent shotgun casings out of the gun, throws them at the body, and pulls two new ones out of the breast pocket of his shirt; he reloads the weapon and says, "I don't know what you got us into, but finish it." Jeremiah nods.

Jeremiah leaves, calls Stefenski from a pay phone, then walks a couple of blocks to the post office. He arrives and asks for a small box, a pen, and a piece of paper. He places the empty can of SPAM in the box and leaves a short note inside. It reads:

I'm coming.

—*The Shadow Walker*

He asks for overnight delivery and mails the can, stuffed with the note, to Eighty-Four Apple Tree Drive, Regal Estates.

Secrets and Repose

October 6, 2:33 p.m.

Jeremiah decides to check in on Heather. He cannot fathom how Shaw located them so quickly; but if he can then others can. Heather is off from work today and should be home. As he walks, Jeremiah is constantly looking over his shoulder to make sure he is not being followed.

The elevator ride to the tenth floor seems like an eternity. The same music is playing as usual. There is a ding, and the elevator doors open. As Jeremiah approaches Heather's apartment door he notices it is slightly ajar.

"Damn it," he says as he pulls out his .45, kicks open the door, and rushes in. He moves quick and checks every room. She is nowhere to be found. Jeremiah is starting to panic when he hears something in the living room. He rushes out. Heather is standing in the doorway; he immediately lowers his gun.

"What the fuck, Jeremiah? What is wrong with you?"

"Are you okay?" he responds with relief.

"Yes, I was taking the garbage to the incinerator. I come back, and you are pointing a gun at me. It seems like every other time you come here, you have that gun in your hand. I can't do this." She starts to cry.

"We need to talk," says Jeremiah sternly.

He tells her everything in great detail. It is necessary that she knows. He decided so on the walk over. She takes it pretty well. Jeremiah has a feeling of relief and tranquility that somehow befuddles him; as if a portion of some heavy weight that he didn't know he carried has been lifted from his shoulders.

"It is almost over," he says.

She hugs him and says, "I know you have to do this. My tears will not help you. Just don't lose yourself in this, lose that sweet and caring man I love. And no more secrets. There is no need to lie to me. I am not your enemy." She kisses him on the forehead.

"Pack a bag. I know a safe place for now. You have to come with me. You are not safe here until this is finished."

They take the bus to ensure that they are surrounded by the public; what better place is there to hide than in plain sight? It is a short but solemn ride. Jeremiah and Heather hold hands, but they don't say a word. He is not sure why she is supporting him. It is as if she has hopped onboard this ship with him, and if it goes down, she's decided they will go down together. And if one of them falls overboard, the other will be there to throw the rescue rope. Heather is stronger than she leads people on to believe.

The Armory: A Lady's Paradise

October 6, 5:27 p.m.

Jeremiah is carrying Heather's bag as they walk through the side door of the office. Stefenski is sitting at one of the steel-type factory-style desks with his feet resting atop it. Ironically, he is drinking a *Harvest Union Oktoberfest* beer. Luke is walking down the stairs.

When Stefenski sees the pretty girl with Jeremiah, he immediately gets up and says, "You must be Heather," as he gently shakes her hand.

Jeremiah gives Luke and Sonny a short introduction, then asks, "Are Jerry and Telisha in the armory?"

"Yes," says Luke, "in the living quarters. Follow me."

"Nice to meet you," says Heather cordially to Stefenski.

They make their way up to the armory. Luke pushes open the heavy door. "Not many people are allowed in here, not even the rabbits," says Luke.

Heather looks at Jeremiah with a perplexed look on her face. He whispers in her ear, "Don't worry. Just never question the rabbits." She nods.

The first room of the armory is the arsenal, and it is quite large. It is mostly adorned with stainless steel. On the right wall, there is a cache of assault rifles, long-range rifles, shotguns, and submachine guns hanging—all of which are well manicured. There is a special section that holds the weapons they had used at the bank. Below the hanging guns is a countertop with an assortment of pistols and revolvers neatly organized atop it. Underneath the countertop is where the ammo boxes are located—thousands of rounds of varying caliber. There is also a workstation area designated for cleaning and maintaining the equipment. On the left wall is the tactical equipment (i.e., flash grenades, tear gas, bulletproof vests, utility belts, etc.). To the rear of the of the room is another heavy steel door. There is an alphanumeric keypad.

"Follow me," says Luke as he makes a waving motion with his hand. "This door can only be opened from the outside with one code. Rabbits2AreRogue." Luke puts in the code and the door creaks open. "Now, every door can be mechanically opened from the inside from this turn wheel. You are not a prisoner here." He points to the steel wheel on the rear side of the door that is reminiscent to one you would find on a vault.

They walk into the next corridor. It is a short hallway about twenty feet deep and six feet wide. Directly to the right is a doorway of the small room that resembles a holding cell. There is a stainless steel toilet and sink inside.

I hope that is not the bathroom, Heather thinks to herself.

There is also another door to the left with an alphanumeric keypad; Luke does not elaborate on its purpose. At the end of the hallway is another steel door. "The code is the same for this one, Rabbits2AreRogue. These are your living quarters," says Luke as he enters the code. The door clicks open.

Telisha and Gonzo greet them as they enter.

"I'll leave you to get acquainted," says Luke as he quickly walks away while closing the door behind him. Telisha is holding Stefenski's daughter. Heather's heart melts. (She still doesn't think it is the right time to tell Jeremiah that she is pregnant.)

The living quarters are quite nice. The main room upon entering is the dining and kitchenette area. There is a gas stove, cabinets stuffed with high-end pots and pans, a refrigerator, and an assortment of appliances sitting on the countertop. The drawers are stuffed with cooking utensils and silverware. Gonzo is sitting at a round dining room table making a list of groceries and other commodities the girls will need.

He's doing pretty well, Jeremiah thinks to himself.

There are two bedrooms that abut the kitchen—one to the left and one to the right. There is a large full bathroom and even a washroom. The place resembles a high-end and fully loaded condo. There is even a common room with leather couches and there are TVs in every room. The ladies will be very comfortable here.

"Let's vamoose, Speedy."

"Roger dodger," responds Gonzo; he winces under his breath as he gets up from the table. "We will have your groceries by the end of the night. The security camera is channel thirty-seven dash one. Do not open the door for anyone but us." Jerry and Telisha exchange a quick kiss on the lips. They both smile. Jeremiah smirks briefly, but he does not have time for feelings right now. He kisses Heather's soft lips before him and Gonzo leave.

Downstairs, Luke, Gonzo, Stefenski, and Jeremiah have a short discussion.

They are all pretty tired from the events of the day and agree to meet again as a group the next afternoon at 2:00 p.m. sharp. Stefenski and Luke are going to sleep on a cot and air mattress, respectively, in the office. It is a cold night and they are going to fire up the wood-burning stove that Luke had insisted they install. It is against city code, but fuck 'em. Jeremiah and Speedy are going to go to *The Main Street Food Market* to get food for the girls before it closes.

They are about to leave when Gonzo suddenly stops them. "Do you know what I just realized?" After a brief pause Speedy says, "We are all millionaires."

They all look at each other as if they are in a Mexican stand-off—perplexed and confused as of how none of them have thought of that yet. Then they all start laughing. Luke giggles.

The Messenger and the Thief

October 7, 1:59 p.m.

What is the opposite of a nightmare? Is not a nightmare a dream? Why must we label one as such and not the other? Maybe all dreams are nightmares—electronic pulses in the form of images and sounds of things we often cannot remember nor describe. But we are always polarized by our own subconscious creation. We are either glad we've awakened or disappointed we can't go back to sleep.

They are standing around the meeting table, eating the last morsels of their sandwiches. The girls came down fifteen minutes before and left them each a sandwich, a pickle wedge, and a glass of cold milk. Heather made Jeremiah his favorite—salami on white bread with black olives, white American cheese, and mayonnaise on both the top and bottom slices of the bread.

"Why do sandwiches always taste better when someone else makes them?" asks Stefenski as he licks his fingers.

By now Jeremiah is looking at his watch. "It is time," he says.

"*Operation Bait and Switch* was perfectly executed despite a couple of mishaps. All the files related to it can be burned." Jeremiah nods toward Luke. "Now we need an exit strategy from these unforeseen repercussions. The most important thing we can do now is stick together and control the chaos. And use it as a weapon of our own device, for our own advantage in this endeavor we must face. Our budget is no longer a question. There are no more excuses. Now I know that my intentions may seem driven by revenge, and part of that might be true. But we all know that we must see this through to the end. Or we and those we love the most will end up hurt, or even worse, dead."

There is suddenly a quick and light knock on the side door of the office. Jeremiah is in no mood and does not check the security monitor before he opens it with his .45 drawn. Looking straight down the barrel of Jeremiah's gun is a small boy. He is ten years old at most. He does not seem frightened by the gun pointing at him. He is wearing a newsboy-style gray apple hat over his red hair. His brown coat is worn and torn in several places. He is more than likely a child of the streets but looks in good health.

"Geez, mister, that is no way to greet someone who knocks on your door."

Jeremiah holsters his gun, then leans out the door and scans the alleyway. His eyes return to the boy. "Who are you?" he asks.

"My name is Jasper, Jasper McBride, mister. But most people call me Redd with two *d*'s," responds the boy in a thick Irish accent.

"What do you want, Redd?"

"Some slicker in a fancy suit paid me ten sawbucks to come here and deliver this." The boy reaches deep into one of his pockets and pulls out a folded piece of paper, and a small package wrapped in a brown paper bag. He hands the note and package to Jeremiah. "The slicker was also wearing a Rolex," says Redd as he is proudly holding up the watch to show Jeremiah. He has a clever little smile on his face. Jeremiah first reads the letter:

Mr. Shadow Walker,

We must meet to discuss business as gentlemen. Saint Paul's Cathedral, 11:00 p.m. tonight.

—Happy Hal

It was the church his father's funeral was held in. Jeremiah crumples the note in his hand. He then unrolls the package and opens the brown paper bag. Inside is his mother's broach that he had left in the pocket of his father's police coat at *The Museum*. Jeremiah stares at it for a brief moment.

"Are you hungry?" he asks the boy.

"Yessir," replies Redd.

"Before you come in, I want my watch back."

"Ah, it is a shitty *Time Saver* anyway," the boy responds as he hands back Jeremiah's watch. He has that same clever smile on his face.

"Come in."

Jeremiah uses the intercom to page the girls. "We have a hungry boy down here. Can you make some food? Someone will come up and get it."

"No problem. Give me a couple of minutes." The voice on the other end is Heather's.

"Sit here," Jeremiah says to the boy as he points to a stool sitting at the meeting table. Stefenski, Luke, and Speedy all stare at the boy.

"Who is he?" asks Gonzo finally.

"He's probably your long-lost son looking for his daddy. His name is Redd. That's two *d*'s," says Jeremiah with a smile on his face.

"Ready," responds a voice on the intercom. Stefenski has a chuckle.

Redd is observantly very hungry. They let him eat the sandwiches the girls have made for him before they ask further questions. In the meantime, Jeremiah explains the note and the broach to the crew. The boy devours the food, as if he will never eat again.

"You're the Blackguards of Charlatan, aren't you? I heard about you. The word on the street is that you are a wild bunch." None of the men acknowledge his question.

"Who's talking?" asks Gonzo.

"Mostly the vags and junkies in *Skid Row*. They say you are evil. Me, I just think you are doing what you think is right. But that is not saying much from a nine-year-old messenger boy and thief." He laughs. The boy is very wise for his age.

"I only have two questions for you, Mr. Shadow Walker. Are you going to go?"

"Maybe," replies Jeremiah. He seems to be thinking about something else.

"And the other question is, What is *rule number 3?*"

All the men laugh. Redd smiles, gets up, and starts walking toward the door.

"If you are ever hungry, there is always food here," says Jeremiah before the boy makes it out the door. "Just hit the buzzer on the intercom next time."

"Thanks, mister."

Family

October 7, 5:47 p.m.

They are all on the roof—Jerry, Telisha, Luke, Stefenski, Jeremiah, and Heather. It is a rare, warm October day. The sunset is brilliant. Stefenski is cradling his daughter. She is softly asleep. The skyline looks as if it is a dark void—a jagged black contour that meets a vibrant hodgepodge of hues that will make God proud of his own creation. The mood is one of solemn comfort. Not much is spoken. How much can one ask of happiness without asking too much?

For once, Jeremiah realizes that he is surrounded by his family. These people are his world. He spent such a long time foolishly thinking that no one cared. He was so scared to let anyone in after his parents died and Heather moved away. She must have climbed back over the wall he had built when he wasn't looking. Women are sneaky like that.

People always say that there is calm before the storm. And sometimes, we take sayings for granted; yet each one holds some truth. This life is not a fairy tale. Like his father, he will become a monster, if necessary, to protect the good things that live inside of those he loves. Everyone deserves their own truth. This is his truth.

Luke drags over a barrel. He builds a fire. The temperature is dropping quickly.

"There is a cold front coming," he says as he scans the horizon while feeling the crisp breeze in his face. "We might get an early snow."

Jeremiah has not decided yet whether he will meet with Happy at the church. However, his inquisitive nature will probably get the best of him; he wants to know what Happy has to say.

All of them stare at the dancing flames, as if mesmerized by their chaotic rhythm. Heather has her head leaning against Jeremiah's shoulder. No one speaks until sometime later when Jeremiah breaks the silence.

"I'm going. Stefenski, I want high ground in the bell tower."

Nothing more is said.

St. Paul's Cathedral

October 7, 10:03 p.m.

Jeremiah has not walked through the arched doors of the church since his mother's funeral. He has no grievance against God, he just hasn't had anything to say to him. The large door creaks as he slowly pulls it open. The sound echoes off the marble arches as if they ruefully whisper, *Where have you been?* Father Winter is walking towards him down the center aisle of the pews as Jeremiah enters. Behind Father Winter and to the right of a stained glass window is a corpus crucifix suspended on the wall. It is as if the eyes of God are staring upon them and keeping a watchful eye. They meet almost exactly halfway down the middle aisle of the cathedral.

"Hello, Father Winter," says Jeremiah as he extends his left hand to shake Father Winter's. Everyone knows that the preacher's right arm was paralyzed in *The Christmas Eve Massacre*. He keeps his hand in his pocket most of the time both to stabilize it, and keep somewhat of a normal posture.

"Hello, Mr. Jeremiah Revel. Are you surprised I remember you?" he says with a smile and in the same rumbling euphonic timbre that Jeremiah remembers. It gives him chills.

"I knew someday you would return to the church. I just did not know under what circumstances. You look like you have something troubling on your mind. Come with me." He motions with his left hand for Jeremiah to follow him. Jeremiah checks his watch: 10:10 p.m. They both take a seat in the front row of the pews, sitting almost directly in front of the crucifix statue.

"What is on your mind, young man?"

Jeremiah hesitates for a moment, then says, "Father Winter, I really don't have much to say. One must do what they think is right. Otherwise, are they not lying to themselves?"

"Ah, Jeremiah, you were always full of riddles. But what is a riddle without an answer?" They both spoke while looking up at the crucifix. The preacher continues:

"There once was a stray dog that would roam through the alleyways surrounding this cathedral. I never paid him much attention. Stray dogs are so common in *The City*. They are so hungry. They will eat anything. This particular dog was a mutt. One could not tell its breed. His hair was matted, but otherwise he seemed to be in good health. One day, I was walking down the south alleyway when that dog came up to me limping. He had a small blanket in his mouth. He sat in front of me. It looked as if he had been in a pretty vicious fight recently. He had many bite marks and scars on him. He suddenly gave me his paw. I noticed that in between two of his paw pads was lodged a canine tooth from another dog. It must have been causing him such discomfort and excruciating pain. With some force, I was able to dislodge it. It was difficult, you know, using one arm and all. The dog seemed to instantly feel better. He rubbed his head on my leg as if he were giving me a thank-you hug. That is when I noticed he was wearing tags. I read the address of the owner. It was only about two blocks away. I decided to pay the owners a visit and tell them that I had found their dog." The preacher laughs for a moment. Jeremiah does not know why.

"An old man opened the door and informed me he was indeed the owner. He said, *'I know exactly where Caesar is. He's in the alleyway behind the cathedral. Every time I'd bring him back here for the last month or so, he would find a way to escape and go back to that same alley. He's a good dog. The door is always open here, but he refuses. So I leave him food.'* I'm not sure why I thought this at the time, but it just seemed as if there was more to this mutt than met the eye." The preacher pauses for a moment in silent reflection, then continues.

"About a week later, I was coming home from the market with some groceries when I heard a ruckus around the next corner. Upon turning it, I saw *Caesar the Mutt* with his teeth clenched around the neck of another stray dog. He did not let go until the other dog was limp and lifeless. It was vicious. There was blood everywhere. There was a small frightened kitten meowing on the ground, covered in what seemed to be the other dog's blood. *Caesar the Mutt*, after viciously killing this other stray dog, suddenly began licking the kitten clean. He gently picked it up in his mouth and carried it to a small wooden vegetable crate with a blanket in it. The same one I saw him carrying the week before. The crate was protected by the elements by an awning above it. *Caesar the Mutt* then just curled up in front of it, maybe waiting for the next predator. When I accidentally got too close to the carcass, *Caesar the Mutt* growled, as if he wanted the carcass of the dog to sit there as a warning to others.

"The point is, Jeremiah Revel, violence is awful. *Caesar the Mutt* had a comfortable life where he was living with his owner. Whether it be natural instinct or born of divine circumstance, he chose to protect those kittens. Even if it meant killing not by choice but necessity. And possibly dying in the process." Father Winter then takes a deep breath and slowly looks up toward the corpus crucifix. He exhales as if disappointed and says, "Self-sacrifice is inevitable to those who give a damn about anything. To the rest, well, they are just puppets. Jeremiah, you were not confirmed nor baptized, right? But you were born because of God's love. And that is enough."

Jeremiah—entrenched in his own thoughts—suddenly looks at his watch, then stands up. He only nods to Father Winter as he turns and walks away toward the marble arched doors of the cathedral's exit and away from the corpus crucifix; there is a cache of words on the tip of his tongue that will go forever unspoken. He has decided that he has nothing to say of God, nor pray to a pagan carving of Nazarene's sacrifice that was donated to St. Paul's Cathedral, as the plaque near the entrance reads, by the generous estate of one R. James Henry.

Renee's Diner

October 7, 10:51 p.m.

After calling Stefenski about the change of plans, Jeremiah stops in *Renee's Diner* for some coffee and a turkey sandwich on rye. He chooses a booth next to the window with a yellow neon sign reading *"Hot Coffee." Renee's* is reminiscent of an old-fashioned diner without attempting to be. Most of the decor is original to its construction. The colors are drab and the stainless steel countertop is worn; but the food is consistently good and fairly priced. There is always the stale smell of cigarette smoke in the air. Smoking was banned in restaurant establishments some time ago, but *Renee's* was grandfathered in. Harriet has been working here for umpteen years and doesn't even take Jeremiah's order. He can remember her looking exactly the same as she did when he used to come here with his parents. She begins to pour his coffee.

"Jeez, you don't look right, kid. You got something on your mind? And what's with the all black?"

"I was born not looking right," responds Jeremiah quickly and with a smirk on his face. "I am fine. Thanks, Harriet."

She is right. He is wearing all black—dress shirt, tie, long peacoat, dress pants, fedora, and hatband. Even his coffee is black. However, he is wearing his signature burgundy shoes as a nice complement of color.

"I thought you would dress more discreetly, Mr. Shadow Walker," says a well-dressed man who is suddenly getting into Jeremiah's booth opposite of him. He knows who it is. He could have guessed so even without Mrs. Olejniczak's photo.

"Hello, Mr. Henry," responds Jeremiah. They both stare into each other's eyes as if trying to gauge each other's courage. Each of them have their hands in lightly clenched fists while resting them on the table.

"I like the can of SPAM. It was a nice touch. Dominick Shaw was a longtime client of ours. We go way back." Jeremiah continues to stare and does not say a word. "You probably don't like me very much. I don't like you. We have that in common, Mr. Shadow Walker."

"Sir, would you like to order anything?" Harriet interrupts as she puts the turkey sandwich in front of Jeremiah.

"No, ma'am, I'm only going to be here a minute," responds Happy without ever looking away from Jeremiah.

"Great, another big spender," mumbles Harriet to herself as she walks away. Happy continues in a mocking tone:

"The end-all of this endeavor you pursue will only end in death, Mr. Shadow Walker. But somehow I don't think you give a damn about that. Of course, I had to see it for myself, and I was right." Happy finally breaks his stare and looks down at the table as if in a daydream. He makes a circular motion with his index finger on it. "Well, I suppose we've all got to die someday," he says as he taps his finger on the table. He then pauses for a moment and looks back up at Jeremiah. "I will offer you the same deal as I did a gentleman by the name of Billingsly—disappear and you live. Poof"—Happy snaps his fingers as his tone becomes more aggressive—"gone like the magic man himself performing his greatest illusion. Your family and friends live. All is antebellum. Hell, I'll even let you keep a brick of gold," says Happy, followed by a sarcastic chuckle. "This can end here. What do you say, buddy old pal?"

Jeremiah finally speaks. "Do you have the time?"

Happy suddenly looks down at his empty wrist where his watch used to be. When he looks back up, Jeremiah is holding his Rolex. Gonzo had stolen it back from Redd. Jeremiah hands it back to Happy and says, "You might need this to keep track of the short time you have left on this earth."

Happy gives Jeremiah a "golf clap," while saying, "Oooh, this is going to be fun." He continues, "You see, men like us can bend words in our favor. We never really tell the truth, but we never actually lie. It is fascinating to meet someone else with such talents." Happy laughs to himself.

"I'm nothing like you. We are done here," sneers Jeremiah.

"Very well, Mr. Shadow Walker. Till we meet again." Happy gets up from the booth and begins to walk away. He then stops and looks back toward Jeremiah. With a seditious smile on his face, he says, "We are very alike. You just lie to yourself every day thinking you give a damn about other people." Happy turns away and casually exits *Renee's Diner*; Jeremiah eats his sandwich.

Here's Looking at You, Kid

October 8, 8:14 a.m.

To be on the precipice of something greater than oneself is both exhilarating and frightening when your only options are victory or death; everything in between is called war. However, both options bring peace in some form or another. Happy said that Jeremiah didn't care if he died. That is not true. He only cares that Happy not live. And if shutting off one's emotional attachment to death to do so is necessary, so be it.

Jeremiah decides to sleep at his apartment for the night. He just wants to be alone. He sips his coffee. It is quite a stale brew, but it's hot and serves its purpose. It is a gloomy morning outside his window. The clouds gather in such a way that the edge of one cannot be differentiated from the other, creating a vast expanse of endless gray. Jeremiah ponders the irony in the fact that on days such as this, there is a lack of shadows; but a sunny day somehow exacerbates them. The brighter the light, the darker the shadow it casts.

There is suddenly a knock on the door. Jeremiah quickly grabs his gun and moves to look through the peephole. There are two police officers standing outside of his door. They look relaxed, however, and don't even have a hand on their gun. Jeremiah opens the door with the safety chain attached.

"May I help you, officers?" he asks.

One of them, by the name of Edwards, speaks, "Yes, we are doing a safety check on a lady down the hall. The landlord has tried to deliver her mail to her the past couple of days, but she will not respond. He said it is unlike her. They have a schedule. He says you are close?"

"Yes, I have a key. Let me get dressed."

Jeremiah recognizes Edwards, Drake Edwards. They graduated the police academy together. He is not that close to him, but on the night of graduation, Drake and a group of cadets went out for celebratory drinks. By happenstance they came to the same bar that Jeremiah and a couple of his classmates were. He and Drake struck up a conversation. They spoke of a bright future—one where they would make a difference and help people. We all thought like that back then. It seems as if it was a lifetime ago.

The officers follow him to her apartment door. He knocks three times, holds once, then once more. There is no answer. He unlocks her door, turns the handle, and slowly opens it. The TV is on, but she is not in her chair.

"Mrs. Olejniczak," says Jeremiah in a loud voice. The police officers follow him. There is a noticeable aroma coming from the master bedroom. The door is slightly ajar. He pushes it open. Upon a neatly made bed lays her frail body.

She is wearing a black dress, black dress gloves, and a black veil over her face. Both hands are resting on her chest. In the right, a rosary; in her left, a folded piece of paper. Officer Edwards removes the paper from her hand and gives it a quick glance. He then says, "It's for you, Jeremiah." Edwards hands him the handwritten note:

Jeremiah,

It is time. I am tired. All I have is yours. It's not much, but it's all I got. See you on the flip side. Thank you for your kindness.

Love,
Helen Geraldine Olejniczak

PS. Do not murder the trust that God has given you.

"Sometimes people just know when their time is up," says Edwards.

"I'll call it in," his partner responds as he leaves the room.

As Jeremiah looks at her lifeless body, he can't but notice how peaceful she looks. The black-and-white family photo on the end table next to the bed shows a beautiful young woman standing next her man. In front of them is their daughter. They look so happy. Happiness is such a fragile thing.

"Will I have to claim the body and fill out the paperwork for cremation?" asks Jeremiah.

"Yeah, you will have to go to the coroner's and fill out form F-9. It is pretty obvious that you are her executor. We'll write that in the report. You can go down there anytime you like and take care of it, even if the body hasn't arrived yet. This is not suspicious, but they will have to perform an autopsy to rule out suicide or foul play before they issue the death certificate."

"Thank you, Drake." Jeremiah walks out of the bedroom.

As he goes to turn the TV off in the living room, he stops to watch it for a moment. There is a man at an airport talking to a beautiful woman. He seems in a hurry. The man puts his fingers on her chin to gently lift her head up so he can see her eyes. There are tears in them. Even in black and white, they still suggest the finest blue.

"Here's looking at you, kid." Jeremiah turns the TV off.

A Picture of Proof

October 8, 9:53 a.m.

Jeremiah stops at the office to check in on things before heading to the coroner. Upon entering, there is a plate sitting upon the meeting table with a few crumbs left on it. There is also an empty glass that looks as if it contained milk. On the couch in the corner near a wood burning stove, Redd is sleeping underneath an old and tattered blanket. He looks very comfortable. The girls must have made him some food and tucked him in.

Suddenly Redd jostles, looks up at Jeremiah, and says, "Mr. Revel, tell Ms. Heather thank you for making me a sandwich. It is the nicest thing anyone has ever done for me."

"I will," he responds.

"There is a guy I know who wants to talk to you. We call him the Wizard. You will know why when you see him. He's a vag but really smart. I mean book smart and on the streets. He lives under *The Pink Panther* whorehouse near *Sycamore* and *Palm* in *Skid Row*."

"What business would he have with me?" asks Jeremiah.

"I don't know. But he told me to give this to you." Redd hands him a photograph, then rubs his eyes. It is a wedding photo. Jeremiah recognizes the bride. It is Mrs. Billingsly. The groom must be Charles.

"Did he say what time?" asks Jeremiah.

"No, but I have never seen him not there. I only know him because he lets me lie low there when it gets really cold out."

"Very well," responds Jeremiah.

"Oh, and Mr. Revel, I will never steal from you. But I might steal Ms. Heather's heart," he says with that same clever look on his face he displayed the previous day. Jeremiah just shakes his head. Redd curls up, wraps the blanket around himself tighter and nods back off to sleep.

Before he leaves, Jeremiah goes up to the armory. He briefs Gonzo about the Billingsly situation. The girls are sleeping.

"They need to stay in here. Things are going to get really dicey. I mean it, Gonzo. This is the beginning of the end." Jeremiah grabs some extra clips of .45 ammo on his way out of the armory just in case.

14

Mr. Billingsly

October 8, 11:37 a.m.

A man is defined by the nature of which he uses his love, kindness, and anger to the benefit of those he loves. A man is not easy to love. But when he knows that she chooses him, he will protect his woman with a vicious rage that he never wants her to see. If he gets angry at her, it only means he cares. A man is also defined by fear. He will fight wars and negotiate with death, just so she won't have to. But love is more frightening to him. So everything that good men do is out of love and should not be misunderstood otherwise.

Jeremiah has called Luke on the rotary phone in the armory and asks him to shadow him. Luke dresses in drag in order to hide in plain sight.

"He's got nice legs for a dude," Jeremiah says as he laughs to himself.

Luke is wearing a tight red dress with an aqua-blue boa scarf around his neck. He is surprisingly spry in high heels. He will fit right in with the colorful characters in *Skid Row*. Jeremiah cannot but ponder the question: Who did Luke's makeup? He looks like a rodeo clown who got fired for scaring the bulls.

Most of the whores keep to themselves. Especially when they know you are not a client. Then you have the ones that are high on some sort of tar-based drug.

"Hey, handsome; lookin' for a good time?"

"Not from you snaggle puss."

"Fuck off, narc." If you can offend a whore, you are doing something right.

As Jeremiah is about to enter the alleyway next to *The Pink Panther*, he can't but somehow feel that he is crossing the threshold of what separates dreams and sorrow. A place where everything is lost, not to the world, but to oneself. It's such a lonely endeavor for one to bear—their own loneliness. The very whisper of silence is empty and has no sympathy for what is void. And thus, the alleyway screams of sorrow not for itself, but for those who enter its unforgiven realm. "Keep Out," the sign reads. Jeremiah enters.

Even death itself will attempt to avoid such a dank place. Maybe it has. Jeremiah is indeed going to meet with a man who has legally been declared dead. The alleyway is dark, and the smell of sewage is pungent in the air. Luckily, the door of his destination is only a few yards into the concrete abyss. The black door is surprisingly clean and well kempt. There is a hand-painted sign on the door. The blue letters read: "The password is my name." Jeremiah knocks on the door. A viewing slide built into it opens up, and a man with piercing green eyes is staring at him.

"What is the password?"

"Billingsly. Maria sent me."

The man's eyes seem to light up with excitement. The door creaks open.

"Come, come. I wasn't sure you would show. The lad tells stories sometimes." Billingsly's hair is snow-white and reaches down to his midback. His beard is of the same hue and has grown to his waist. He is, however, a well-manicured man. He is wearing a white robe and leather sandals. The humble abode of which the Wizard calls home is small but quite efficiently kept. "Hello, Mr. Shadow Walker. Welcome to a dead man's home. Make yourself comfortable," says Billingsly with a coy smile on his face. His accent is neutral. He points to a brown leather chair with a matching ottoman. It sits next to a fireplace that is hand-chiseled into the cobblestone wall of the basement.

"What is the nature of the business you wish to discuss?" asks Jeremiah.

"The streets speak, Mr. Shadow Walker. One can learn a great deal by listening to them. I want in on your little plan. I have been preparing my revenge for six years now. I gave up everything to protect my family. Now, I am going to take it back."

"Revenge is a dangerous thing—for everyone involved," responds Jeremiah.

"I am already dead, Mr. Shadow Walker. The doctors gave me three months. The time for me is now. But if I am going to go, it will be on my own terms." Billingsly's green eyes are resolute. He walks over to a bookshelf and fumbles with a lever. There is a click, and Billingsly slides the heavy bookcase to the side; it's a hidden room—an armory. The Wizard then turns to address Jeremiah.

"There is an underground route into Happy's compound. It is through the sewers and some maintenance shafts. There are not many rats in the sewers of the Northern Regal Estates. I am the only one who can get you in. It will be a firefight, but we will have the element of surprise on our side. How is Patricia?"

"She seems okay. She said she just wants closure for the boys."

"Well, she will get it. This will be my final curtain call. My last hurrah," he says with hint of dark romance resonating in his voice.

There is a sudden knock on the door. The Wizard quickly walks over and opens the slide. "We do not want any of your disgusting services!" yells Billingsly in a disgruntled manner.

"I need to speak with—" The slide is shut.

Jeremiah recognizes Luke's voice. "Hold on. Open it back up." Confused but trusting, Billingsly opens the slide back up. It is indeed Luke, in drag, on the other side of the door.

"I called to check in on the office. There was no answer—both lines."

"That's not good," responds Jeremiah. "Luke, call Stefenski. We'll meet ASAP." He looks at the Wizard and says, "Well, Mr. Billingsly. You wanted to be part of this. Welcome to the team. It is time."

Billingsly grabs a military-style duffle bag from his armory. "Let's do this."

The Sage and the Envy of Hatred

October 8, 12:47 p.m.

Neither Jeremiah nor Billingsly say a word for most of the ride back to the office. Luke is shadowing them. He is sitting in the back row. Jeremiah and Billingsly are toward the front and side by side in the same row; they are the lone travelers on the bus. Finally, Jeremiah breaks the silence.

"I wonder why Happy Hal didn't just kill us all?"

The Wizard ponders for a moment while grooming his beard with his hand and finally responds, "Well, I think it is probably for the same reason you didn't go public with the evidence you had on him. You see, this thing is personal. He has been untouchable for so long. Maybe he is just getting bored. You can only cage the animal, feed it, and pamper it for so long before it misses the thrill of the hunt. This is a game to him. He is looking for a showdown, just as much as you are. He probably envies you for your hatred of him. You have more than him—a cause."

"A cause? Revenge is not a cause. Revenge is not worthy of a hero's decree. It only creates a different monster. The thing is, I haven't quite figured out what I am," responds Jeremiah in an eloquent rant. It seems as though this has been on his mind for some time. "I don't know if I am the leader of the rats in the corner or the monster in the room."

The Wizard responds, "The absence of humanity can only exist in humans. And sympathy for the devil is our greatest fault, but it's what makes us human and separates us from the animals—having that choice." A small buzzer sounds off as Luke pulls the signal cord to let the driver know that they wish to get off at the ensuing stop. They are a block away from their destination. The worst feeling a man can have is to disappoint the ones he loves even when he knows he has done the right thing. They just don't know it yet.

The door to the office is smashed in. Luke ditches his high heels. He is bearing an assault rifle from Billingsly's arsenal. Billingsly wields a 12-gauge. Jeremiah kicks in the door. He is in first, followed by Billingsly then Luke. The first floor seems empty. There is a half-eaten sandwich and a glass of milk on the meeting table. It is still cold. Luke and Billingsly clear the first floor while Jeremiah covers the stairwell. There is a noise. It sounds as if the armory door is opening. The moment is tense.

"Yo, hombre. It's me, Gonzo. Telisha and I are coming out. They are gone!" yells Speedy. Jerry is holding Telisha's hand as they enter Jeremiah's gunsight. As they begin to walk down the stairs, Jeremiah lowers his gun. Telisha is crying.

"Heather was giving the boy a sandwich when they busted in. It happened quick. There was nothing I could do," says Gonzo.

"They took her and the boy." He is breathing heavily as he speaks. Suddenly, Stefenski walks in and startles everyone.

"Jesus, don't shoot," he says with three guns pointed at him. As he stands there for a moment with his hands up, he says, "Holy shit, Luke, what the fuck are you wearing? And who the fuck is that guy?" He points to Billingsly.

"This is Charles Billingsly," Jeremiah says, as he points back with his thumb.

"I knew you were alive. C'mon, Luke, pay up." Luke pulls a one-hundred-dollar bill from his cleavage and hands it to Sonny. Despite the situation, Jeremiah can't help but smirk at this spectacle. Stefenski then shakes the Wizard's hand.

"You shouldn't bet on a man's life," says Billingsly. His piercing green eyes are once again stern and resolute. It catches Stefenski off guard.

"I'm sorry. But I did, and I won," he responds with a smirk.

A Woman's Scorn

October 8, 1:23 p.m.

Stefenski quickly realizes the dark cloud hanging over the room. "So what's going on?"

"They took Heather and Redd. We are going to take them back. Knowing Happy, they are his collateral. The Wizard and I are going."

"My fiancée is there. I am going too," says Luke. Jeremiah, Stefenski, and the Wizard all turn their heads without moving their shoulders. They have a perplexed look on their face. "Her name is Melanie. She is his daughter. I didn't know. I didn't know. Until a couple of days ago. She is his bookkeeper and assistant. She cannot be hurt," Luke avers in a loud voice. Sonny and Jeremiah are unsure how to process this one. Luke is still wearing the dress and boa.

"Will she come willingly?"

"Yes," he responds immediately.

"Well, I guess we've all got our secrets," mutters Billingsly.

"Is anyone hungry?" Telisha interrupts.

Jeremiah nods, and almost in unison, the rest say, "Yes."

"If you're going to die, you might as well have some fried chicken," she says in a disappointed tone as she is walking away; a way in which you never want to see a woman walk away. Her hands are on her hips. For a moment, they are more afraid of her than their future endeavor. Gonzo is enamored.

Jeremiah has no patience for planning anymore. "Listen, Stefenski, Jerry, you have no obligations. So I hereby relieve you of your duties."

"I'm in," says Speedy as he looks over his shoulder to make sure Telisha cannot hear him. Stefenski hesitates to answer. Jeremiah knows that they will need someone on the outside.

"Sonny, we will need a ghost rider. Just keep a loop."

"Roger. So this one is for free, huh?"

Jeremiah is done with jokes and does not even gesture to the comment. His mind is on Heather.

Fried Chicken

October 8, 2:07 p.m.

The mood is somber. The food is delicious. They are all sitting at the meeting table eating—Jeremiah, Charles, Luke, Sonny, and Telisha.

"My father gave me a small cigar box when I was twelve. He figured I was old enough to understand. Inside it were some belongings of my mother's. This recipe was one of them. This meal is all I have left of her. All that I can possibly share," says Telisha with a deserted smile and a distant stare; but every women is satisfied when she can feed those she loves.

What should a man feel in such a moment of uncertainty? Jeremiah can only comprehend darkness. Heather is his only light. As he eats, reality has become almost surreal to him; as if his eyes are self-aware. His being has become primal and direct. However, the feeling he holds is not born of destructive rage but of instinct and self-sacrifice of one's soul. This will be the end—fried chicken.

Fire and Beauty

October 8, 4:41 p.m.

She can hear two men talking. One voice is deep, aged, and calm. The other seems younger and has a nervous inflection. Everything is dark.

"We have all men at their posts, sir. We are ready for anything."

The door can be heard closing. The sound of the latch suggests a heavy but archaic door. The hood is pulled off. The sudden burst of light is blinding.

"Where is the boy?" asks Heather to the man who is sitting across from her. Her hands are not bound, but her feet are secured to the floor with shackles. Her naturally born motherly instinct has kicked in. The room is small and seems as though its main purpose is to serve as an interview room. The rafters of the floor above are showing, and the infrastructure of the building's electrical work and plumbing is exposed. There is a single table and two metal chairs. The man just stares at her. "Do you talk, or are you just going to sit there and look like a moron?"

"You are prettier than I thought you would be, Heather," says Happy with a slightly amused expression on his face.

"Fuck you. I asked you a question. Did I stutter?" responds Heather.

Happy now has a smile on his face. "The boy is fine. Well, let's just say he will be leaving here with less appendages than he came with." Happy looks at his watch to check the time. "You know the funny thing about time is? Everyone keeps track of it, but no one ever really has it."

"What is the purpose of all this? Why are you so hell-bent on destruction and evildoing?" asks Heather nervously but with authority.

Happy laughs again with a big grin and responds raucously: "It's just too goddamn fun."

He is seemingly intrigued by his own words. Happy goes on. "Ms. Heather, this world was not built for heroes. It was not built for people like the Shadow Walker. He cares too much about others. That's what gets people killed. That's what gets a lovely woman like you in shackles, sitting in front of the Puppet Master."

"I thought you'd be taller," she responds. "I am getting the vibe of Napoleon complex. I bet you make up for your little dick with an oversize ego." Happy is happy. He gives her a golf clap, then slaps her in the face.

"And there's the proof," she avers quickly and angrily while staring back at him with justification in her raging blue eyes. In some indescribable irony, she does not fear Happy; albeit strange and unexplainable, Jeremiah Revel is the only one that can frighten her.

"He's coming. He is going to kill you," she says in a somber tone.

"Ah, we'll see," responds Happy as he gets up and leaves. He turns to look at her before he closes the door.

He eyes her down and says, "Fire and beauty. The perfect combination." The large door clanks shut. Heather cries not for herself, but for Redd and her unborn baby.

A Fleeting Joke

October 8, 5:15 p.m.

As Jeremiah is about to hop into the side door of the van, he stops for a moment. He has his foot on the footboard, and both hands grasp either side of the opened sliding door. He looks through the eyeholes of Happy's mask. He can see his own breath evaporate toward the fading light of *The City's* gray skyline. It gives him chills.

Is this about love or revenge? he asks to himself. No matter what the answer is, this battle with Happy was always inevitable. He hops in the van. They will enter a manhole in the Northern Ports area.

It is Jerry's idea that they wear their disguises. That is, everyone except the Wizard; he looks like that all the time. Jeremiah is wielding the tommy gun with the hundred-round drum magazine and his .45. Luke is carrying an AR15 assault rifle and a Glock 19. Gonzo wields a pistol grip 12-gauge shotgun with 00 9-pellet ammo and also a Glock 19. The Wizard has a long-barreled 12-gauge hunting shotgun with slugs for ammo and a S&W .38 Special with a four-inch barrel. They do not have any diversionary devices in their satchels, only more ammo and a couple of frag grenades each. The weight of the extra ammo is noticeable, but none of them seem to care. The Wizard decides to forego wearing a bulletproof vest. No one questions him. He is not expecting to leave Happy's compound alive.

The ride up to the Northern Ports is wrought with suspense and anxiety. Some men will question the very nature of their intent, and others will become overwhelmed with fear. Jeremiah does neither. No one speaks. Silence is their revelation. Jeremiah catches the Wizard's eyes. They nod to each other only in a way that men can understand; a single nod can solve all men's problems without ever having to say a word. The loud ride in the back of the van is comforting. It makes one realize why they invented elevator music.

The Wizard pulls out a pipe, packs it, and lights it with a match. The tobacco's aroma reminds Jeremiah of his father. His mother would not let Isaiah smoke tobacco unless it was a holiday. Somehow the aromatic mix of tobacco and apple pie resonates within the lovely memories of the short time he knew them. Jeremiah lowers his head and stares at the floor of the van.

"Here," says Gonzo. Jeremiah looks up. He hands him a cigarette, then hands Luke one. They all have to lift their masks up. Each use a *Renee's Diner* match. The nicotine demands focus and temporarily removes stress.

"How much do you love her?" asks Jeremiah.

Luke takes a long drag from his cigarette, then responds, "Enough to be in this van right now dressed like a clown with a bunch of morons." They all laugh. It is one of those moments that humor and laughter truly become one, and the world is just a fleeting joke.

How much can one speak of and endeavor to understand the very thing that is love? When will the ideas run out? When will man exhaust the library of human words that try to describe it? I surmise, never. We will invent new words in a frivolous attempt to describe something that cannot be defined; it can only be experienced and adored.

The Maintenance Shafts

October 8, 6:32 p.m.

So goes the Blackguards of Charlatan, traversing the maze of twists and turns that make up *The City's Northern Ports Sewer System.* Coupled with the dampness, it is much colder in the subsurface sewer than at the ground level. Jack Frost seems to be in his element, but the rest can't help but feel the chill.

"It took me months to map out this route. See that marking on the wall." The Wizard points to a blue spray-painted symbol on the stone wall. The symbol resembles a wizard-style hat with arrows passing through it that seem to point in random directions. "The symbols are coded. Only I know which ones to follow and which to ignore," explains Billingsly.

The sewers look similar to those near *The People's Trust Company and Bank*, except they are cleaner and so far, they have only come across a single rat. The ceiling lights actually work. Billingsly flips a lever switch, and a one-hundred-yard section lights up like a Christmas tree. They continue to flip the switches as they progress. Jack Frost is on point with the Wizard; shotguns tend to clear a hallway pretty quick. The Shadow Walker is next. The Thompson can throw a lot of lead downrange to keep the enemy under cover, but it's not very accurate. Pewee the Clown is last with the AR15. It is the most accurate gun of the group's and can hit small targets farther downrange.

Occasionally, they pass under a sewer grate where one can hear a group of people holding casual conversations about work or maybe what their plans are for the weekend. This baffles Jeremiah. He has been, for so long, estranged from the concept of simple life pleasures. The people above know nothing of what lurks below in the shadows, nor does he know what lies upon the surface. There is no duality. There is them, and there is him. Neither can ever truly understand each other.

Their footsteps echo off the walls and arched ceiling of the tunnel. The Wizard does not seem concerned with what may be waiting around each corner. He promises that they will not meet any resistance in the sewers. However, he cannot guarantee the maintenance shafts are clear. Jeremiah realizes why it took Billingsly so long to map it out; with all the twists and turns, no one can possibly distinguish one right turn from the last left. Finally, after a half hour, they reach a metal door. It is solid with no window. It has a robust dead bolt lock on it.

"I can pick it," says Luke.

"No, you can't," says the Wizard. "It has six vertical tumblers and three side ones."

"I see," responds Luke.

"But luckily I have the key," says the Wizard with a sly look on his face as he is holding a thick brass key up in the air in between his thumb and index finger. No one can even ponder how he got the key. "Is everyone ready?" The Wizard looks intently into the eyes of each man as his gaze pans between them.

"Remember, no matter what, keep moving forward as you fire," instructs Jeremiah.

They all grip their weapons tighter and fine-tune their bodies into a hone position. The key slips in effortlessly, and the dead bolt can be heard sliding. The Wizard removes the key and places it back in his pocket. He slowly turns the handle. The door creaks as

Billingsly pulls it open; the squealing pitch grows higher as the door opens farther. Suddenly, all is silent.

The Wizard stares down the barrel of his 12-gauge shotgun into the maintenance corridor of Happy's compound. He will be on point from here on out. He squints through the dim light to try to make anything out in the distance. All seems calm. He makes a motion with his hand to move forward without losing focus of what is on the end of his barrel. They enter—the Wizard, Jack Frost, the Shadow Walker, and finally, Pewee the Clown. They move as one organism; quite well for a team that has not trained together. However, they do not know if they are the hunters or the hunted.

The corridor is only about six feet wide. There is an assortment of pipes lining the cinder block walls on either side. There does not seem to be any of Happy's men in the shafts.

"She is probably in the lower-level holding room. It is up through the vent," the Wizard says as he points up to an industrial-sized heating duct; there was no money spared in the construction of the heating system. Jeremiah is not a small man, but he should be able to shimmy through it. Meanwhile, the Wizard has propped himself up on one of the pipes on the wall and is using the screwdriver on his Swiss Army knife to remove the screws of the ridged heating vent; it's about eight feet high. Jeremiah removes his shoulder holster, satchel, and fedora. He will also leave the tommy gun behind. He then puts an extra clip of ammo and a frag grenade in his coat pocket. The Wizard hands Jeremiah a small flashlight, then points as he iterates, "Just go that way about twenty feet. There will be a vertical rise, then it should be the first opening on your right after that. You are far enough away from the heat source that it should not be too hot if the heat turns on. But it will definitely be warm."

Suddenly, Luke starts singing through his clown mask in a surprisingly operatic voice, *"Chestnuts roasting on an open fire."*

They all have a chuckle. Gonzo cups his hands. Jeremiah steps into them. The Wizard supports his back. They lift him up into the vent opening. He throws his .45 in first, then finagles his way fully into the bosom of the duct.

It isn't like in the movies. Although there is ample space to maneuver, there is a half inch of dust that has accumulated throughout time. He does not have far to go, but he has to go slow as to not disturb the dust too much. He utilizes an elbow crawl. The vent walls seem to close in on him as claustrophobia gnaws at his psyche. It is strange that a man holding a gun can feel so alone and helpless. Luke had taught him a coping mechanism awhile back. *Spend all your mental energy focusing not on what you are doing but why you are doing it.*

"Heather," he says out loud. Jeremiah moves forward—the only way go. *What if she's not there? What if he has hurt her? What if… What if she is dead?* He shimmies his way up the small vertical rise. He can now see the light of the outlet vent ahead. There is also the soft murmur of two voices. Jeremiah crawls up very slowly. As he reaches the ridged vent grate, the heater blower motor suddenly turns on. All the dust he has disturbed behind him suddenly creates a cloud of dander and dirt that surrounds him. He can do nothing but wait and curse silently under his breath.

Jeremiah waits with his head buried in his arms for the blower to turn off and the air to clear. After about ten minutes, he can make out the silhouette of a girl in a chair. She is not facing him but he knows it is Heather. The heavy door suddenly opens. A woman walks in. She is a thin brunette with brown eyes exacerbated by a set of thick glasses. She is wearing a pink dress with black polka dots. *That has to be Melanie,* Jeremiah thinks to himself. He observes a pricy engagement ring, then notices she is wearing ballerina-type shoes. *She is actually quite cute. The best kind of cute—nerd cute. Nice job, Luke.* The woman sits down in front of Heather.

"Are you hungry or thirsty?" the lady asks in a soothing voice. Heather does not respond, nor does she even acknowledge the presence of the lady. "My name is Melanie. You've met my father. You must be Heather." Melanie looks down at the table and taps her index finger twice on it. "I know more about you and Jeremiah than you think." Jeremiah is surprised; it is the first time he's been acknowledged by his real name by someone in Happy's clan. "Give me your hands. You must trust me. I'm a palm reader." Melanie reaches out

125

both her hands toward Heather, with her palms facing the ceiling. Heather finally looks at her. There is something calm in Melanie's eyes; something trustworthy. Heather reaches out her hands with her palms toward the ceiling, suggesting trust and submission. Melanie places four fingers from each hand into the palms of Heather, including a key for the shackles. "I see darkness in your future, followed by freedom, peace, and new life." There is a subtle noise outside of the door. "I am not supposed to be here," says Melanie frantically as she instantly translates every noise into some impending doom. That is Jeremiah's cue. With three painful elbow whacks to the outlet vent, it pops open and Jeremiah crawls into the room.

He stands before the two women in a cloud of dust. He is completely covered in it. It is unnerving to Heather and Melanie; first, he startled them with a quick entrance. And now they are staring at a figure with a metallic hockey mask who is completely ashen in color.

"You're him, aren't you?" asks Melanie.

"I am," responds Jeremiah without really knowing what she means. Melanie reaches back from her chair and locks the door. Meanwhile, Heather is fumbling with the key to unlock her shackles. Melanie notices and immediately crawls under the table in haste.

She takes the key from Heather and says, "I used to play with these things as a kid." She unfastens them in less than three seconds.

Jeremiah looks up toward the back corner of the room and notices a security camera mounted on the ceiling. He turns toward it and stares directly into it with his head slightly cocked to the right. He raises his .45, fires, and watches it shatter into a thousand pieces. He turns to the girls who are rubbing their ears and avers, "Go in the vent to the left. It's not far. Just head straight and there will be a dip. A little farther then, the guys will help you down." Jeremiah then throws them the flashlight; he can make it in the dark. The two girls reluctantly enter the ducts; Melanie first, then Heather.

However, before Heather enters, she asks, "What about Redd?"

"We'll get the boy. One thing at a time."

The women are in the ductwork. The door is being compromised by what sounds likes some sort of breaching ram. Large gaps are starting to develop where the heavy oakwood panels are being separated within their steel support strips. Jeremiah fires three rounds at center mass. The breaching attempt momentarily stops. Two shots are fired back through it; they hit him in the vest. The door has absorbed most of the lethality of the rounds; they barely stun him. Jeremiah empties his gun into the doorway as he backs up toward the ductwork vent entrance. The last three rounds are fired from his back as he slides into the vent headfirst. He struggles to free the frag grenade from his pocket. When he is finally able to negotiate it out of his pocket, he realizes the pin has been pulled.

"Ah, shit!" he yells in a pissed off tone. He throws it out the vent entrance into the interview room and hastily moves himself farther into the vent way. He hears voices just before the concussion.

When one hears the expression that a person has gotten their "bell rung," unless you have had it happen to you, you will not understand. Jeremiah cannot see straight nor hear anything but a high-pitched ringing sound in his ears for about five seconds. When this occurs, the outside world is no longer something cognitive nor important. Everything is a blur and can only be recollected after the fact, maybe. The moment seems as if it is a missing puzzle piece in the fabric of space and time.

Jeremiah only comes to after he slips down the vertical drop of the ductwork. He has continued to crawl backward, even in his state of comatose. He catches himself somehow, even amid the darkness of the vent. Luckily, he is still holding his .45. He rolls onto his stomach and elbow crawls the rest of the way. The dim light of the opened access vent is a beacon of hope. Jeremiah just wants to be out of the coffin-like feeling of the ductwork. It is no place for a man.

Jeremiah looks down from the opened vent door. Even though they can hear him banging against the vent walls as he crawls, the group has a look of relief on their faces when a figure appears and a voice says, "What's up, assholes? Why do I have to do all the dirty work?"

"I thought you liked it dirty?" responds Gonzo. The men laugh. The girls don't. Jeremiah hands his gun down to the Wizard and exits the ductwork headfirst with the help of Jerry and Luke. Luke and Jeremiah begin to dust off their women.

"You were shot?" asks Heather. Luke, Gonzo, and Billingsly briefly observe the damage then continue on with their own agendas.

"Yeah. If it was serious, I would tell you," responds Jeremiah. He brushes her hair out of her eyes with his hand and looks into them in such a way that is reserved for her alone. His fingers are on the back of her neck; his thumb is on her cheek. He can only muster up the words "I'm sorry, but I love you. And it scares the shit out of me, Heather." It is the first time he has said it to her before she said it first. Jeremiah then puts his fedora back on and attempts to brush as much dust off himself as possible. Gonzo sneezes and winces in pain once again. "Damn it! That hurts," he blurts out as he has his hand on his rib.

Happy Hal is watching everything from his office. He sees his daughter's actions as they unfold. He slams his fist on the table and yells, "Damn it, Melanie!" He cannot blame her, however. He brought her up to be her own person and to do whatever she thinks is right. He smirks slightly as if proud of her, even though she is dead to him.

The Betrayal

October 8, 7:42 p.m.

Happy is sitting at his desk. One leg is crossed over the other, and the corresponding fingertips on each hand are pressed against one another, including the thumbs. Melanie's treason has hit him hard. When he finally breaks his daydream, he pulls a *Havana-Hur* brand cigar from the humidor that sits on his desk. He lights it with a customized silver-plated flip-top lighter. The ivory plates on either side of the lighter's facade read RJH, written in calligraphy font. It was a Christmas gift from Melanie. The smell of the butane flame is somehow rewarding. Happy takes a couple of drags from his cigar as he leans back in his chair. He stares at the fire that one of his assistants had built earlier in the evening. Upon the mantle sits a framed piece of artwork that Melanie had created for him when she was only ten. It was produced using black ink, pencil, and a touch of scarlet-red paint.

Surrounded by a white background is a black rose. The stem curves down toward the bottom right corner of the piece. Each thorn has a small touch of blood on it. Melanie has created many other drawings, paintings, and various artworks; but this, this by far is his favorite. He does not know why.

Happy gets up from his desk and approaches the mantle. He stands with his hands clasped behind his back and his face less than a foot from the picture. He studies the contour and shape of every dark petal; it's the varying hues and the contrast of the scarlet red that somehow become absorbed within the irises of each eye in such a way that he becomes intoxicated with wandering thoughts. He can still see her little hand carefully and delicately maneuvering its way across the paper; her smile, the bedtime stories, and the laughter. She dubbed the piece, of all things, *The Betrayal*. And in the bottom-left corner, it reads, "For Daddy. Love Melanie."

Happy, in a moment of sudden fury, picks it up from the mantle and tosses it into the fire. "Fuck this world," he says out loud. It is sitting faceup among the flames as he stares at it. The white background begins to brown and blister from the heat. "Damn this," says Happy, suddenly angry with himself. He quickly removes the artwork from the fire, brushes it off, and places it back on the mantle where it belongs. It is as if he has now added his personal touch to the piece.

He then walks back to his desk, opens the drawer, and pulls out a S&W Model 29 .44 Magnum with a four-inch barrel in a leather holster and a box of extra rounds. He unloops his belt, attaches the gun to his hip, then walks to the coatrack in the corner. He slips into his tan trench coat. It is going be a long, cold night.

Where does the devil hide his soul? Why does he care for his craft of wicked enterprise? How weary one must become with their own endeavor, when there is no hope for peace, only further destruction and desecration of anything good? What is good? What is bad? Is hatred like a lonely tornado that can only destroy everything in its path—something that has no conscience? And is hated, for only existing, built to annihilate the very systems of nature it was born of? Yes, conscious thought will attempt to provoke, create, and preserve an answer. But in the end, love is love, and hate is hate; both are parasites of the heart.

The Fate of Hate and Cowards

October 8, 7:42 p.m.

"Follow me, I know where the boy is," says Melanie suddenly. "This way," she says as she summons them with her hand.

"Slow down. You don't know what is around that corner!" yells the Wizard frantically.

Melanie stops just before the corner, turns around with her hands on her hips and says in an almost condescending tone, "Don't you think I know what I am doing?"

Suddenly, there is a loud bang. As if it were in slow motion, a bullet passes over her right shoulder next to her ear and hits Jeremiah in the forehead, bouncing off his mask. A chunk of Melanie's hair was ripped out from the passing bullet; it gently floats to the ground unnoticed and with wandering beauty.

For the second time in ten minutes, Jeremiah's bell is rung. Luke jumps on Melanie. Jeremiah, despite his condition, tackles Heather by instinct. Jack Frost and the Wizard open fire downrange. Their shotguns are so loud in the tight quarters that Heather is certain that she has busted her eardrums; she, too, now hears the ringing of the bell that tolls within the voice of death's whisper.

Melanie wrestles free from Luke, stands up, and starts walking toward where the shots are coming from. The gunfire momentarily stops. Melanie is noticeably angry.

"Is that you, Habs and Levi?" she yells.

There is one more shot that is blindly fired around the corner. It ricochets past the group. Melanie does not waver and reiterates, "Habs, Levi, is that you?"

"Is that you, Mel?" responds a voice that sounds like Levi.

"Everyone, stop firing," avers Melanie as she stands, looking at Speedy and Billingsly with one palm facing them and the other in the opposite direction, suggesting peace.

Levi nervously pokes his head around the corner. He can see she is serious.

Jeremiah helps Heather to her feet and quickly searches her body while asking, "Are you okay?"

"Yes," she responds.

Levi steps out from the corner with his weapon holstered. He motions for Habs to follow him. Melanie looks back at Frost and the Wizard, who still have their weapons trained on the men. With fury in her eyes, she instructs them to lower their weapons. Reluctantly, they do so.

Levi approaches Melanie and stops roughly six feet away; Habs follows. Levi is wearing a dark blue mechanic's uniform stained with both fresh and old oil stains. His pulled-up sleeves reveal forearms that are gnarled like twisted rope. His hands are large, scarred, and strong in appearance. They suggest a life of hard work. Accompanying his rusty-red hair is a set of blue eyes; they hold sympathy and peace. He speaks with a hint of Bavarian in his accent.

"Melanie, why are you with these people?" asks Levy with a look of sadness on his face as he points with his hands, palms open toward the ceiling.

"Because she is a two-faced whore." Habs interrupts.

"Shut your mouth," sneers Levi suddenly.

"Everyone, shut your mouths," says Melanie with resolute authority as she pushes her thick glasses back up to the proper position upon the bridge of her nose.

If she and Luke have a child, the poor kid is going to be blind, Jeremiah thinks to himself in a moment of detached self-candor.

Levi has known Melanie since she was a little girl. He thinks of her as a daughter. Habs never liked her. He always thought she was spoiled and detrimental to their operations. She was a freethinker and a kindred spirit to others. From day one, as head of the lower-level security, he knew something was up. He could smell a rat from a mile away. Jeremiah wants to kill them both in the moment but can tell that Levi seems to have an intimate attachment to Melanie.

"Fuck this!" yells Habs as he puts his left hand back on his lowered weapon. Jeremiah is growing impatient. He steps forward, nudges Melanie out of the way, and approaches Levi.

"We don't have time for this," says Jeremiah. He stands awkwardly close in front of Levi. He towers over the two men. Jeremiah's shoulders are prone and his presence is foreboding. "We both have two options—leave or die. I'm in no mood to die, and I'm not leaving. So it seems as though it's your decision." Jeremiah's tone invokes chills in the spines of all those present. The air is still. He divided what is right and wrong, and contradicts the conundrum of what lives in between. Habs will decide the endgame for all involved.

Through his mask, Jeremiah's eyes are studying and wandering back and forth in between the other men's; eyes always tell the truth; they have a voice within them. Levi's still speak of bewilderment and love. However, Habs' eyes have become dilated. There is a void that develops in one's eyes when they become absent of thought. This is when rage rips through the irises like a hurricane wind and exploits their secrets, unknowingly giving them to the world. Jeremiah knows this all too well. He has seen this in his own reflection in the mirror.

Jeremiah speaks while staring directly into Habs' eyes, "Death can only be the beginning of the end. You have shadows in your eyes. And they haunt your secrets. Mr. Habs, death is upon us. Drop your weapon and no one dies."

"Let them go," suggests Levi nervously; he is a coward when he is blinded by earnest love; but he means well.

"If you raise that gun, you are outnumbered and will die," Jeremiah says as he makes a point to shield Melanie from Habs' periphery. Her betrayal is what Habs hates. Something so simple as loyalty can warp one's intentions; yes, hate can only be learned, and love can only be earned, but betrayal commits treason upon one's soul. Habs no longer knows the idea of peace and lets rage dictate his broken cause. He is no longer worth the price of sympathy and he is numb to his own guilt.

The crack of the .38 revolver is startling. It catches Jeremiah off guard; everything seems to do so lately. The shot is at center mass in the forehead of Habs. His body becomes limp; subjugated to the laws of nature, it slumps to the ground of the cold concrete floor of the maintenance shaft. His blood evacuates from his nose and mouth in surprisingly quick fashion. It's as if the blood knows it no longer has a purpose and should return to the earth where it belongs. His eyes suddenly lack the presence of life, but his heart still beats for a moment, seemingly sympathetic to this sordid endeavor.

So stands the Wizard, gun in hand. It is now raised and pointed at Levi. Levi is shaking. His fear has become his god. Jeremiah does not want this man dead, but he cannot trust him. If Billingsly wanted Levi dead, the trigger would have already been pulled. Jeremiah must make the decision. Levi steps back with his hands raised. He stares at Melanie with sympathetic and loving eyes.

"Melanie, c'mon. I...I...I—"

Jeremiah interrupts. And while staring into the eyes of fear he solemnly declares, "I'm sorry, but we cannot trust a coward." He turns away from Levi, faces the rest, and nods to Billingsly.

Crack. Levi is dead. He slumps as he falls and eventually rests atop Habs' body. They are no more and belong to the unknown. In times of peril, a leader must make difficult decisions to protect those they love or to protect their cause. Whether that cause be for good or bad, one constant is that you can never trust a coward.

16

Charlemagne

October 8, 7:42 p.m.

Stefenski has been making circles around the blocks surrounding Happy's compound at random intervals in an attempt to go unnoticed. He is aggravated that, like normal, he is not with the others. But he understands that he must do his part. He admires the houses in the *Regal Estates* as he passes them. In a moment of self-revelation, he realizes that he can now afford one if he likes. But he decides he wants nothing more than to raise his daughter modestly.

Her mother was a whore in *Skid Row*. She was seventeen when Stefenski bought her. Her name was Charlemagne. She went by Charlie. Charlie was beautiful and, therefore, expensive. Her brown eyes could capture love, anger, and sadness all at the same time; personifying them and giving them to you in subtle ways that only a woman can.

She was so delicate. He could not have sex with her that first time in that dirty hotel room. He just wanted to know her for reasons he could not understand. Maybe her beauty frightened him. She just sat there bewildered when he said he just wanted to talk. Her answers were vague to his questions at first. But eventually, she opened up. Stefenski fell in love with Charlie that first day. He could not decipher whether it was pity or his own loneliness in just needing someone to talk to. One cannot choose their thoughts. One cannot choose love; love chooses them.

Stefenski stole a car a day for a month to buy her from her pimp. It was not greed that drove him; it was earnest love. They were to be married, but he got caught. She was pregnant with Lillian by then. He was sentenced to a year in prison for her freedom. He would have done it all over again if necessary.

"Sacrifice is a part of a life that's worth living," the judge told him; he was unusually sympathetic to Stefenski's cause after his testimony. Stefenski was let out after six months of good behavior.

They were eloped by that same judge that sentenced him. Soon after this, she was shot by her ex-pimp for reasons unknown. Speculation suggests he was jealous of her happiness; he died of a drug overdose before he was arrested. She held onto life for a week. The final days were the hardest for Stefenski. He felt foolish to be sad, when she was the one dying. Lillian was lying on her chest when Charlie finally passed. In some way, he wanted Lillian to know her mother's heartbeat not only as it was in the womb, but as it was in life; even if she won't remember either. That was his only solace. He tried to hate God, but he could not. This was not God's work—one cannot blame a blueprint—and they will try to blame the one who built the machine, but in the end, it is humans who destroy one another.

Subtle Rage

October 8, 7:45 p.m.

Melanie is in shock. The group is hastily moving toward the exit of the compound she once called home. She is leading them there. As she passes Habs' and Levi's entangled dead bodies, she finally realizes how far this must go to end. A thousand thoughts pass through her mind. Her allegiance now rests in the reckless hearts of strangers. She knows little of their past. She can only devote herself to the moment. They reach the door.

Jeremiah speaks, "Stop for a moment."

Melanie turns around. Jeremiah's eyes hold a subtle rage in them. She feels as if they stare through her. They are both frightening and compassionate. The man in the mask and black fedora is human after all. He is just covered in dust and looks ridiculous. Yet his presence is regal. She now knows why Luke will die for Jeremiah if necessary; as will she, in honor of Luke's love. A people can be united by a cause, even if they fight for different reasons.

"Where is the boy?" asks Jeremiah sternly. Melanie stumbles with her words. She has never done that. Jeremiah's presence is intimidating. Suddenly he realizes he has frightened her. He slumps his shoulders and puts his left arm on hers. He says in a soft tone, "I'm sorry. It is just we need to get you girls and the boy out of here. His name is Redd. He is a good kid. He is one of us." Even with his compassionate words, Jeremiah still seems detached to Melanie.

She composes herself. "If you create a diversion, Heather and I can get the boy."

Her brown eyes are now demanding attention. Jeremiah does not entertain overly dramatic eyes; they are not truthful. Melanie's, however, are resolute.

Jeremiah speaks, "Melanie, one fights for love, revenge, or both. I don't think you have made your choice yet. Why are you doing this for us?"

"We need to keep moving," she responds.

Jeremiah turns to Peewee the Clown and tells him, "I can see why you love her."

His smirk cannot be seen beneath the mask, but his body language suggests that he is impressed.

"Billingsly, go with the girls."

Who is Melanie?

October 8, 7:53 p.m.

"There are two ways we can do this, boy. You can stand still so I can do this right, or I will just swing and see how it goes. It might be a couple of fingers—a hand—I don't know." Redd stares in defiance back at the very large man holding a meat clever. He has an eye patch and a thick brown mustache. Redd knows he is probably not going to leave the compound without something missing but has decided that he will show one last act of defiance.

"You're a disgusting human being, you know that?" says Redd. The man does not speak. He is growing impatient. "Who is Melanie?" asks Redd.

"How do you know that name?" responds that man, viciously. Redd points at the wall.

When Redd was first brought into the room, chained to the floor, and had his hood removed, he thought it was odd that it resembled a nursery. There was a chalkboard, stuffed animals and toys in the corner, and a bookshelf with children's novels.

The walls are generally light blue. However, they have artwork and poems written on them. The content seems to grow in complexity and height as one looks from each wall in a clockwise motion. The first drawing is closest to the floor near the entrance. It is a cliché set of stick figures—mother, father, and daughter, with a sun above them. The most striking part of the mural, however, is the sun. It seems that the artist spent most of their effort in perfecting it. It is as if they wanted it to be the focal point of the piece and is signed *Melanie Antoinette Henry*.

As one continues to move their attention clockwise around the room, they will notice the murals becoming darker in their hue and their content alike; as if the room, in some subtle way, tells the life story of the artist. What seems to be the last thing written by the artist is an obscure quote that reads as follows:

"No more can one hate people more than they love money."

The man has grown impatient with Redd. He raises the meat cleaver as Redd points his pinky finger out, places it on the table, and closes his eyes. He figures that his pinky is the least important finger if he has a choice.

Muffled gunshots and yelling can suddenly be heard. It distracts the man's attention momentarily. He moves closer to the door with his right ear at attention to try and make out the commotion.

"It is the Blackguards of Charlatan. You are going to die today, sir," says Redd in a monotone and foreboding voice. He then smiles.

The door is suddenly kicked open. The man is startled and stumbles backward as the Wizard stares at him. Billingsly recognizes the man. He was one of the two that dragged him out of his house that rainy fateful night. "I will soon join you in the unknown, but not right now."

As the pellets rip through the man's flesh, they hurl blood, splattering it against the wall. He is pushed backward and settles, sitting on the floor with his back against the wall. He is struggling for breath and gurgling when the Wizard pulls out his .38.

"No, leave him there!" yells Redd. Billingsly nods at the boy, reholsters his gun, and checks the man for weapons.

Melanie kneels down quickly to remove Redd's shackles while Heather checks him over. She is relieved to see all his fingers still attached and in place.

"Did you make that?" asks Redd. He points to the mural above the dying man.

It is a caricature of the Archangel Michael who seems to be looking down at him with his sword raised. The man's blood is the final addition to the piece.

"I guess I did," she responds.

"Who are you," asks Redd.

"I am Melanie."

Fearlessness is Empty

October 8, 7:51 p.m.

Happy hears the gunshots. He knew this was coming. He takes a long drag from his cigar before putting it out, then puts his hand on the door handle. He suddenly hesitates and looks back at the picture of *The Betrayal* on the mantle. Happy pulls out his .44, steadily aims, and fires. The large-caliber bullet destroys the artwork. It shatters into an oblivion of pieces, much like his life has. He is no longer angry; he is empty. He never knew he could love something more than power and money. Now that she is gone, Happy realizes that he took Melanie's love for granted. He always wants what is best for her, yet always seems detached from her in some way. *Levi is more of a father to her than I am,* he says to himself. They say that love lost is better than never having it; Happy no longer knows if it was ever his to lose.

He turns the handle, pulls the door open, and will never look back. It is ironic how close love and fear are attached; does one fear because they have something to live for? Do they become fearless when there is nothing left? Happy's sentiment will suggest the latter. Sometimes, such answers can only be found within.

The devil and his friends

October 8, 7:59 p.m.

The bottom level of the compound contains an abnormally wide and long hallway. It still has some fancy decor but is used mostly by the staff. There is a kitchen, a utility room, a laundry room, and the nursery. The door where Redd is located is just across the hallway from them. Jeremiah and Luke have taken refuge in the kitchen. Speedy is pinned down farther back and is taking cover behind a marble statue of Caesar. Luke suddenly turns his head and realizes the cooks are still in the kitchen. He quickly turns his gun toward the two men and one woman. They are paralyzed with fear by the sudden chaos as Luke yells to them, "Do you like swiss cheese?"

One of the men nervously responds, "Yes."

"Do you want to be it?"

Trembling, the man responds, "No."

"Then get the fuck out of here. But before you do, make me a PBJ sandwich." Luke laughs while he watches them run away and escape through the rear door of the kitchen. "Some service. I hope they have a complaint box." He is hungry.

"Stay focused, Luke," says the Shadow Walker with a hint of comical inflection.

Jeremiah is taking sporadic fire as he leans out the doorway to return suppressing fire with the Thompson. He can see that Heather is holding Redd's hand while Melanie follows. They are crouched and low to the ground, still inside the nursery. The Wizard begins to lean out and fire.

"It sounds like we have a firefight!" he yells.

His shotguns litters the hallway with pellets, sending fragments of wood and glass everywhere.

"We need to get out of here now. Luke, hand me a frag!" yells Jeremiah.

Luke responds, "Now this is getting fun."

Jeremiah pulls the pin and throws it as far as he can toward the direction of the gunfire.

The boom is deafening. Then there is nothing but pieces of things that once were whole, now broken apart, scattering throughout the hallway with no plan or self-awareness of their cause. Jeremiah makes a motion for everyone to follow him. Melanie pushes herself out first to ensure they all make it back to the maintenance shafts' entrance. Heather is next, followed by Luke, Jeremiah, and finally Billingsly. Jerry is hastily approaching them.

"Is everyone okay, hombres? I'm sorry I got pinned down. There was not much I could do." No one can hear because of the concussion of the frag grenade.

As if in slow motion, Jack Frost points toward their rear as he runs past the group. He begins to pump off shots from his shotgun down the hallway. Happy Hal is toward the end of it. He does not react to Gonzo's shots; a shotgun is not as effective at that range. Happy Hal stands there for a moment, then raises his .44 Magnum. By then, everyone has become aware of the situation. Jeremiah motions for the girls to take Redd and run. Melanie looks back for a moment as she, Heather, and Redd begin to beeline toward the maintenance shafts. She figures it will be the last time she will see her father; she can see that all-too-familiar face full of smug rage.

Melanie no longer has any reservations regarding her decision to aid in her father's downfall.

Speedy takes one more shot, to no affect. He begins to retreat, still pointing his gun downrange. Happy fires. The crack of the large-caliber bullet is intimidating. The bullet barely misses Gonzo as it passes by his right ear. His future recollection of this moment will be in slow motion.

Gonzo is taking cover with others. The four are aligned with their backs against the wall behind the marble statue of Caesar. Jeremiah is at point; it is as if they are mimicking the statue's pose for better cover. Happy Hal begins to run toward the men while continuing to fire. There are large chunks of marble being fragmented from it. Jeremiah reaches around the statue with his Thompson and blindly fires at full auto. The gun is uncontrollable, and he just focuses on maintaining his grip. He is so full of adrenaline that he does not notice a bullet rip through the upper part of his right forearm, barely grazing him, but leaving a large flesh wound nonetheless. Meanwhile, Jack Frost retrieves a frag grenade out of his pouch, pulls the pin out with his teeth, and haphazardly rolls it down the hallway as if it were a bowling ball.

"Frag out!" he yells.

They are all ready to brace for the explosion as the grenade rolls back toward their position; Happy Hal has thrown it back. In a split second and instinctively, the Wizard jumps out from their cover, grabs the rolling grenade, and in one motion throws it back. It explodes less than a second later. Debris flies everywhere. All in witness must wait for the dust cloud to settle before they know the fate of Billingsly.

There is only silence. Billingsly is curled up in the fetal position in the middle of the hallway and parallel to the statue. They take a brief moment to recollect themselves.

Jeremiah looks back and asks, "Is everyone okay?"

Luke and Gonzo nod. "Luke, Gonzo, get ready to provide cover. I'll give suppressing fire. Ready. Go."

Jeremiah jumps from cover and unloads a fury of lead down the hallway. Luke and Speedy follow.

When he reaches Billingsly, Jeremiah stops firing. All three drop to one knee and focus their fear down the hallway, searching and waiting for any movement. The moment is tense. But there is nothing. Jeremiah slings his Thompson around to his back and puts his hand on Billingsly's shoulder; he lightly shakes him. Billingsly does not respond. Jeremiah slowly rolls him onto his back. His robe is tattered and his nose is bleeding. Jeremiah takes off his glove to check Billingsly's pulse below his jaw and on his neck. Jeremiah realizes he is wounded; there is blood dripping from his fingertips onto the Wizard's robe. Regardless, he proceeds—bloody hand and all. Suddenly, Billingsly grabs Jeremiah's arm as he opens his eyes. Their green hues embrace life.

He stares into Jeremiah's for a moment and suddenly says, "What does a guy got to do to get killed around here?" All four share a chuckle.

"You'd have to join the other guy's team," responds Jeremiah as he helps the Wizard to his feet.

"Hombre, you look like hammered shit," says Gonzo.

Besides the bloody nose, he has shrapnel wounds in various places on his body with small blood spots forming on his robe; his messy hair epitomizes his condition. "That fuckin' hurt," says the Wizard, as he is lifted to his feet. "Where's my gun? I saw him run into the kitchen before the grenade went off."

"Here," says Luke as he hands Billingsly his shotgun. The Wizard begins to inspect it and checks if it needs reloading.

"Let's end this tonight," he says as he slides two more rounds into the shotgun's magazine tube.

"What about the girls and Redd?" asks Luke. The three observe Jeremiah lower his head. He is deep in thought. His eyes once again stare into nothing.

Suddenly, he responds, "Melanie knows this place like the back of her hand. She will keep them safe. Tonight, we will have our final dance with the devil and his friends." They all nod in agreement.

A Kiss

October 8, 8:21 p.m.

Heather, Melanie, and Redd are in the maintenance shafts. "They probably came through the sewers, but there is another way," says Melanie. "I used to play down here when I was a kid."

"You had a strange childhood, didn't you?" asks Heather.

"Stranger than you'd think," responds Melanie.

"Are we going to get food soon?" asks Redd.

"We are all hungry. We will eat as soon as we can," responds Heather. The muffled gunfire behind them is disconcerting.

Heather is torn apart inside. She is worried about Jeremiah. She never thought that in her lifetime she would be kidnapped, chained to a floor, shot at, and living in hiding. She does not know if she is part of something greater than herself or just someone caught in the wrong place at the wrong time with the right people. The thought passes through her mind for a brief moment that Jeremiah can be dead. She then hates herself for thinking that way. Heather knows in her heart that he will make it out. She just wishes she told him she was pregnant. So if he did die, it will not only be for the woman he loves or his friends, but also his future child. There is no greater cause that a man can ever have in life; and if death were to call his name, he will go in peace.

"We will have to fit in with the crowd when we get out there. We are going to have to clean up as best we can and get this dust off us. I had a secret hiding place when I was a child down here. I still go in there from time to time. I couldn't stand the screams coming through the vents. It's right around this corner," says Melanie as her pace hastens.

There is a pink door with black polka dots on it. "I can see you were trying to be subtle," says Heather as she lets out a short laugh.

"Subtlety was never part of my design," responds Melanie as she tosses her hair with her hand. She opens the door and flips the light switch on. All three enter.

To no one's surprise, the room is painted pink on all four walls. There is a vanity with various hairbrushes atop it, a small twin-size bed adorned with a houndstooth-patterned comforter, and a light-green sink. I have some extra dresses in the closet over there. Heather observes that they all have polka dots.

"Redd, you're going have to wait outside while we get cleaned up and change."

"You sure I can't stay?" he asks with a devious smirk.

"Get out," Heather and Melanie say simultaneously. He laughs and steps outside.

Melanie and Heather undress down to their bra and panties. They wash all the dust off themselves. They have to wring out the washcloths many times. Melanie is looking at Heather as she is brushing her hair.

"I wish I had your blue eyes," she suddenly says as she breaks the silence.

"What is this?" she then asks.

"What is what?" responds Heather.

Melanie walks up to Heather and is awkwardly close to her. She softly places her right hand on Heather's belly. "You have a little baby bump here. You're pregnant?" inquires Melanie.

Heather turns her head away as she responds, "Yes."

Melanie gently puts her left hand on Heather's chin and directs her head until they make eye contact. Melanie kisses her. She softly bites Heather's upper lip in a moment of sympathetic passion and need. Heather is surprised but does not stop her. Instead, she softly returns the kiss.

Melanie then looks into Heather's eyes and whispers, "Our men will be fine. We will see them soon."

Heather cries not because of the kiss, but because there has been so much bloodshed, fear, and pain in her world lately. Melanie's lips are so soft, delicate, and thoughtful; Heather realizes that she has forgotten what those simple pleasures feel like. A whirlwind of emotions devour all the fear and uncertainty that has been weighing on her heart, even if it's but only for a moment. That is Melanie's intention. She has never kissed a girl before, nor does she intend to do so again.

It was just necessary; as if somewhere in the realm of God's love, they've been given a sacred permission to embrace each other's courage. Heather and Melanie hug as they cry together, and somehow feel closer to God.

They get dressed. Heather is wearing a green sundress with abnormally large, white polka dots; Melanie said it's her favorite. Melanie also gives her a woman's long, black peacoat.

"It is going to snow tonight," she says.

"At least it will cover up most of this dress," Heather mumbles to herself.

Melanie's outfit is similar, but her dress is red with small black polka dots. "What about Redd? Won't he be cold?" asks Heather.

"I'll be fine. I practically live outside," responds Redd in a muffled voice from behind the door. "Can we go now? I'm hungry."

Sympathy for the Cook

October 8, 8:23 p.m.

Happy is making his way past the reserve walk-in coolers, heading toward the cook's sleeping quarters. He is limping while he reloads his Magnum. He had caught shrapnel from the frag grenade in his upper-right leg and buttocks. He is not happy, but he says nothing. He knows now what he is up against and must move fast. The door to the head chef's quarters is up the hallway to the left. He tries to open the door, but it is locked. He knows there is an in-house rotary phone in each of the chef's rooms in case he needs late night or unexpected food service. Happy looks down at the worn-down doormat. It reads, *"I can see your sausage from here."* He rolls his eyes as he lifts a corner of it up and finds the spare key.

Inside, there is a small cot, a cache of cookbooks scattered about, and an old wooden table with a black-and-white tube TV upon it. The antennas are wrapped with tinfoil. The TV is playing an old episode of *My Mother the Car*. Next to it is the phone. Happy calls the in-house emergency number. A man's voice on the other end answers.

"We need to meet at the Alamo. All hands on deck," says Happy.

"Who authorized this?" asks the voice.

"This is Happy."

"Geez, what the hell are you doing in the head chef's room. This is bad, ain't it?" the voice asks.

Happy has lost his patience and roars into the phone, "Just do it now." He then slams phone against the table, breaking it in half before hearing someone make a noise from underneath the cot.

"Who is under there?" asks Happy.

There is no response. He reiterates with anger and authority.

"My name is Hextal. I am the head chef here," responds a voice that stutters and trembles.

"Get out from under there. I am Happy Hal."

"Yes, sir," replies Hextal as he slowly crawls out.

"Stand up." Hextal obeys.

Happy is not a tall man, but he towers over Hextal who is standing feebly before him. "Hextal, do you know how to use a gun?"

"No, sir," he responds, still shaking.

"Then you are useless to me." Happy raises his Magnum, pulls the hammer back, and points it at Hextal's head.

Hextal begins to retreat with his hands raised and begs, "Please, let me say my prayer first. I am not a killer. I am a cook."

Happy ponders for a moment all the delicious meals that this man has made for him. Hextal is the finest chef in *The City*.

He uncocks the Magnum and says, "I might need you after all. Get the hell out of here and take that floor mat with you."

Happy makes a waving motion with the gun toward the door. Hextal stumbles as he runs out of the room. Happy follows. He must get to the Alamo.

17

The Branches of the Elms

October 8, 8:43 p.m.

There is something within the crisp air of a calm, cool fall night that provides comfort to one who is troubled. Mother nature is not shy. She does not care. She will take what she pleases and give what she wants. Her timing is not your timing. But on some nights such as this, she will whisper in your ear thoughts of kindness and tranquility, and incite one's reflections upon a better time—a happier time. It's as if she can put *The City* into a slumber and let it rest its weary eyes, even if but for a moment. Maybe it is her gift, or maybe it is her warning of an impending storm.

Redd is holding Heather's right hand. Melanie is to the left of her. They have made their way away from the compound. Both Heather and Redd are reveling at the mansions of *The Regal Estates*. Redd has never seen trees so large. They dwarf those that are in *The City Park*. Their leaves are a hodgepodge of red, yellow, and brown. The branches of the elms arch over the street, creating what seems like an entryway to some beautiful cathedral ordained by mother nature herself.

They see car lights turn from the corner ahead. Their beams cut through the darkness of the night. Heather's grip on Redd's hand tightens.

"Just act natural," avers Melanie.

The vehicle slows down as it approaches them. The window rolls down. All stare forward as if they don't notice; they continue to walk.

"Heather!" yells a familiar voice. It is Stefenski.

"Sonny, is that you?"

"Yeah, I'm so glad you guys got out. I can't believe we did it." Stefenski suddenly notices that no one is jovial. He tries to break the silence. "Who is she?" asks Sonny while motioning toward Melanie.

"This is Melanie. She got us out of there," responds Heather, finally in a dry tone.

"So this is Luke's fiancée, huh?" Stefenski reaches out the window to shake her hand. Melanie does not move.

"Shit hit the fan in there. They are in a huge firefight." Redd interrupts, subliminally hinting to quit the unnecessary small talk.

"Ah, damn it. I saw that coming. You guys better get in," says Sonny.

"No. The guys will need you here. I know someone up the road that can help us," responds Melanie. Sonny looks at Heather.

She nods and says, "Melanie knows what she is doing. We will go back to the armory."

Stefenski hesitates for a moment, then responds in an emoting soft tone, "All right, just be careful." He casually drives off.

"There is a professor that lives up the road. He's retired now, but he was head of *The Modern Arts* department of *City University* in the *Museum District*. My father paid him to refine my skills at painting. He stopped taking money after a while. I would just show up whenever, and we would talk about anything and everything besides art. We just laughed all the time." Melanie smirks slightly as she momentarily reminisces.

"It's getting colder out. And we need to eat," says Heather suddenly.

"It's just up the road. We will get food there," responds Melanie.

No one speaks anymore. They walk in silence, juxtaposed, listening to the subtle creaking and moaning of the elms and the rustling of every leaf, which is amplified in the stillness of this cold October night.

A Bullet and A Sandwich

October 8, 8:37 p.m.

The hallway is swiss cheese. Every footstep sounds as if they are walking on eggshells made of fragmented splinters of wood, glass, and other unrecognizable debris. Gonzo enters the kitchen first. The frag grenade has loosened most of the pots and pans from their hanging hooks above the center island of the kitchen. They are strewn about on the floor. Jerry pans the room for a moment. It quickly becomes obvious that Happy is not in the kitchen. He keeps his weapon trained on the restaurant kitchen-style door to the back left while the others enter.

"Take a look," says Speedy as he points to the floor; there is a trail of blood droplets leading to the kitchen's door.

"He's got to be wounded," says the Wizard.

"Well, he certainly ain't dead yet," quips Jeremiah. "Get in position and ready to move."

"Hold on," says Luke suddenly. They all turn back and observe him run over to the fragment-riddled stainless steel fridge. He opens the door and rummages through it. Luke pulls out an egg salad sandwich wrapped in plastic wrap. "It isn't PBJ, but it will have to do. The rabbits are hungry." They watch as he unwraps it, lifts up his clown mask, and shoves the entire sandwich in his mouth at one time. He then sticks his fingers into his mouth and pulls out a 00 size shotgun pellet and throws it on the ground without hesitation. Luke then returns to the fridge, pulls out a half-gallon carton of milk, and washes the rest of the sandwich down.

"You're a strange guy, Pewee," remarks the Wizard.

"Alright, I'm ready," responds Luke.

Darkness

October 8, 8:42 p.m.

Gonzo demands to be on point. He kicks open the door. It swings back, hitting him in the face and knocking off his fedora.

Jeremiah laughs, picks up Jerry's hat, and says, "Didn't you know that restaurant kitchen doors swing both ways, just like your last girlfriend?" Frustrated, Jerry rubs his nose, puts his hat back on, and enters without responding. The rest follow. Luke is last. The door hits him in the back bumping him slightly forward into the Wizard.

Suddenly, everything goes dark. The power has been cut to the compound; they are immediately blinded by complete darkness. There is no natural light in the lower levels, so their eyes will not even be able to adjust.

"Luke, turn on your flashlight," says Jeremiah.

"I thought you had one," he responds.

"Does anyone have one?" asks the Wizard. No one responds.

"Does anyone have a lighter?" asks Jeremiah.

"I only have some matches from *Renee's Diner*," responds Luke. He fumbles in one of the pockets of his pants for a moment, then lights one up.

The small flame is surprisingly bright in the abyss of darkness that surrounds them. They all have their left hand on each other's shoulder, while their right hand keeps contact with the wall as they move forward. Luke is now on point. The matches only last a short time, so he must continually light a new one. Their ears are fixated on every sound, as if their sudden blindness has heightened their audible sensory capabilities. They all know that their situation is dire; they can be ambushed at any time. The moment is tense. Luke suddenly breaks the silence after they progress about twenty yards down the hallway, based on Jeremiah's estimated count.

"This door is the janitor's office. See?" Luke redundantly holds a match up to the sign on the door and reiterates as he reads, "Janitor's Office." He turns the handle. Surprisingly, the door is unlocked.

"There has to be something in there we can use for light," suggests Jeremiah. They all enter.

Luke hurries to find something to make a torch with; he is running out of matches. The others wait in darkness. There is a four-tier metal shelf with an assortment of neatly organized tools. He finds a *Hokanson's* brand butane torch. The tank is nearly full. After lighting it, he searches further and finds an old butane lantern behind an old *Park's and Co. Petrol* oil can. Its tank is empty, but Luke is sure the tank from the torch will fit the lantern. It does. The lantern lights up the entire room to the relief of the others. Somehow, it almost seems too bright as their eyes adjust. Luke hangs it from a hook attached to a ceiling rafter. They all explore further for something that can be useful for their cause.

The Wizard inspects the ceiling, looking for security cameras. He finds one and covers it with an old mechanic's rag to simulate that the room is still dark, just in case. Gonzo finds an old tin first aid kit hanging on the wall. Luke, meanwhile, is rummaging through the other shelves.

Jeremiah walks over to an industrial-style steel desk that sits to the left when you first walk into the office. On it, he observes an assortment of maintenance logs, schematics of the compound, and a photograph with a handmade frame constructed of balsa wood; in the photograph, Melanie is sitting on Levy's lap. She must be eight years old or so. It looks as though Levy is braiding her hair. Their smiles are true and deeply intimate, as if he loved her like a father would love his own daughter; smiles of that nature cannot be fabricated.

For a moment, Jeremiah questions his own thoughts on Melanie. She witnessed a man who meant so much to her die; not by her hands, but being indirectly responsible, and held her composure without breaking down. *There really wasn't any time to grieve,* he thinks to himself. Will it hit her later? Jeremiah hopes so. However, she is her father's daughter after all.

Jeremiah stares intently at the photograph, specifically Levy. His thoughts wander; he is responsible for giving the order to kill this man after all. It was necessary; but at the same time, he was not emotionally bound to Levy such as Melanie was. Suddenly, and for unknown reasons, Jeremiah reminisces about a quote his father had handwritten on poster paper and tacked to the ceiling above Jeremiah's bed so it would be the first thing he saw when he woke up in the morning:

"All is as it was and can only be what it will become. Our fate is bound to our own choices."

"What is that?" asks Gonzo. Jeremiah suddenly breaks his daydream.

"It's nothing," he responds as he places the picture facedown on the table.

"Take off your coat. I am going to bandage your wound."

"Okay. Hey, Luke. Take a look at these schematics." Jeremiah gathers the drafts off the table and hands them to Luke who is already beside him.

"You've gotten blood all over them," says Luke as he takes them to where there is better light, underneath the hanging lantern. The Wizard drags over an old wooden table from the corner and joins Luke to inspect them.

Jeremiah takes off his coat and sits in Levy's chair. He looks at his forearm. From the wound down to his fingertips is completely covered in dry and coagulated blood. The wound itself is worse than he thought. The skin is torn to pieces and the muscle exposed. There are fragments of fabric from his coat within it, and more blood seems to seep out in synchronization with every one of Jeremiah's heartbeats. Gonzo uses a small squeeze bottle of iodine to flush out the wound and sterilize the surrounding area. After putting on the dressing pad, he wraps the wound tightly with gauze, and exhausts the entire roll of medical tape to make sure the bleeding stops.

"That feels so much better," says Jeremiah as he opens and closes his fist several times. "Thanks, Jerry."

"No problem, Shadow Man."

"I think we have something here, fellas," says the Wizard as he and Luke are staring at them. Luke's index finger is firmly pressed upon the schematic. Jeremiah stands up, puts his coat back on, and buttons it up. He and Gonzo walk to the table. They have a plan.

Professor Tjaden

October 8, 8:55 p.m.

Melanie knows the pass code to open the gates to the professor's estate. She says, "Professor Tjaden changed it to my birthday so I would always remember it. When I was younger, I didn't even have to use the code. I would just squeeze through the bars." Melanie puts in the code—0916. The gates make a droning-like electric hum as they slowly open.

The driveway is made of gray cobblestone. The house is large and eloquent. Yet, it is forgetful. Like the tenements that litter *Skid Row*, the houses in this neighborhood tend to all look the same to Heather. Redd is still fixated on the trees. The driveway leads to a large double-door garage. They take the brick pathway through a white lattice arch to the front door.

"Normally, I would just walk in, but I have not been over in a while."

There is no doorbell; only a large and seemingly archaic cast-iron knocker. It squeaks and clanks loudly as Melanie knocks three times.

A man of average height opens the door. His eyes are a rare shade of gray. He is wearing a brown wool cardigan and tan slacks. His hair is thick and mostly gray with random patches of brown locks.

"Melanie, it's been too long," he says excitedly as he reaches out his arms. Melanie and Tjaden embrace. "What brings you here so late?" he finally asks after a long hug.

"We need your help. We have trouble," she softly responds.

"Come in, come in. Who are your friends?"

"This is Heather, and this is Redd," says Melanie as Heather extends her hand. Tjaden accepts her handshake.

"I am really hungry," says Redd.

Tjaden squats down to make eye contact with the boy and says, "Well then, I guess we'll have to make you guys some grub then, huh?"

"Please, sir," responds Redd.

As they enter Tjaden's home, Heather whispers in Redd's ear, "Don't steal anything from this nice man."

"I have to," he responds.

They go directly left through an open doorway; the room resembles an oversize living room. The fireplace is aglow with hot embers and flames. The iron firewood crib is stacked with dry, aged logs. Melanie and Heather take off their coats and leave them on a recliner. They sit next to each other on the twin sofa. Redd is sitting cross-legged on the floor in front of the fireplace. Tjaden takes a seat in what Melanie knows to be as his thinking chair. He rings a small handbell to beckon his longtime maid. She arrives in the room immediately with a pitcher of ice water and four glasses.

"Doris, how are you?" asks Melanie excitedly.

"Oh, Mel, it is so nice to see you! I thought that was your voice I heard," responds Doris. They, too, share a long hug.

"Doris, she is pregnant and needs to eat. The boy has been through a long day. He is really hungry. Could you make us some of your famous Polish cuisine?"

"Of course, Melabean," responds Doris as she still has her hands on Melanie's shoulders. Doris is so happy to see her.

"What is the nature of your predicament?" asks Tjaden, attempting to prevent digression. Melanie refocuses. She sits back down on the twin sofa and quickly begins to go through, in detail and truthfulness, the events of the day and what led to them. Tjaden has known few details of Melanie's father but has always had reservations regarding the nature of his income. He has only known him as Bob Jameson. Tjaden listens both intently and with a careful balance of sympathy and anger.

"That is quite a story," says Tjaden as he adjusts his round spectacles. Doris comes in and serves perogies, kielbasas in sauerkraut, and Melanie's favorite, celery sticks stuffed with cream cheese. All four indulge themselves. Redd devours his milk, and Doris keeps his glass full. In her pregnancy, Heather has a constant craving for orange juice and drinks three glasses while Melanie and Tjaden sip an aged Merlot. Both the food and atmosphere is hearty and soothing. However, they know they must be on their way.

"Tjaden, we need some transportation. We came here for your help. But we have to do this ourselves," says Melanie. Tjaden rubs his chin with his index finger and thumb while Heather and Redd wait intently for his response.

"I assume you are going to need to be discreet," he finally says. "Take the *Dodge Destiny*. It's old and drab, but it runs great."

"That should do the trick, Tjaden," says Melanie in a loving tone as she excitedly opens her arms to give him a big hug.

"Doris will give you the keys," he says as they finish their embrace.

Heather stands up to wake up Redd, who has fallen asleep in front of the fireplace. "We have to go," says Melanie.

The garage door is already open when they get outside. "Do you have a license?" asks Melanie to Heather.

"No. Do you?" she responds.

Melanie just smiles without answering. The *Dodge Destiny* is a smaller sedan adorned with faded maroon paint, a peeling after-coating, and an assortment of scratches and surface dents. Tjaden's words were true. The jalopy starts immediately. The four cylinders clink and clank as it fires up on the first crank. Heather makes sure Redd is buckled in properly in the back seat before sitting in the passenger seat. She fumbles with the seat belt for a moment before it finally locks into position.

For Melanie, there is a sense of freedom in the moment. She has never driven a car without one of her father's chauffeurs before. This car can take her far, far away—away from everything. She thinks for a moment of just driving off and leaving this all behind. She adjusts the rearview mirror and catches Redd in its reflection. He is just staring out the window—a blank stare. Melanie begins to feel some form of selfish guilt; she was given everything she ever wanted, but never indulged. All she ever really wanted was what she didn't have—someone who understood her. She suddenly feels lonely and detached. Redd has never known that form of selfishness. All he's ever known is how to scratch and claw his way through life. *Maybe he's the lucky one,* she thinks to herself.

The Alamo

October 8, 9:12 p.m.

Whispers of silent repose never entertained Happy's intentions, nor could they ever. Chaos is his god, fear is his mistress, and death is his masterpiece. He views kindness as pagan and love as weakness. He cares so little for life that he does not even put value on his own. The only thing he ever foolishly come close to loving is Melanie. Now she is gone. Happy's rage has made him blind of emotions and deaf to the pleas of mercy.

The Alamo is a detached building in the rear of Happy's compound. It resembles a large four-door garage from the outside, adorned with expensive cedar wood shingles atop antique brick exterior walls. The bricks were salvaged from the *Old Main Train Station*. There was protest from some people in *The City* against tearing the station down as it was protected by *The City Historical Coalition*. They were silenced, and Happy got his way.

Like Happy himself, the exterior of the Alamo is just a fancy shell of the truth that lies within. Behind the brick is a two-foot-thick concrete wall reinforced with rebar. There is a large arsenal of varying weapons in the armory to the rear. Behind the first garage door is a white four-door limousine that was custom-built to be bulletproof. Looking at it, one would find it unassuming, reflecting Happy's never-ending battle to keep a low profile. There is also the compound's command center to the aft and left of the garage structure. That is where they cut the power upon Happy's instruction. He did so knowing it will slow down the Blackguards of Charlatan and buy him and his henchmen more time to get organized and plan their counterattack.

"Gentlemen, have we reached the climax of *The Harvest Union's* empire? I think not." Happy slams his right fist on the table. He speaks in a direct and angry tone. "Incompetence has become rampant through our lackadaisical approach to progress. Instead of moving forward, we have become content in our constant and easily obtained decadence. Business has become a routine, and therefore, we let ourselves become numb to what is important—power, sub-jugation, and obedience." Happy pans his eyes from left to right, observing his nine henchmen who are listening intently. "Everything we have worked so hard for is under attack by these fools. *The City* would be in disarray without our control. We need to save our city, and save our livelihood." All the men agree. One of them, Liberto, actually gets teary-eyed.

Happy continues. "As you all probably know by now, we are under attack by a bunch of amateurs who are hell-bent on destroying what we worked so hard for." Happy pauses for a moment and looks around. "Does anyone know where Levy and Habs are?" he asks.

"Last I knew, Habs was heading down to the maintenance shafts with Levy," responds Liberto. "Levy heard some noises and went and got Habs. That is the last I heard from them."

"Then, they are probably dead," says Happy solemnly. "Those assholes got Bull's-Eye in the nursery too. Trevor, go get the medical kit. I need someone to pull this shrapnel out of my ass and patch me up."

"Yes, sir," responds Trevor from across the room.

"I know some of you are pretty beat up, but we don't have much time. And if we are going down, we are going to take *The City* down with us. Gear up and get ready to move."

The Ghost that Haunts the October Sky

October 8, 9:17 p.m.

Luckily, the kitchen has an abnormally large dumbwaiter. They each take turns; first is Jack Frost, then the weapons, followed by the Wizard, Pewee the Clown, and finally, the Shadow Walker. The ride up to the third floor is relatively quick.

They must have spent a lot of money on this thing to have a backup battery, Jeremiah thinks to himself. Luke and the Wizard suggest that their best course of action will be to start on the highest floor and work their way down so they would always have the high ground. The roof will have to be cleared first, however.

The dumbwaiter jerks to a stop. The door slides open from the outside. Luke is standing there with the lantern. Seeing a man in a clown mask holding a lantern surrounded by almost complete darkness catches Jeremiah off guard. Luke holds out his hand and helps Jeremiah out.

"This should be it," says Luke as he lifts the lantern up in the air and pans the room. They are in Happy's office.

The embers of the once lit fire are now barely aglow. They illuminate the room in a soft orange hue, accompanied by darkness and the aroma of spent cedar. Jeremiah walks over to the fireplace and bends at both knees. He momentarily puts his palms out to feel its warmth, but is suddenly distracted by a picture frame sitting on the floor. He observes the broken glass and the bullet hole through the middle. The shattered glass makes the picture unrecognizable. So he flips it over, takes off the back cover, and removes it. It is the picture of *The Betrayal.* Jeremiah reads the inscription: "For Daddy. Love Melanie." He thinks for a moment of folding it up and placing it in his pocket. Instead, Jeremiah throws it into the embers. As he watches it burn, he somehow feels that it is what Melanie would want. He decides he will never tell her about this moment, even if he were to get the chance.

"You ready to move?" asks Billingsly suddenly.

"Yeah. Let's go," responds Jeremiah. Luke opens the door while Gonzo covers. There is only silence and darkness on the other side.

"It doesn't seem like anybody's home," says the Wizard as he squints in a futile attempt to see down the hallway. He has a slight smirk on his face.

"We need to get to the roof." Jeremiah interrupts. They move. Luke hands the lantern to Gonzo, who will be on point again.

The lantern only shines roughly ten feet in front of them. Luke has memorized the floor plans like usual, but Gonzo is still nervous being on point. He does not want to get shot again. He hasn't even recovered from the first time. He is tense. Sweat is pouring down his face and stinging his eyes.

Suddenly, Jeremiah aggressively grabs the lantern from him while saying, "We need to move quicker." Gonzo is both angry and relieved at the same time. The group follows.

As Jeremiah walks down the hallway on point, he kicks open every door haphazardly while holding up his tommy gun and the lantern. He fires a short burst down the hallway in frustration; it startles everyone. The bullets make thumping noises as they hit their unintended targets.

"Do you see something?" asks Luke in a nervous tone. Jeremiah does not answer.

"Save your bullets for the enemy, Mr. Shadow Man," avers Billingsly in an aggressive tone. "Your mind has become separated from your soul. We don't need this nonsense at this point. If you want to die for whatever reason, that is fine. Just don't take us with you."

"Then leave," responds Jeremiah as he keeps moving.

The Wizard suddenly lurches forward, grabs Jeremiah by the shoulder, and turns him around in a fit of rage. The Shadow Walker and the Wizard are in a showdown.

"Look at me. Look into my eyes," commands Billingsly as he points with his index and middle fingers toward them. Jeremiah does not speak or move for several seconds. Speedy and Luke are frozen. It is a moment of uncertainty. One thing they know is that Jeremiah does not like to be touched. He suddenly lifts the lantern up next to Billingsly's face in a quick motion. The soft glow exacerbates every contour the man's face, as if every shadow of every wrinkle tells its own story. The metallic mask of the Shadow Walker does so as well—every scratch, dent, divot, and scar.

The men are face-to-face, less than a foot away from each other. Their eyes differ in many ways within the glow of the lantern light; Billingsly's are fiery, and their green hues have become reminiscent of the burning lights of Aurora. Jeremiah's are distant and detached; they have become a deep-blue void. Both men are angry but for different reasons.

"I've had enough of this bullshit," says the Wizard suddenly and violently.

"I am the one dying. You are walking around in this selfish rage trying to get yourself killed." Billingsly pauses for a moment then continues, "Do you know how precious life is? Do you know what it's like to be told you have three months to live and your family cannot even be by your side because you have to protect them? You are selfish. I have more life in my dying eyes than you do."

Jeremiah has just been staring at Billingsly while remaining motionless. He suddenly slings around his tommy gun so it's resting to his rear. He puts his right hand on the Wizard's shoulder and asks, "Are you afraid of dying?"

"Of course," responds Billingsly immediately. Jeremiah momentarily stares off into the dark abyss that seemingly absorbs all light; sans that which is reflecting in his eyes.

Finally, he says, "Sadness has ruled most of my life. There is peace in the unknown. So I do not fear death, nor do I welcome it. It is just there. Why should we fear the inevitable?" attests Jeremiah.

"You're a fool," blurts Billingsly as Jeremiah readies his tommy gun and walks away.

Suddenly and unexpectedly, however, he stops, turns around, and walks back toward Billingsly while still holding up the lantern. He speaks in a vicious tone as he rhythmically pokes his index finger into the Wizard's chest:

You lost your family, yes, but they are still alive. Mine are gone and dead at the hands of this monster. Stefenski lost his girl to this death-monger's drugs when that asshole pimp killed her. I have no idea where Heather, the boy, and Melanie are. Death and misery follows everything Happy touches, but he does not indulge. So I am going to introduce him to it. I will do it for my parents, and I will do it for Charlemagne. But I will not do it for you, Billingsly. We are only here together because we are united by the same cause. So shut your fucking mouth and get ready to move so we can see this thing through to its bitter end."

The Wizard has nothing left to say. He knows Jeremiah is right. They all get into single-line formation; Jeremiah on point. They reach the door leading to the roof without incident; it is locked. Gonzo breaks off the handle quite easily with the four-pound sledgehammer he found in the janitor's office. The stairwell to the roof is narrow.

There is a red door at its peak. Gonzo passes the hammer up the line to the Wizard, who is second from point. He breaks the handle to the roof access door while Jeremiah covers.

The group enters the rooftop with intrepid guile, moving like a ghost that haunts the October sky. A motley assemblage of shadows disguise the light that should surround them. But they are the Blackguards of Charlatan, led by the Shadow Walker himself; this is where they belong, and they all know it.

Thoughts of Brutus

October 8, 9:43 p.m.

There is a small noise heard by all, similar to the sound of a wineglass breaking. It is subtle and barely audible. But it is there, and it is frightening to those of who know its source. There is then a thud, followed by immediate trepidation within the group. Knox is hit. He stumbles forward before falling to his knees. A mist of blood sprays onto some of the others. Knox grasps his shoulder and roars out in pain before attempting to stand once again. His attempt is futile as he falls back to the ground. It is a survivable wound to the shoulder but debilitating nonetheless.

The Blackguards of Charlatan literally catches Happy Hal with his pants down. Trevor is still attempting to pull shrapnel out of Happy's buttocks when Knox is hit. And as bullets from automatic gunfire begin to ricochet off various objects within the Alamo, Happy quickly pulls up his pants, loops his belt, and takes cover behind the Limousine. He is amused. He misjudged how much time they had to get organized, but Happy loves chaos. It is his drug and his purpose.

They are pinned down and have become self-aware of this fact. Their only option is to escape in the armored limousine. Happy is in first, followed by Knox, Trevor, then the others. Burkowski will be driving.

The mood in the vehicle is mixed among the men. Some are focused and alert, grasping their weapons with confidence; others have eyes that hold noticeable fear. Happy hates this. He stares at those men from the back seat of the limo with disgust and abhorrence. His eyes pierce them. It is as if they have already betrayed him, like Brutus had done to Caesar. His thumb is on the hammer of his pistol. He wants to kill the weak ones but knows he needs them as bait, if nothing else. Happy has accepted his own evil. It is pure; he is no longer capable of remorse, love, or any quality that exists in humans that separates us from the animals.

The limo crashes through the front iron gates of the compound with ferocity. Stefenski has to swerve to avoid the collision. His attempt is unsuccessful; the back bumper of the limo catches the front edge of the van as it fishtails through a right turn. The chrome bumper sparks as it spins and skids across the black pavement. It finally settles across the road in a neighbor's lawn. The commotion, however, has stirred up the neighborhood. Lights begin to turn on, and people can be observed peeking out of their windows taking the form of dark silhouettes caped in curiosity. In his periphery, Stefenski sees Jeremiah, the Wizard, Luke, and Gonzo hurrying down the driveway toward him. He is dazed by the adrenaline rush incited by the near miss with the limo. From his perspective, it is as if they are running in slow motion and taking an eternity to reach the van. Their very presence should invoke thoughts of impending troubles. However, he is comforted in some indescribable way that only he can know and experience; words will always fail to define such moments. But even death enjoys a companion because loneliness is worse. If so it must be, he will not die alone, and that is somehow comforting.

Thaddeus Bismire

October 8, 10:27 p.m.

The City Redd has called home the entirety of his life, although be it short, suddenly seems so foreign to him. He has only known wandering, scavenging, and haggling with the vile creatures that inhabit its dark shadows. For the first time, the hands that grasp his on either side bring a solemn comfort to his troubled young soul. He never noticed the beauty of a moment, nor the kindness of people, until now. His endeavors for survival have blinded him of all things of that nature. However, sometimes one must play the cards they are dealt, fold, and then wait for that perfect hand before they go all in.

They have run out of gas. Apparently and without their knowledge, the gas gauge is broken. The vehicle gurgles and suffocates as it comes to a stop. Its electrical systems are the only thing working as the headlights dim, running solely on battery power. Heather, Redd, and Melanie decide it will be best to walk. They are only about a mile away from the office anyway, and the crisp air is refreshing.

"I know a shortcut," says Redd as he motions with his hand. "This way." They make a left turn onto a street named *Via Tripodi*.

"This isn't a good neighborhood," says Heather immediately.

"Ms. Heather, Ms. Melanie, I trusted you before when we were in that compound. Now, it is your turn to trust me," responds Redd. His baby face is momentarily absent and replaced by unwavering determination that can only be manufactured by subconscious guile. He ungrasps both of their hands, turns toward them, and stares into the women intently while waiting for the answer to a question he never asked, but craftily implied. They both look at him, exchange a brief glance, and apprehensively nod to each other in agreement. They walk.

Via Tripodi is in one of the oldest and original parts of *The City*. The archaic streetlamps are unchanged from the day they were installed, other than the fact that they were converted from gas to electric some time ago. Their chipped paint manifests their age with subtle variances, almost like the rings of a tree—truthful but less accurate. The colors of every layer seem to reflect the mood of the era in which they were painted; each grow darker as they reach their most current and topmost hue—matte black.

It begins to snow; it is a light flurry. The snowflakes have just crystallized and are small. They swirl at the will of a breeze that seems to always be present in this area of *The City*. The sidewalks are in disrepair. The old water and precipitation management systems leak, creating ice beneath them. The ice lifts and distorts the concrete slabs of the sidewalk creating a pattern of raised and concaved cracks. Redd avoids stepping on such cracks. He does not want to break his mother's back, even if he does not know who she is.

"Here, this way," says Redd with confidence. He is pointing down an alleyway. It is completely dark, other than a distant flame from what looks like a barrel fire. Before they even enter the alleyway, they hear a voice. It is an inaudible whisper followed by a sadistic cackle. Echoing footsteps can then be heard clamoring away into the darkness. Redd is undeterred and proceeds to walk forward toward the fire. Reluctantly, the girls follow. Along the way, they can hear sordid coughs and occasional mumbles of beggars who feel entitled to indulge within their own sorrow, thinking someone will give a damn. Maybe someone does; just not them, not tonight.

"Who is coming from over there, walking toward old Teddy Bear?" The words resonate throughout the alleyway. If *The City* has a voice, one could be certain that it would sound as such. The wheels squeak as a figure in a wheelchair slowly makes its way toward them. Meanwhile, Melanie, Heather, and Redd have become subconsciously drawn to the warmth of the barrel fire; they huddle around it while waiting as the features of an older black man with gray hair and a grizzled beard slowly manifest from the darkness. He has no legs below the knees and is missing the index finger on his right hand. He is adorned in a shirt the color of jade and a Zulu hat the color of purple, which is accented with gold trim and red patterns. On his lap is a gray cat with drab yellow eyes.

"It's me, Redd. We are just passing through."

"You know I don't entertain guests, young Jasper," says the man as he strokes his cat. The cat does not take its eyes off them.

"Give us a break. We have trouble. We need to pass," responds Redd.

"Your trouble is not my trouble. But I can make yours double. You know the score, Master Jasper, so it need be that you better talk faster."

"I can pay our way. Here." Redd pulls from under his coat a sterling silver candleholder he stole from Professor Tjaden's fireplace mantle and hands it over to the man. Melanie looks at Heather with a livid expression on her face. Heather does not make eye contact with her. She just shakes her head while looking away, disappointed.

"This is Melanie, and this is Heather," says Redd firmly, as the man inspects the candleholder. Redd continues in an even more affirming voice, "Don't be rude. Introduce yourself."

The man pauses momentarily and stares at him with a look of rage, as if he has been extremely offended by the boy's tone. Then, and suddenly, he looks up at them. While panning with his eyes, he says with a slithering inflection, "Of course, Jasper, my little Redd friend. Where are my manners? Ladies, my name is Thaddeus Bismire, but you can call me Teddy if so you're ready to be my acquaintance."

"Nice to meet you, Mr. Bismire," responds Melanie in a noticeably uninspired attempt to be cordial. Heather once again does not even respond. She is still seething in anger over Redd's thievery of Tjaden, and Thaddeus notices.

"Well, ratta tat tat, said the man with the bat. It wasn't me who stole the fat from the cat. Of course we all know that. It's always the one-armed man with the hockey stick," says Thaddeus. He shares with himself a short chuckle, as if he is amused by his own cryptic words. He then continues in an unlikely solemn voice: "Don't be mad at the boy. You see, we are all thieves and liars when we needs to be."

Thaddeus then pulls a large cigar from his coat and lights it. He takes a deep drag and immediately exhales a thick white smoke ring. He smirks, as if entertained, while not taking his eyes off them. He then focuses directly on Redd and says, "Jasper, you know as I know, the streets talk more than a gossiping midwife with a dirty butter knife. If its trouble you seek, then its trouble you'll find. But these alleyways, these are mine. You may pass. But first you must help me with a task. You see my little furry friend doesn't have a name. Maybe I'm to blame, but all the same, will you help me with thisss simple endeavor?"

"Prudence. Her name is Prudence," blurts out Melanie immediately. As if in a moment of pondering, Thaddeus slowly rubs his four fingers through his knotted beard.

"I like it, I must admit. You know she is a cat of the streets—a gray, a fray, a Machiavellian stray, now named Prudence. So her story goes. One day, I found her in a litter in an alleyway by *St. Paul's Cathedral*. There was a dog that didn't want to give her away. But I had a look and took her anyway. Old Teddy Bear always gets whats he wants. That dog was a damn fool of a mutt. Go now. You've exhausted your stay."

As they proceed down the alleyway with Redd, they can hear Prudence purring. And in a low tone, they can hear Thaddeus Bismire give one last piece of advice: "Cat, scat, matter of fact, it's nice we had this little chat. But do not wander from the path."

An obnoxious and hellacious laugh fades away as Melanie, Heather, and Redd hurriedly make a pass through the maze of back alleyways. Redd knows that if they pleased Thaddeus, there will be no trouble; it is the rest of *The City* he is worried about.

Whiskey Run

October 8, 10:01 p.m.

The two rear tires of the van squeal and scream in protest as they spin on the cold blacktop, each fighting for grip and sharing their struggle with the suddenly awakened neighborhood. The large V8 rumbles and churns in perfect cadence with its powerful design. The men are quiet at first. There is really nothing for them to say. In speculation and speculation only, they can each agree that they are glad to be out of the compound, and that they are glad to see their friend Stefenski. These things are known but unspoken.

Sonny breaks the silence. "Are we chasing down these fucks or what?"

"Yes," responds Jeremiah dryly.

Sonny's voice grows louder and more intense in order to be heard above the ambient noise in the van. "I saw Heather and Redd, and the other girl too. Melanie, I think. They were walking down the road toward someone's house that they said was safe." Jeremiah and the rest share an internal sigh of relief.

"Turn the fucking heat down, man. I'm sweating my gonads off here, hombre. Do we have any water?" asks Gonzo.

"Here," responds Luke as he hands him a bottle of aged whiskey and calmly says, "Water is for horses. Men drink whiskey."

Gonzo grudgingly agrees, spins the cap off, and indulges with a large swig. He replaces the cap, then gestures to hand the bottle to Jeremiah, but Jeremiah does not notice; he is once again staring off into space. Billingsly observes this and quickly takes the bottle from Gonzo's hand. He treats himself to an even larger swig than Gonzo's before twisting the cap back on and handing the bottle back to Luke.

"Jeremiah, you shouldn't think too much all the time. Thinking will drive a man crazy," says Luke as he is holding the bottle up in front of Jeremiah's face. "Here, this will help calm you down." Suddenly, and without looking directly at him, Jeremiah haphazardly snags the bottle out of Luke's hand. He lifts his mask up with his left hand, and with his right hand, he uses only his thumb to spin the cap off the bottle. It slingshots down onto to the floor of the van and continues to spin.

For a brief moment, the bottle cap catches the eye of the Wizard. He is mesmerized by the rotating object, unlikely brought to life by the carelessness of someone else's actions. And unlikely landing on the only spot of the floor where physics are an accessory to its cause and friction is nil. It spins carelessly. It will never be self-aware. It will never concede to its own endeavor. It is just there, riding the momentum of its circumstantial beginning, and obligated to succumb to its inevitable end.

The Wizard's daydream is broken as Jeremiah stomps his foot on the spinning cap. Billingsly instinctively looks up. Jeremiah Revel's face is comforting. It is human again. His eyes care. It seems as if it has been a lifetime since they have seen their friend. They watch as he bottoms up and guzzles down the remainder of the whiskey.

"Crazy, you say? Have you looked around this van lately?" says Jeremiah unexpectedly and with an impish grin on his face. He then cocks his head in a downward motion to make the mask flip back down, once again becoming the thing that is the Shadow Walker. They all briefly share his smile that they hope still exists underneath the mask.

"You better strap in. It's going to get rough." Sonny implies in a foreboding tone. The approaching yelps and blares of police sirens can be heard muffled in the distance.

Sonny's hands grip the steering wheel with anxious authority. Driving the van is like driving a tank as far as maneuverability is concerned. He knows that he will not be able to keep up with the modified limo; he will have to use his knowledge of the back roads to cut them off. What happens then? There is no plan.

19

Dreamville Borough

He was a lost boy; a young heart is not designed to carry such a burden. Very few, if anyone at all, could ever understand his point of view. *The City* had lost a hero; the boy had lost his father. He no longer seemed to fit in anywhere and felt as if he was an outsider looking in; perplexed by a world he couldn't understand, nor it him.

"It's not your fault," his mother would say as he watched her wither away. She seemed to have aged overnight after Isaiah was killed. And in the cadence of typical human condition, the young boy's sorrow soon turned into an elixir of anger and selfish rage.

The first time he got into a fistfight was for her. In retrospect, he cannot recall details of what set him off. Maybe the other guy just had the wrong tone. He didn't even know he liked her, but Jeremiah got his ass kicked on Heather's behalf by an older boy that day. And she eventually annoyed him so much that he couldn't stop thinking about her.

He had passed by the place many times before, paying it little attention. But now, he had a purpose. He entered *Al's Boxing Academy* with the intention of learning how to defend himself but gained so much more.

Al knew his father, Isaiah, and took it upon himself to teach Jeremiah the art of sparring. There was no charge. Jeremiah was a natural, but novice. Al's first lesson seemed odd and uninspiring to him at first, but the young man slowly accepted the program: Do not fight with anger; use it as a weapon with calm and calculated precision.

"Be the hammer, not the nail!" Al would always yell from the ringside with a raucous timbre.

Jeremiah's first ring fight was sloppy—full of haymakers and little strategic grace. By happenstance, he had won by a small margin in a judge's decision but paid the price physically; his fifteen-year-old body took a month to recover. He wore his bruises as badges of courage, of course, like any young man would. After he recovered, he went on to compete in four other fights, finally losing the fifth one; he was devastated because Heather was there. He had somehow convinced her to come watch him, even though she said that boxing was stupid and only morons will hit each other for sport. But her eyes were transparent at times. He could see through them—even if only occasionally—and at her own will. They built legacies he thought he could never live up to. Yet he was the legend to her, even if unintentionally and misunderstood.

That was the first time they kissed; it was his first kiss. Her lips absorbed his pain. How could someone love such a bloody and battered body, let alone a soul? His words were rambling at first, and he was almost able to muster up the courage to say how he felt, but he had truly exhausted his knowledge of words that could ever define her beauty. Everything else could only exist on the edge of her lips. Even then, he would not want to understand. He knew that she is everything he is not. Sadness had ruled his life. Her smile, her eyes—they became the cure to his world. She was her. Her heart, her lips, and her eyes; her breath was a gift. And such as the truths held within earnest love, she wanted his pain to be hers; she would make it her own. And if she could not, then they would share it. But they said nothing. Their guile had not yet matured.

They were an item. Even though they went to different schools, their districts were close, so Jeremiah made it a habit of walking the two blocks to catch her on her way out of *PS16* (his school let out fifteen minutes earlier than hers), and he liked to walk her home. They talked about anything and everything. By then his mother had been gone for two years, and he stayed with Al much of the time—*The*

City Social Services Department agreed to let Al become Jeremiah's legal guardian until he was eighteen, as long as he maintained good grades in school. Sometimes he would stay at Heather's house, but her father was not thrilled about the fact that Jeremiah was older than her. So that did not happen often. Occasionally, he did sneak in at night, never getting caught. There was that one time, however, he almost did; but he dove out of her window and onto the fire escape located on the second-floor tenement apartment. He still, to this day, bears the scar on his eyebrow from hitting his head on the railing. Heather just laughed with an uninhibited giggle when he told her about it the next day.

By the time Jeremiah was eighteen, Heather's parents knew that *The City* had become far too dangerous and decided to send her upstate to live with her grandmother to finish high school in a small town named *Dreamville Borough*. This was in preparation for her to attend an Ivy League college bearing the same name of the town—*Dreamville Borough University.*

That last night Jeremiah and Heather spent together was bittersweet. She was moving on to a brighter place, and they both knew it was best for her. But he could feel it in her kiss and the way that she wrapped herself up in his arms that the distance would drift them apart. Her heart and mind was already elsewhere. Suddenly, he was alone again, and she was gone, chasing something in *Dreamville Borough* that he could not give her.

Beautiful, Defiant, and Steady

October 8, 10:26 p.m.

Their footsteps seem to be the only noise forgotten by the restless *City*. They echo throughout the concrete jungle like a ticking timepiece in an empty room; *The City* has a way of devouring the individual like that. Strangers become stranger, and friends become rearranged memories of abandoned acquaintance. An occasional nod and an empty smile produce a brief glimpse into the human condition of otherwise faceless beings passing by like lost apparitions haunting their own forgotten dreams.

"Do you hate him?" asks Heather.

"Hate is a strong word," responds Melanie immediately. She then elaborates, "One shouldn't hate anything. They should only love what's right. Tjaden told me that one time."

"I don't know the difference between what's right or wrong anymore," responds Heather under her breath and almost inaudibly. "Do you think they are doing what is right?"

"At this point, does it really matter? We are already in too deep. Look, just because something is right does not mean it's all polka dots and pixie dust," responds Melanie in a way that seems as if she has something else on her mind.

"So how did you and Luke get together?" asks Heather in a subtle attempt at digression.

"You ask a lot of questions, you know that?" Melanie is annoyed.

"Well, it's just that he's a little eccentric. I mean, he is different. That's all," says Heather as she is muddled to find the appropriate combination of words that reflect her curiosity, while not offending Melanie at the same time.

To her relief, Melanie lets out a wholehearted laugh and sweetly responds, "You just don't know him like I do. That is all."

Heather is not satisfied with her answer, and her uncommitted smile reflects it. She comments, "Your whole life is one big riddle, isn't it?"

The snow is now falling more aggressively. It is blanketing the sidewalk beneath their route. And every step they take generates a muffled and thudded crunch in an asymmetrical rhythm that only exists in the beautiful cacophonic symphony composed by mother nature and her wandering melodies. A trill here, a rumble there; the howl of the droning winds that whisper in one's ear the secrets of *The City* that she's supposed to keep but cannot. It is neither her purpose, nor her will.

Jasper has been quiet. He is perplexed by the passing shops, delis, boutiques, thrifts, and other establishments of which he does not know their purpose. Some are vacant and boarded up—casualties of bad management or unfortunate circumstance, perhaps. He ponders what the lives of the owners and inhabitants are like; what is their favorite color, what is their life story, did they ever love, can they hate, and are they happy? And he finds himself longing for the smell and sound of the elms once again that, even if ever so briefly, made him feel like a vulnerable child who needs love and attention. He's angry with himself that he let his guard down, let himself feel. That is dangerous thinking to a boy of the streets after all.

A hand softly grabs his. He pushes it away in disgust, not with her, but with himself. He does not know what to feel anymore. He does not want to feel anymore. Redd is blue and confused. His comfort zone has always been his indifference toward others. His clever young mind, although wise beyond its years, cannot comprehend his own mistrust. So he just grabs Heather's hand and rests his head against her as they continue to walk down *Providence Boulevard*.

The distant blares of sirens are not uncommon in *The City*. Most of the time, they are lost within her droned hum. The fact that they are growing louder is what catches Melanie's ear. There also seems to be many more than usual; a hodgepodge of blended yelps and horns suddenly devour the tranquil air and the humble silence that has surrounded their short walk.

"Something is going on. Listen," she says.

They all stop. The rumble of a large engine is slowly growing more audible and beginning to drown out the noise of the sirens.

A white limousine suddenly whips around the corner from *Kismet Avenue* and onto *Providence Boulevard*. Its tires screech, and the suspension bends, moans, and creaks as designed under the weight of the aftermarket heavy armor of the vehicle, keeping it true on its course. Melanie recognizes it; she had ridden in it many times.

"Hide your face," she says, as the vehicle begins to slow down. It's too late. She knows they have already recognized them.

The brakes squeak as the limo comes to a halt. Heather's heart drops into her stomach as Redd pulls himself closer into her motherly bosom. They are paralyzed with fear. Melanie quickly pushes them aside, so they are behind her, acting as a human shield. She then pulls a .357 Magnum from her purse and holds it by her side.

Her posture is beautifully defiant and steady. She is outgunned, but not outwitted. So as long as there is a heart that beats in her body, she will fight to destroy the monsters her father has created.

Ungoverned Mischief

October 8, 10:38 p.m.

There is nothing sacred in a showdown. It is merely the beast inside of one person pitting war against the beast in the other. Sympathy is unbecoming and useless when the threshold of reason is no longer discernable. Anger is sometimes manufactured from mis-understanding, mistrust, or misinformation. Melanie's does not fall under any of those categories. Is she angry with herself for not doing something sooner? Maybe, but she wasn't ready. That time that she was forced to pull that man's fingernails out with needle-nose pliers is still fresh in her memory; she was only thirteen. She stayed locked up in her room for three days after that. When she finally decided to confront her father about her abhorrence with what she had done, he just laughed and said, "The louder they scream, the more they'll obey." It was a futile attempt by Happy to teach her to be numb to torture and things of that nature. But that only exacerbated her long-ing for kindness. In retrospect, her rebellion was her father's inven-tion. Her love was inevitable, and she forgot how to hate. Yet here she stands, holding a gun, ready and self-obligated to defend people she has only met just hours before.

Suddenly, a van appears from the alleyway that runs perpendicu-lar to *Providence Boulevard.* Like a three-ton battering ram, it T-bones the limo with a deafening and crunching blow. The momentum of the crash pushes the limo toward Melanie, Heather, and Redd with such force that it almost hits them; saved only by the large light pole they are standing behind. The occupants of both vehicles are dazed. Human instinct would suggest that Melanie, Heather, and Redd should flee, but they are intimately invested in the surrounding cir-cumstances, and stand their ground for reasons only they can know.

The silence is broken by a kick on the door from within the limo. The thud is once soft, and the second and third grow ominously with audible intensity. It is coming from the rear driver's side door; only ten feet away from and facing Melanie, Heather, and Redd. Melanie raises her .357 Magnum and waits. The movement stops. The gears of the transmission begin to grind and clank. The limo begins to move. It peels itself from the lamp pole with a slow and spine-tingling screech. The engine begins to hobble as it gains momentum and suddenly releases from the pole. It travels a short way down the street, then unexpectedly comes to a stop. The rear door is kicked open, and a limp body is pushed out of it. The body settles with its legs still underneath the vehicle; they crunch with a muffled thud as the limo runs them over. Melanie recognizes the man as Knox. He's dead.

The van can be heard turning over as the starter motor grinds in attempt to get the pistons of the large V8 motor firing. Not without demur from the damaged vehicle, the engine fires up. It is leaking radiator fluid as it makes a two-point turn and drives off in the direction of the limo.

Melanie quickly puts the Magnum revolver back in her purse as four *City Police* cars haphazardly turn onto *Providence Boulevard* from *Kismet Avenue*. With sirens blaring, the first three pass by them in a blur of black, white, red, and blue, creating a cold draft in their stead that manifests a penetrating chill up their spines. The fourth pulls up beside them and the figure in the car asks if they are okay as he quickly opens the door.

Melanie responds, "Yes."

"Is he with you?" asks the officer as he points toward Knox's dead body.

"No. A limo hit him as he was crossing the street. He's probably a vag," says Heather instinctively as she comically recreates the accident with hand gestures.

With a look of disappointment on his face, the officer calmly responds, "It doesn't matter what he is, ma'am. He's a person and needs help." Lieutenant Edwards slowly beelines toward Knox to check on the man. Unbeknownst to him and mistakenly, he left the police cruiser's driver-side door open. Melanie and Heather immediately share a subtle, savvy, and sagacious glance with each other. They smirk slyly and nod in agreement; a contract unspoken but rather inked by the steady hand of ungoverned mischief.

"Now it's getting fun," says Redd.

An Unsympathetic Hum

October 8, 10:45 p.m.

Edwards approaches the lifeless body of Knox. The seventeen-foot walk seems as if it could be seventeen miles. He knows the man. Knox was the one who trained him when he first graduated from the academy and became a *City Police Officer*. They eventually became beat partners via a referral from Knox himself. They were a stereotypical good-cop-bad-cop duo. Edwards was calm, cool, and collected, while Knox was experienced, fiery, and hotheaded. They called him Foxy Knoxy because of his gift of craftily inciting quarrels out of nothing while claiming—and inevitably proving—his innocence of such *egregious and banterous allegations*. Although it was useful at times, Knox's temper always seemed to escalate otherwise modestly peaceful situations into violent confrontations. Edwards tried to be the voice of reason, but it went unheard. In actuality, he was subconsciously envious of the man; a man who literally lived by no rules. Knox was not much into thievery, but he could steal the words off the tip of your tongue and use them against you.

As expected, everyone in the department had some exaggerated story of Knox's antics that Edwards gladly lived in the shadow of. But after *The City Police Union* decided to strike, demanding higher wages and better death benefits, Knox never came back to work. He signed his resignation papers and became a recluse of sorts. Edwards eventually did run into him by happenstance, but only once afterward. It was several months later at the *Marcinkiewicz Meat Market* on Third Avenue. The encounter was awkward. Knox was wearing a high-end *DiPirro*-brand gray pinstripe suit and shoes made of the finest *Blue Heather* suede. He seemed regal yet detached to Edwards. Their conversation was short; Knox asked how his wife was doing, made small talk about the stocks, and went on his way. However, the one thing that perplexed Edwards the most was why he was buying cases of SPAM from *The Marcinkiewicz Meat Market*.

Officer Edwards arrives at Knox's body and checks his vitals. His body is broken, yet he looks peaceful. His face holds no grievance against his life's violent end. It is almost as if his slightly arched grin suggests subtle hints of joy and defiance; like he had bowed out of his final act doing what he loved. Yes, Knox truly lived by none others' rules, not even his own.

"Tango Charlie Delta, we have a three zero four, code black. Subject is deceased. Uh, approximately twenty-three hundred block of *Providence Boulevard* near *Kismet Avenue*. Send medical." As dispatch responds, Edwards is distracted by his own police car passing by him. The cruiser is moving at a slow speed at first, then accelerates as it maneuvers around him and Knox's body before disappearing into the darkness of an alleyway. The red, blue, and white lights bounce off every reflective material that the concrete jungle can possibly provide, passing through some to get to the others, before being absorbed and forgotten by all but their own provenance.

Edwards is perplexed and can only watch in disbelief. Perhaps in a state of confusion, he looks back down at Knox with compassion. The snow is already beginning to blanket the dead man's body. Edwards brushes him off. He does not know why. All is silent, less the distant sirens and *The City's* unsympathetic hum.

An Elephant Among Men

October 8, 10:51 p.m.

The ways of the desperate are fiery, ungoverned by reason, and only worship the gods of chance. They flip double-sided coins to buy themselves time, but will always lose in the end. Happy has bought time, but as every gambler of souls knows, there will eventually be someone coming to collect a debt that money can't buy.

They all stare at Happy holding confusion, mistrust, and bottomless sorrow in the gaze of their sullen eyes. The truth is, they had started as thugs under Happy's tutelage and slowly moved up. Along the way, they had grown accustomed to the lifestyle that he had provided them—good wages, stability, and even a chance at retirement. They had taken wives, bought houses, and started families. Only months before, they had all shared a toast with Knox, including Happy himself, on behalf of his pregnant wife Cynthia who was absent due to illness. He said it was a boy, and he'd name him Samuel. And now he was just pushed out of the car door like a discarded piece of garbage, scattered among the cigarette butts and crushed Styrofoam coffee cups that litter the street.

Happy looks at his men. He sees them, and he listens to their silence. He finally says, "You cannot invest your emotions into mortality, but strive to become one among the gods." He pans. There is only blank stares that intentionally avoid his eyes' contact. It's as if he is speaking into stagnant air, and to the elephant in the room that took a huge dump on his bullshit parade. The men remain uninspired. Happy realizes his thoughts are trivial to their anguish. Knox was their friend. He can only use their anger to his own device; he knows that good people can do bad things if they are hated by a common enemy, and bad people can do even worse.

A Jealous Sun and The Misfit Moon

October 8, 10:54 p.m.

The stars only shine when the beautiful sun no longer blinds us of their very existence. There is an old saying that goes, "Go, go, and reach for the stars." Is it so intrinsic that we as humans should strive to reach beyond the star that walks beside us every day, providing life and comfort? Is it possible that the sun only rises because it is jealous of the stars, and them of it? Maybe, but the sun is always shining somewhere, and the stars elsewhere. While one hides her beauty for the day, the others shine in her stead as glamour among the darkness. And the clouds roll in trying to steal the show, the winds blow in with nowhere special to go, while the sky weeps because none of them can get along. And the moon is forced to stare upon them all—knowing it does not belong—even as it shines the brightest in the night sky.

There is no sun; there is no moon; there are no stars. There is only the snow wandering chaotically in front of Stefenski's windshield, making it difficult to distinguish where the road ends and the sidewalk begins. His eyelids flicker to maintain focus as they share time between the road and the dashboard gauges of the van, specifically, the engine's thermostat gauge.

"We only have five minutes, at most, before this shaggin' wagon runs out of flower power," he says loudly and without looking back at them; Stefenski is focused on the limo that is swerving in front of him as its rear wheels struggle for traction.

"Did you fix that hatch?" asks Jeremiah as he nods upward toward the roof of the van.

"No, I forgot, or, uh, just ran out of time I guess," responds Luke.

"Damn it, Luke. As soon as you got that girl, you started slacking on your priorities," says Jeremiah. No one can tell if he is joking or not.

"Gonzo, do you still have that four-pounder?" he then asks. Gonzo reaches under his seat without saying a word and hands the small sledgehammer to Jeremiah.

"I thought it would be bigger," quips Jeremiah. No one laughs.

"No, you'll ruin the hinges," pleads Luke, as Jeremiah starts banging on the seized roof hatch. His thrusts are violent, and the boom reverberates within the steel form of the van with deafening consequence. After the fourth hit, the hatch pops fully open, and the pivot ladder Luke had fashioned to extend down hits Jeremiah on the forehead of his mask, producing a metallic-sounding thud. Gonzo laughs, the Wizard smirks, and Luke giggles. Jeremiah is not amused.

The Shadow Walker sits back down in his seat for a moment. They all watch as he struggles to remove the stubborn drum magazine from his tommy gun. He swears and mumbles underneath his breath, as if hexing the very design of the weapon and those responsible for its blueprint.

Jeremiah tosses the empty magazine toward Luke for reloading. Luke drops it. After making some indiscernible comment regarding butter fingers, Jeremiah reaches under his seat and pulls a full one-hundred-round magazine from a duffel bag; it attaches flawlessly and without issue. He chambers a round and takes a deep breath. He looks down at his ailing arm and opens and closes his fist to gauge the pain. It hurts.

"Is the pain getting worse?" asks Billingsly. Without letting Jeremiah answer, he says, "That thing is going to get funky if you don't get stitches soon."

Jeremiah only responds, "Easy around the corners, Silver Fox."

Ode to The Hapless at The End of The Tommy Gun

October 8, 11:11 p.m.

The cold air makes the endeavor uncomfortable. The snow seems hell-bent on blinding him, making his periphery nil and focus blurred solely upon the soft glow of two red brake lights that wander in the distance. The echoes of *The City* are null, and her structures void. Time and space are relevant only to this moment, and nothing else matters. God can only watch, and the devil can only whisper. Ode to the hapless at the end of the tommy gun.

Some of the bullets riddle the outer panels of the of the limo, while others are absorbed by *The City's* bosom as lost and forgotten fragments embedded in some brick facade or front-load refuse dumpster. *The City* can only beseech silently in a futile attempt at protest; a protest that will go unheard and be forever unforgiven.

The sparks spark, and the ricochets echo. Jeremiah's body is tossed side to side with every subtle movement of the van. The smell of the gunpowder and spent brass shell casings is pungent, yet somehow comforting. The kick of the short bursts from the tommy gun are taking a toll on his injured arm. Jeremiah switches hands. He has never shot left-handed before. It doesn't matter. He is only throwing lead anyway.

For some reason, his thoughts momentarily focus on Heather. He attempts to persuade himself to sway away from such foolish thoughts at a time like this. But she is there. He can feel her. It is so foreign to him; he has felt alone in this world for so long and feels stupid that he cannot comprehend her kindness and love. Love was always tangible to him before her. Now, it is something different. Her beauty is something that could never be worshiped, nor considered pagan. And carefully crafted words are only a foolish attempt by the dumbfounded to describe the indescribable. Jeremiah's okay with that, he surmises.

A loud clank and a sharp pain dissolves Jeremiah's illusions of happiness. A bullet rips through the right shoulder of his peacoat. It catches him enough to force him to retreat back into the van. Against his wishes, the Wizard pulls Jeremiah closer to himself to inspect the wound. Jeremiah submits and sits down. Gonzo joins the Wizard as Luke climbs the drop ladder and tries to poke his head out of the hatch.

The cold air is suffocating at first, but his ambition is unrelenting. Luke can see the muzzle flashes for brief moments as he plays hide-and-seek with the passing bullets, bobbing up and down like a gofer poking its head out of a hole. Luke knows he can't get a true aim with his assault rifle. He is under too much suppressing fire and the ride is too bumpy. A strong arm suddenly pulls him down from the drop ladder and back into the van. He complies. Jeremiah climbs the ladder with reckless bravado. Gonzo tries to stop him, but Jeremiah shakes him off.

The van makes a hard left turn down an alleyway slamming Jeremiah's ribs into the frame of the hatch. It hurts. He knows that familiar feeling of dislocated ribs from when he was a boxer. The injury is the least of his worries. Jeremiah knows that firing aimlessly at the fortified vehicle is a fruitless endeavor. *One more burst,* he thinks to himself. But the tommy gun jams, and the barrel has become red-hot. He is not amused. Jeremiah is pissed off and cold as hell as the passing air makes it way up the sleeves of his peacoat that are acting like a vacuum system to the rest of his body. He once again retreats back into the van.

"This isn't going to work," says the Silver Fox. Jeremiah nods in agreement.

"What are we going to do about the police?" asks the Wizard.

"I don't know. We are not shooting at them. I don't care how dirty they are," responds Jeremiah. They all agree.

"Happy is probably heading to a safe house by the docks. This van is about to die. Gather your gear and prepare to abandon ship." As they begin to gather the rest of their ammunition and scurry to take whatever else they can, Jeremiah can't help but think about *rule number 3*.

Sonny makes a quick right turn, and is able to shake the police by entering a parking ramp through a seldom-used rear entrance. They make it to the top tier before the engine overheats and begins to boil over. This will be the vehicle's last voyage. It sputters and gargles as steam evacuates from underneath the hood and rises into the crisp, cool air. Stefenski cuts the engine. The vehicle is dead. Everything is ominously silent.

Beauty is Reckless

October 8, 11:55 p.m.

The Blackguards of Charlatan stand silent before *The City*—a vantage point like no other. The skyline resembles a craggy cold outline of stone and mortar, placed one by one by the skilled hands of forgotten craftsmen in the name of progress, the visions of the dreamers, and the pocketbooks of the greedy. The pointed steeples are the only relief from the right angles and flat facades—save the patinaed dome of *City Hall*—all of which are barely visible silhouettes on this snowy October night, besides a distant amber glow.

There is beauty in the reckless. There is poetry in the shadows. Perception is an angle ungoverned by rules. Why is it that everything that is beautiful must also be so fleeting? Maybe that is the purpose of beauty. Maybe it is in our nature to respect a moment so precious, that it can only be recollected in dreams where the colors hold brighter hues, even if they are blurred and indecisive. Beauty is reckless and will never ask for forgiveness.

The Fall of the House of Abominable Horrors

October 8, 11:55 p.m.

"Where did they go?" blurts Melanie in a subtle tone that suggests it is both a statement and a question.

"I'm not sure. They were there a second ago," responds Heather.

"I didn't see where they went either," jabbers Redd from the peanut gallery.

"Well, we can't drive around aimlessly, and we are going to have to ditch this *Peace Wagon* soon," says Melanie.

"Turn the police radio back on," suggests Redd persuasively. "We might be able to get some cross talk." Heather complies with the suggestion; she presses several knobs and turns others until the radio finally turns on.

The scanner scans. It is busy with conversations concerning *The City Fire Department* and their ongoing battle with a large house fire in *The Regal Estates* area. Heather and Melanie immediately share a brief glance that holds astonishment and unadulterated amusement. Melanie smiles to herself as her eyes focus back on the road. To her, that place was a *House of Abominable Horrors*.

"I hope it burns and there is nothing left. Not even the ashes belong in this world," says Melanie angrily. Her smile fades as she turns her head solemnly toward Heather. Melanie's beautiful brown eyes noticeably bereave and falter in their attempt to remain mysterious and defiant.

Heather can only respond, "Me too, Melanie. Me too."

"There was this guy named Warren Liszt that owed *him* some money. It wasn't much, maybe a couple of thousand," says Melanie unsolicited; her voice monotone and droning. She continues. "He was a Hungarian immigrant and struggled to get work. He took a loan to start a food service cart business. After he couldn't pay my father back in time, he was picked up by some henchmen and taken to that same room Redd was in. I can still hear him pleading through the air vent, 'Not my fingers. Not my fingers. My wife is deaf. It is the only way we can talk to each other.' His screams still echo in my dreams. My father is a monster." Melanie's voice is shaky. She begins to cry as she pulls the police cruiser over. Heather does not know how to respond, and Redd is silent.

"Let me tell you something my *dziadzia* told me one time. He said that 'tears only exist because there was something worth loving.' It is okay to cry." Melanie looks at Heather, and her eyes refocus.

"That is so cheesy," she responds as she regains composure. "We'll ditch it up here in the alleyway. The vags will strip it down to a shell. They are crafty little minions."

The car comes to a stop in an anonymous snowy alleyway. Melanie gets out abruptly. Without explanation, she walks a stone's throw into it. Heather and Redd are caught off guard. As they catch up with her, she is struggling to pull down a rusted sliding fire escape ladder. It squeals and grinds as all three make a concerted effort to pull it down; their effort is successful.

Past the ladder, the rise turns to stairs. The ascent is easy but cold. The breeze seems to ambush them in the narrow alleyway. The snowflakes are the size of dimes, and the stairs are steps of five. The rooftop is coated with snow, a quarter inch or two.

"East should be this way," says Melanie, as she heads west to make her way to the rooftop's edge. The clouds are low and seem to veil the place where the earth ends and the sky begins.

They look north. There is a soft glow of flickering amber and orange that is lighting up the gray. Melanie has to see it for herself, even if blurred and distant. *The House of Abominable Horrors* is engulfed in fire.

Heather instinctively puts her left hand on her belly. And with her right, she points toward nowhere in particular. Words are failing her, but she spontaneously says, "Out there, Mel. Out there in all that darkness, there is always something worth loving."

20

Copper Grove Part 1

October 8, 11:55 p.m.

"When we get there, call Emerson Bandy. Let him know that *The Harvest Union* has a favor to cash in," says Happy; his words are directed towards Burkowski. Happy continues, "Tell them to meet us at the *Copper Grove Marina* safe house."

"Well, that is nice of you to tell me, sir. I had no clue where the fuck we were going," replies Burkowski sarcastically.

"I tell you things on a need-to-know basis, Burkowski. Now you know, and it would be wise to watch your tone," replies Happy raucously.

The safe house is an unassuming storage warehouse for boats and other marine vehicles. It is named after the first boat Happy ever bought, dubbed *The Copper Grove*; and its namesake was from the town he grew up in—a town he never returned to after *The War* ended. It never felt right. *The War* had ruined Happy. There was a time when he considered taking Melanie to meet some of her cousins there, but he couldn't bring himself to go. Perhaps his memories of the place are worth more to him than the place itself.

The boat is his pride and joy, despite having several others that are larger and more luxurious. *The Copper Grove* was his first big purchase from when he finally made it. Happy briefly reminisces of the sunny afternoons he would spend with Melanie out in *The Harbor*. She was such a happy little girl. For the same reasons he prefers to keep *Copper Grove* in his past, he quickly decides to subdue his thoughts of Melanie.

There is so little in this world Happy loves. Now, it is all gone, and all that is left is an empty void, an absence of light, and petrified memories that sicken him forever even caring at all. Happy has become a shell of even the terrible human being he was. Neither death nor life entertain him any longer. He is nothing more; he is nothing less. And now his own happiness haunts him as a wandering apparition—vague, unwanted, and unwilling to cease. One will never outrun the things that haunt them.

The Fourth of July

October 9, 12:22 a.m.

Not much is spoken. It was Stefenski's choice regarding which vehicle to borrow. His skill was impeccable; he had the vehicle unlocked and hot-wired in less than twenty seconds.

The rumble of the *Power Wagon's* large V8 humbles their uneasiness with a comforting din. The Wizard packs his mahogany tobacco pipe. The sudden orange glow of the match briefly reveals the details of the man's sullen face—every line and contour becoming a road map of past trials and tribulations; all of which seem to lead to the eyes of Aurora—their phenomenon gentle, yet pagan; a verdant abyss that is unbecoming at first, yet infinitely beautiful upon reflection.

Jeremiah's arm is searing with pain. In fact, his whole body is battered and sore. The night has been long, tense, and taxing. Billingsly seems unfazed by his shrapnel wounds, but Jeremiah is certain that he is quite uncomfortable. Jerry's sore ribs seem a trivial matter at this point. Sonny and Luke are the only ones unscathed. Luke, meanwhile, begins to whistle *"Oh, Danny Boy"* to himself within his clown mask. "The acoustics are really good in this thing," he says in passing before continuing. The melody penetrates the air with solitude;

it is ethereal yet clumsy and rogue. Jeremiah finds himself silently mouthing the words:

> *But come ye back when summer's in the meadow*
> *Or when the valley's hushed and white with snow*
> *'Tis I'll be here in sunshine or in shadow*
> *Oh, Danny boy, oh, Danny boy, I love you so.*

"Where are we going anyway?" asks Billingsly. The whistling stops.

Pewee the Clown slowly turns his head toward the Wizard and says, "We're going to the Land of Misfit Toys, motherfucker. But we ain't going to play. Ratta-tat-tat, bing bang boom."

Luke makes a comical motion with his hands that suggest a large explosion of nuclear proportions followed by a troubling laugh. The Wizard shakes his head, as if baffled and intrigued at the same time.

Jeremiah reaches into his duffel bag and produces the *Teddy Bear*. He hands it to Luke without question nor comment. Luke grabs it tight and holds it against his chest.

His head slumps as he says, "I don't feel like dying tonight, is all."

Speedy, the Wizard, and Stefenski heed their own silence within the convictions unintentionally designed by such solemn honesty. Jeremiah looks at the others and then within himself. He must speak, but he knows that words are trivial when given to a broken man.

In a moment of whim, he reaches back into his duffel bag, and secretively uses a *Renee's Diner* match to light a small assemblage of *Wolfpack Firecrackers*. He throws them at Luke. They land on his lap. The *Power Wagon* becomes the Fourth of July.

The *Teddy Bear* flies through the air like a superhero on a bender. It tosses and turns with no plan of a final destination. All watch in awe and surprise while Luke's arms flail. He then begins to frantically pat himself down as if a colony of ants are invading his pants. Then there is silence which lasts far too long for comfort's sake.

Finally, Gonzo says, "I always wanted to see that, hombre. It was worth the wait." Everyone laughs. Luke giggles. The *Copper Grove Marina* is just around the corner.

A Snowball of Awakening

October 9, 12:16 a.m.

Perhaps subliminally suggested by embarrassment, Lieutenant Drake Edwards does not immediately radio into dispatch that his police cruiser has been stolen. As he looks upon the person that once was Knox, he realizes that there is nothing more he can do for the man. So he decides that he will flag down the next vehicle that passes; vehicles are far and few between on this particular stretch of this particular boulevard on this particularly lonesome night. And people don't care much for an officer-in-need in *The City*.

However, by happenstance and luck alone, the lights of a *Taxicab* appear at the corner of *Kismet Avenue* and *Providence Boulevard*. Edwards waves with one arm, and with the other, toggles his flashlight on and off to get the driver's attention. The *Taxicab* slows and comes to a stop. As he opens door, the hinges creak and moan with an obnoxiously loud squeak. The ID tag says A. A. Amble. Amble looks at Knox's body lying on the ground in the road, then back at Edwards quizzically. To his relief, the driver is sympathetic and does not ask the lieutenant the details surrounding his circumstance. Perhaps he has seen worse in *The City*.

"Where to, Officer," he only asks. Amble's brown eyes wander mistrustfully.

"That way," responds Edwards as he points toward the direction his cruiser has sped off in.

The vehicle's heater is on its maximum setting, and makes the officer immediately uncomfortable.

"Can I roll the window down? I'm looking for something out there."

Amble nods. Edwards aggressively turns the window's crank. The cold October air is both refreshing and a betrayal of one's senses, as if the debate between what is too warm and what is too cold becomes trivial, and perfection is mother nature's only available rebuttal.

The tire tracks are still fresh in the road. Time is of the essence; the tracks are fading quickly as the accumulating snow buries them. The cab is eerily silent. Every ambient noise is amplified—the knock of the abused engine, the crunching of the snow beneath its path, and the whining noise coming from a steering wheel that is in need of repair. Their path is true, and within a short time, Edwards finds his police cruiser. It is empty and still running in the alleyway with three of its four doors opened.

He notices immediately as he exits the cab that the fire escape in the alleyway has been pulled down. Considering his previous predicament, Edwards is torn whether or not to investigate. Reluctantly, he slowly moves toward it. He puts his right hand on the ladder; it seems colder than ice. He looks up the ascent; he is still debating his course of action. Instinctively and without intention, his right foot is already on the first rung. As he begins to pull himself up, his radio suddenly erupts with ominous chatter from other units and dispatch. Edwards grounds himself with a short hop from the ladder.

"All available units, respond to a niner two five, code three. Multiple shots fired from automatic weapons and small arms at the Copper Grove Marina. Gunfire is still in progress. Be careful out there, boys."

"What the hell is going on in *The City* tonight?" asks Edwards out loud to himself as he shakes his head. He looks inside his police cruiser as the radio continues its clamor. His shotgun is still in its place near the center console. He somberly enters the vehicle. The car engages into reverse, and Edwards pulls from the alleyway. He puts the car in drive and says, "Well, here we go to the shit show."

Redd is listening to the commotion from the rooftop. He watches as the cruiser drives away and disappears into the fading cityscape. He then turns to Melanie and Heather and says, "It sounds like there is a po-po-row at some marina."

"It's *The Copper Grove*," responds Melanie immediately. "We must go now." She grabs Redd by the hand and begins to walk toward the fire escape. Heather does not move. She is torn by something she does not understand. She can hear Redd or Melanie saying something along the lines of "We need to go," but she is vacant. Her mind thoughtfully wanders.

The snowball Redd throws hits Heather in the back of the head. It implodes, then explodes in a cloud of neon-white crystals. Reality is a potent elixir, and her eyes immediately focus intently back upon him and Melanie. It's as if she has experienced some sort of awakening; their faces have become resolute and beautiful. She knows their intent is good, even if their process pagan. They will see this thing through to its dreadful end—so be it—and embrace their own courage through the darkness of this sordid endeavor.

Silence is for the Wolves

October 9, 12:33 a.m.

Burkowski's voice is already trembling as he tries to convince himself that this is no big deal—only a phone call. He has never spoken to Emerson Bandy before; not directly anyway and especially not after waking the man from a slumber on a cold night such as this. To him, Bandy is a fable, a ghost. Even Happy Hal has never spoken to the man in person. Burkowski reluctantly dials. The varied beeping tones whisper in his ear a forbidden melody, seemingly composed by the devil's dogged hand himself. It is Bandy's direct line. Burkowski pauses, takes a deep breath, and dials the last number, *six*. The sweaty palm of his right hand grips the phone even tighter, as the other line begins to ring.

A raspy drone of a voice answers on the opposite end. It has a drawl, but not a southern one. Burkowski can't pinpoint its origin.

"This is Bandy."

An awkward silence occurs, seemingly lasting eternally, even if only for a moment. He suddenly realizes he is supposed to speak.

"Uh, er, the name is Burkowski." His voice becomes crisp. "*The Harvest Union* has a favor to call in. We are at the *Copper Grove Marina* safe house."

There is no immediate response from the other end, only a disconcerting silence interrupted by rhythmic cadences of someone's breath wheezing in and out.

"Twenty-three minutes," responds Bandy, finally and quite abruptly. The phone clicks. The conversation is over as quickly as it began. The dead phone tone fades as Burkowski slowly places the handset back on its base.

Burkowski did not notice Happy hovering above him and to the left. "How long?" he asks sternly.

"He said twenty-three minutes." Happy looks down at his watch as he rubs his bearded chin with the other hand.

"That's not quick enough." He slams his fist down on the oakwood desk; his voice like a roaring freight train about to derail. "We are not winning. We are running!"

All look upon him at once. Happy has caught the men's attention unintentionally. Their eyes seek direction. There is concern, fear, and a lack of confidence in them. Happy hates this even more than he hates disobedience. Weakness is not part of his prerogative. It is an unfortunate and common occurrence of late; he once again feels like a misfit among cowards. He does not trust the will of his men.

"They will never be an Oscar Olejniczak," he says under his breath. The memories of both the grandeur and losses of *The War* briefly wander through his mind for reasons even he could never explain.

Happy had reached out to Oscar after *The War*. He even sent him postcards on his birthday. Oscar never responded. This hurt Happy, even if he would take that truth to the grave. Their bond was one-sided. Oscar moved on and lived a good life for the most part. Happy, however, couldn't shake the highs of instinctive survival, nor that of instinctive killing. Oscar's silence was somehow Happy's downfall.

Silence is for the wolves. It preys upon the conscience of the thinkers and reminds the thoughtless of the faculties they lack. It is creative to its own device and haunts its victims from within. But even the wolf will occasionally howl to warn its prey; silence has no such sympathy.

Peace is Broken

October 12, 12:40 a.m.

The Harvest Union will be expecting company. The Shadow Walker and his friends know this. The docks of the *Copper Grove Marina* are empty and cold. Both the yachts of the privileged and those of the middle have been dry-docked for the winter. The moorings are vacant, and the water seems a black abyss on this moonless night. It ripples calmly against the floating walkways going unnoticed.

Stefenski parked the *Power Wagon* outside of the east gate near an abandoned slipway. There is no lighting there, and they can follow the shadows toward the main storage building. Their movements are steady yet fumbling, as if choreographed by deception but performed in burlesque.

The Wizard is on point. He is intimately familiar with the layout of the *Copper Grove Marina*. In what seems like a lifetime ago, he hosted galas and other social gatherings in the *Chapman-Ferr Clubhouse*. They were mostly funded by Patricia's inheritance. His meager journalist's salary could never afford such delicacies, but he enjoyed the attention nonetheless. In retrospect, Billingsly is certain that Happy had actually attended one of his events with a little brown-haired girl. He recalls how she had such striking and honest eyes. They were brown, yet bright as the sun. She stood there; her tiny hand consumed by her proud father's. Billingsly never spoke to the man on the other end of the girl, but again and in retrospect, he is certain that it was Melanie.

"You know they know that we will be coming from this way, right, hombre?" says Gonzo nervously.

"Yeah, and they will hear us coming from this way too if you don't shut the fuck up," says the Wizard, uncharacteristically. The tension is high. They know Happy Hal is no fool, and they are likely walking into an ambush.

"How many frags do we have left?" asks Pewee the Clown suddenly.

"Couldn't you have asked that on the way here?" suggests Gonzo begrudgingly.

"Both of you, shut your filthy heathen-loving mouths. I don't want to die before the fight begins because Tweedledee and Tweedledum can't get along. I will knock out every one of your teeth and mail them to you. And when you put them under your pillow, I will sneak into your room while you are sleeping and steal all the whore money the tooth fairy left you," says Billingsly sarcastically.

"Don't call my mom a whore," says Luke unexpectedly. "Just sayin'."

Jeremiah has had enough. He pushes Billingsly out of the way and moves forward recklessly from their makeshift cover into the open. He stops abruptly and turns around. He motions as if he is about to speak but says nothing. Jeremiah is torn by something.

The Shadow Walker wants his revenge, while Jeremiah wants this all to end. Both are fearless; both are misunderstood. Both exist in front of their men as a dark silhouette; their presence august on this troubling October morning. The metallic mask feigns the human qualities of the deranged demigod that is before them. The moment is sublime, yet subdued and elegant. The snow falls quietly, reflecting all around him within a softly lit backdrop surrounded by endless darkness. The snow gathers on his fedora and on the shoulders of his peacoat. His left hand rests on the barrel of his slung tommy gun. Each breath becomes a white fog that lofts, and seems to return to its rightful place in the heavens where it does not belong.

The Shadow Walker suddenly turns back around. No words are welcome and none exchanged. He only nods before abruptly moving back into the cover of darkness. The others follow. The spotlights of the *Marina*'s safe house serve as an ominous beacon across the snowy platform. Their destination is near.

The Blackguards of Charlatan are now within a stone's throw from the *Copper Grove* safe house's entrance. All is quiet and suspect yet somehow peaceful. They knew this was going to be a close quarters firefight, and for the most part, their chosen weaponry is designed for this method of battle. That, however, is their only solace. Pewee the Clown looks over toward Jeremiah. He reaches into his side satchel and produces a frag grenade, which he abruptly rolls toward Jeremiah. It bounces and tumbles across the warped boards of the dock, but its destination is true, albeit reckless. Jeremiah picks it up, tips up his mask, and as if straight from a scene from some action movie, pulls the pin out with his teeth. He spits it out and smiles back at his friends. Luke giggles, the Wizard smirks, Gonzo plugs his ears, and Sonny simply gives him a thumbs-up.

"I always wanted to do that."

The grenade flies proudly toward its final destination. After bouncing twice off the dock, it gently ricochets off the green oak-wood door of the safe house's main entrance and settles. The concussion splits the door upright and in half. The splinters disappear into a ball of dust and fire. Peace has been broken and cannot be undone.

The Unforgiven

October 12, 01:13 a.m.

The explosion is predictable, as is the ensuing firefight. The rooftop lights up with muzzle fire, and anything that was beautiful a moment ago has turned to sulfur and dread. A bob here, a weave there; the bullet is not impressed nor does it care. The flesh tears; the skull cracks. The laws of physics are ungoverned and godless.

Sonny Stefenski is the first to fall. He felt nothing. The sound of the thud comes first, then the echo of the round. His feet collapse below him and he is no more. Perhaps the unknown will reunite him with Charlemagne, but those are dangerous thoughts for the unforgiven. Sonny never knew what hit him.

The Wizard drops to one knee and instinctively checks the vitals of a man who is obviously dead. He looks upon Sonny's body with hopeless eyes. He has only known him briefly, yet a piece of himself now seems vacant. A thousand emotions consume Billingsly within a single moment, yet he has naught the courage to feel them. So he fights.

Gonzo is oblivious to the fate of his brother. Fractions of millisecond divide what can be his own violent end or a story of unlikely survival. He flanks to the right and takes cover behind a wood pillar. He makes himself small and uses the lack of light to his advantage.

Pewee the Clown is juxtaposed to the left, recklessly out in the open. Gonzo observes him and is mesmerized by a man in a clown mask firing an automatic assault rifle from his hip while stoically yelling in between comical laughs, "The rabbits whilst have their revenge!"

Never in Gonzo's life could he ever have ever imagined he would see such a sight to behold. It is as if life is in slow motion; the snowflakes fall peacefully around him, becoming a beautiful blitzkrieg of exploding bombs as they land on the boards of the dock and splinter below Pewee the Clown's feet.

Suddenly, from the darkness, appears the Shadow Walker. The tommy gun rages on with a carnivorous roar. The beast hunts without trepidation, as if it will not be satisfied without blood. Jeremiah reaches out with his left hand to grab the fabric that rests upon his friend's shoulder and pulls Luke into cover, all the while throwing lead toward the *Marina* safe house.

"Don't get yourself killed, Luke," says Jeremiah as they settle behind a group of hardwood benches.

"I can't see a fuckin' thing from here," says Luke in rebuttal to a comment that is never made. An object seems to catch both of their peripheries at the same time.

"Do you have a quarter?"

"No, but I have two dimes and a nickel," responds Luke as he unexpectedly pulls the exact change from his thigh pocket. Jeremiah inserts a nickel into the pier binoculars and hands the remaining two dimes back to Luke.

"I guess it only costs a nickel."

"That is a good deal," responds Luke.

The pier binoculars only pivot so far, but far enough to get a closer view of the *Marina Safe House*. Jeremiah becomes the spotter. They must be quick and precise; they both know that their muzzle flash will attract immediate attention, and that the hardwood benches are poor cover.

"They are hunkered low, only head shots available. If I can get them to fire toward us, you can aim directly at the muzzle flash. No pressure," says Jeremiah, as he turns his head from the pier binoculars; he stares at Luke without refrain.

"Ready?" asks the Shadow Walker. He slings his tommy gun around to his back and winces in pain as he pulls his Colt 45 from his shoulder holster. The adrenaline is struggling to overcome his injuries.

The Shadow Walker's blood is cold as he steps into the light. He turns to Luke and says, "I'm probably too old to die young, you think?" Suddenly and recklessly, he beelines toward the *Marina Safe House*. His Colt 45 cracks with rhythmic deaf tones. Death has become audible, as it whispers in his ear the secrets of life, and the glory of the unknown—both of which it hates the most. Luke aims.

The Forgiven

October 12, 1:13 a.m.

The City seems foreign and distant to Heather. She holds both Melanie and Redd's hand as they walk, yet wonders if they feel as lonely as her. She worries, she loves, she hates—all in a single breath. No one can understand, nor words prosper without beguile. Her solace will only be in the arms of Jeremiah Revel. She knows that he will burn the world for her, but she will never let him.

"What are we going to do?" asks Heather.

"I'm not sure," responds Melanie; it is as if they have simultaneously realized that they are walking about aimlessly. Heather looks up at Melanie. Her brown hair is graceful and simple. Each individual strand somehow absorbs the neon lights of *The City* and refracts them in various auburn hues, becoming more beautiful than they were before.

Heather's hand grips Redd's tighter. Somewhere through the darkness that exists on the other side of the wall of snow that is blanketing them, there is only chaos that awaits. This, they know. Yet despite the promises that death keeps, they are drawn toward the things they love the most.

Of Rage, Revelry, and Thoughts of the Broken

October 12, 1:13 a.m.

"You hear that, men? That is the sound of victory," says Happy. Even with a slight limp, he paces stoically. The ambient sound of ricocheting bullets, breaking glass, and splintering wood suggest otherwise. Happy is oblivious to all the chaos around him; he is where he belongs. It is the first time he has truly felt alive since *The War*.

Happy, in a fit of unkempt and spontaneous candor, empties all six rounds from his .44 Magnum into nowhere in particular. His eyes are suddenly withdrawn and lack any qualities that humans expect from one another. He is lost to this world and belongs to the unknown—the place where God no longer forgives and the devil has no interests; the void is empty, and its vacuum complete.

As the Magnum's hammer clicks one last time upon a spent shell, the Shadow Walker breaches the compromised and splintered front door of the *Copper Grove Marina*. The moment is frozen in time. Happy finally sees his protégé, the Shadow Walker—a younger version of his broken soul.

What is the difference between one beast or another? Happy mutters to himself with a smirk for reasons unknown even to himself.

The Blackguards of Charlatan, sans one, follow in Jeremiah's stead. They administer death. They are no longer Jeremiah, Luke, Jerry, nor Charles. They are the Shadow Walker, Pewee the Clown, Jack Frost, and the Wizard. Everything left that is beautiful in them now belongs only to those they love. The rest is of rage and revelry.

"Where is Bandy's men?" asks Happy to himself aggravatingly, as he and Burkowski retreat back to the office area along with several others; some wounded, others vacant and befuddled from the attack they just endured. Happy realizes quickly that they are not outgunned; they are out-willed. They have found themselves taking cover in the farthest room to the rear of the *Copper Grove Marina* complex. Burkowski is in the center of the room, squatting down and hunkered low while tightly gripping a willing and able 20-gauge shotgun; Happy is upright to the left with his left hand resting on a dark ash wood desk. His right hand rubs his chin with the thumb and index finger; his gun holstered.

Just as quickly it began, it ends. The gunfire becomes less sporadic and finally ceases entirely. Inaudible and muffled banter can then be heard. The Blackguards of Charlatan are closing in. Happy knows this. He hates retreating as much as he hates disobedience, as if they are one and the same. Suddenly, he composes himself, unholsters his Magnum and flips open the drum in one motion. Happy releases the spent casings from the weapon. He watches as they fall to the ground and listens affectionately to the symphony of chatters and chimes they produce against the concrete floor.

Burkowski is baffled as he watches Happy bend down and pick up one of the spent casings from the floor. He holds it to his nose and sniffs it while making a swirling motion, as if it were fine wine. The smell of brass, copper, lead, and sulfur permeate through his nostrils—all elements of nature yet used in unnatural ways. The aroma is arousing. Suddenly, Happy aggressively throws the casing back onto the floor and clears his throat.

"Why must every man's finest moment seem to come in his darkest hour? Why must we wait and bereave our lives of that simple pleasure?" Happy slides the sixth and final round into the drum of his .44 Magnum. "I suppose a man's darkest hour could be his finest in the end." Happy seems to hesitate for a moment before mumbling to himself, "Oscar would be proud."

"Sir, we are wasting time. We need to go. We—" Burkowski's entreaty is interrupted midsentence by the gun barrel of a Magnum pressed against his forehead.

"I give the orders. Have you forgotten?" says Happy raucously as he pulls the hammer back. Burkowski stares up at him defiantly. Happy's features are rigid, yet seem noticeably worn in the dim light of the room. Burkowski speaks.

"That trigger ain't going to pull itself."

Happy is both impressed and somehow proud; he uncocks the hammer and reholsters his gun. Burkowski can be trusted. Happy turns away from him abruptly while softly saying, "Just like his father."

How far can one man be pushed until he no longer cares? Is there a dividing line—a line where pride and ignorance no longer has influence and anger is all that is left? Is there anything on the other side of that line worth caring for in the first place? Anger is useful, but only when one cares enough to give sympathy to all that is damned. These are the thoughts of the broken.

Thoughts of the Loved

Heather looked beautiful with her shoulders drowning in Jeremiah's white T-shirt; her frame so slender within the broad shoulders of its design. The aroma of him wrapped itself around her, yet all he could smell was her. Each breath gave him purpose; there were no questions left to ask; there were no answers to be given. Her beauty was so simple, yet defiant and lovely. Jeremiah wanted to tell her of how he enjoyed the way the sunshine walked beside her, but he could never get the words right.

Simplicity is love's nectar. It nourishes without regret. It rues when foolish tongues complicate it; words will always fail where love begins. However, one must love themselves first, lest they consume others within their sorrow. Heather wanted to tell Jeremiah of how she carried his love for him, keeping it safe until he was ready for it. But she could never get the words right. These are the thoughts of *The Loved*.

The Opposite Side of Racism

October 12, 1:13 a.m.

The police cruiser's engine revs up, then down, then up again, as it bobs and weaves through *The City's* gridded maze of boulevards, avenues, and alleyways. There are one thousand ways to get anywhere, but not one seems faster than the other. Slowing Edwards' progress further is the slippery condition of the roads; an October snowstorm of this intensity is rare, and *The City DOT* has only installed a handful of plow assemblies onto their fleet of work trucks. It is unlikely that the snow will be cleared anytime soon.

Officer Drake Edwards' mind is focused far beyond conditions of the road. It seems the mansion fire, the limo, the firefight, the stolen police cruiser, they are all connected; they must be. He is certain that there is something strange and profound bustling in *The City* tonight.

Edwards mouth is dry and his palms are sweating; he tightly grasps the steering wheel. His adjustments are immediate and rhythmic as the rear wheels of his cruiser fishtail behind him. Around each corner, another mystery awaits. The cityscape that has been comforting and predicable now seems reckless, hollow, and vacant. The siren wails, and the light bar flickers and glows in soft hues of red, white, blue, and amber that bounce off the facades of storefronts and tenements, seemingly unwanted.

The cruiser slows, and all four wheels lock before it slides to a complete stop. Edwards turns the siren off and lets his mind wander briefly. He exhales what was once a deep breath and aggressively puts the vehicle into park. The steering wheel column shifter is stiff, but it engages. He and his wife are not on good terms, but he can really use the sound of her voice right now.

The coin clanks through the mechanism of the pay phone. Edwards reluctantly dials his own phone number. The sound of the ringing on the other end is unexpectedly dreadful to him. Why should one be afraid to call their own home?

A soft and groggy hello greets Edwards from the other end of the line. It seems a lifetime ago that he would make her laugh endlessly, or he would kiss her forehead before she fell asleep. How could two people fall together into the deepest chasms of love, and then find the effort to climb out from those chasms, and stand on the edge, looking down at something they no longer recognize?

"Hey, Sophia, it's me," Edwards mumbles, as his voice cracks.

She knows something is wrong. "Drake, are you okay?" she responds immediately in a voice so kind and euphonic, that her persuasion could certainly end the need for wars.

Edwards is at a loss for words. The timbre of her voice somehow heals all the bad things nagging his troubled soul. He questions for a moment why he decided to call her, but does not have a viable answer. Perhaps the words that hold the answer have yet to be invented.

"Do you remember that time we were walking the docks near the *Copper Grove*? You were wearing that white sundress with the yellow flowers."

"Drake, please stop," responds Sophia.

"No, I have to say this." She exhales with protest. "You remember when your parents found out I was white? We had only been dating for a week, and your dad was so angry." Drake chuckles to himself briefly, then continues, "I never thought that I'd ever find myself on the opposite side of racism. I just wanted to be on the opposite side of the girl."

"What do you want, Drake? It's almost one-thirty in the morning," responds Sophia. Drake's tongue is muddled, as if his heart and mind are struggling to communicate. His eyes shift to the left and stare into a brief memory, where her smile is as bright as the sun and, her lips as soft as her delicate ebony frame; a place where he can lose himself in the varied dark-auburn hues of her brown eyes.

"I love you, Sophia. That is all." The phone clicks.

Naught a Penny's Worth

October 12, 1:22 a.m.

"Where is Sonny?" asks Luke.

Jeremiah looks up suddenly. He makes eye contact with the others, before they all quickly scan the room while looking for their friend. The Wizard seems distant. Jeremiah notices this immediately. His eyes look downward and stare into nothing in particular. He opens the drum of his .38 revolver and releases the spent shell casings onto the tile floor of the *Copper Grove Marina* safe house. Billingsly begins to reload the weapon. Each round slides into the drum effortlessly. Words do not exist that can entertain his disposition; yet he must speak. So he slides the fifth and final round into the gun, and without looking away from it, solemnly says, "He is dead. He's out on the docks. Never knew what hit him."

Billingsly's voice trails off. Jeremiah's eyes now share Billingsly's vacancies, as he looks down at the smoking barrel of his own tommy gun, and then at the several dead henchmen strewn about the bloodied floor of *The Marina*.

After endless silence, Speedy speaks, "Let's just finish this for Charlemagne and never let Lillian know of this moment. *Umrą za nią. Kocham Cię, mój bracie.*" The room is heavy. The weight is almost unbearable. Jack Frost asks a question that catches everyone off guard.

"So, broseph, why does the devil fear God anyway?" Gonzo's inflection is contrite.

The Shadow Walker, not knowing how to answer, responds instinctively and without hesitation, "I don't know, but we're going to find out." Gonzo, and the group as a whole are satisfied with Jeremiah's answer.

"*Rule number 3,*" says Luke abruptly, cutting through the tension in the room like a nunchuck through a pierogi.

"*Rule number 3,*" respond the rest in an uncoordinated and fumbling cadence. Somehow, the cryptic ritual helps The Blackguards of Charlatan regain composure and steady themselves to press on.

Luke, inspired by his own guile, mumbles to himself, "Oh, man, the rabbits aren't going to like this at all, not one penny's worth."

Cold Feet

October 12, 1:13 a.m.

Upon the shoulders of her regal form rests the fabric of a simple coat—a colorless coat. And upon that coat, the snow gathers in random crystalline patterns that somehow absorb enough light to briefly shimmer within the darkness of *The City*. Melanie appears to walk blindly, but with intent. The snowflakes that catch her long brown eyelashes seem as if they are trying to shield her from the abominable things that await ahead.

Melanie's pace hastens as her hands simultaneously slip from both Redd and Heather's. They watch as she slowly distances herself, until something appears to catch her eye. She reaches down and picks up an unidentifiable blunt object. Heather and Redd have no recourse other than to stop, stand silent, and observe.

The backlighting of a flickering streetlamp is enough to create a mirror image of herself, as Melanie stares beyond the bars of the closed storefront window. And for a brief moment, she can see hints of her father in the contours of her own reflection—all the best parts of her, all the worst of him. She is her father's daughter after all.

Melanie's turns away. Suddenly, she is uncomfortable within her own skin. In her periphery, her eyes catch the vague forms of Heather and Redd; they are standing outside of the threshold of the light's reach. Redd, on a whim, boldly steps forward and enters the light. Melanie's shoulder is slightly slumped downward and to the right as she holds the object.

Redd is no more than a peasant boy thief from the streets. But on this October night, in front of this particular storefront, in this particular moment, Melanie only sees an innocent red-haired boy looking back at her with perplexed, kind, and worried eyes. Yes, Melanie is her father's daughter after all. However, she is stronger in will and in her courage to reinvent her heart. She will always be closer to love than he will be to hate. She sees this now as she turns away from sweet Redd, and looks back into her own reflection. The image shatters as the brick makes it pass through the window.

As the store's alarm awakens the hibernating *City*, Heather and Redd watch bewilderingly as Melanie carefully reaches in between the bars of the storefront's windows, and retrieves a pair of *Felcher-Mudd* women's winter boots that are on display. She mutters, "My feet got cold for a second there," as she slips them on. They fit perfectly. Perhaps the shoes her father bought for her no longer feel right.

Damning Relics

October 12, 1:49 a.m.

The Harvest Union is on the run once again. Emerson Bandy's help is unpredictable and sporadic. It seems he has his own agenda to attend to. And to top off Happy's cocktail of idiocy, he does not believe his men are capable of bringing order back to this wretched *City*. Even the desperate vags don't seem interested in salvation.

"What did I miss?" asks Happy to himself softly and almost inaudibly. His mind wanders. Logical matters have never muddled his thoughts before. If you pull the trigger, the gun fires. If you shake the thief, the thief cowers; if you drown the swine, the pig dies.

"These misfits have no place among the heroes. They do not belong with us," he says aloud and raucously.

"Sir, we are criminals," responds Burkowski.

"So are they," responds Happy casually.

The remaining and capable members of *The Harvest Union* had slipped out of a delivery entrance toward the rear docks during the short lull in the firefight. Happy's cache of collectable cars is only a couple of buildings away. With Burkowski on point and Happy just behind, they negotiate the shadows carefully toward the *Hoover-Nowe* complex. Their last communication to Bandy was that they are going to head to *The City Square* to regroup at the Charles Armor Building; there is a discreet rear entrance along the building's eastern alleyway that can be accessed from the main northern one.

Happy never cared much for collecting cars. Burkowski, on the other hand, is an avid enthusiast of all things with motors and four wheels. Happy would send him to auctions with the trust that he would make sound investments. Burkowski did well for the most part. However, on rare occasions, he would indulge in what Happy unceremoniously dubbed "grease monkey investments." One time, Burkowski came back with a title for a *Z423 IRok Duster* coupe. Happy was not pleased, but Burkowski promised that he would pay him back. However, Happy never asked for the money. It held sentimental value to Burkowski and Happy knew this; it was the same car that Burkowski used to work on with his father as a teenager.

Burkowski knew the intimate details of the car's design—every fitting, every bolt, and every hum of its intrinsic idle. Happy subconsciously envied Burkowski for this connection to his father, but never acknowledged it. He always considered it dangerous to have tangible connections to the kinder parts of one's past.

There is a quick buzz, followed by an echoing thud and a soft droning hum as the storage complex slowly illuminates. The carefully aligned rows of tan-and-gray canvas-covered forms seem inconspicuous at first. There are no windows in the complex and only one way in or out. This is comforting to the hobbled ranks of *The Harvest Union*; if they are ambushed, at least they will know which way to shoot.

Burkowski glances over toward Happy; he watches as the wounded man limps toward the back corner of the complex, slowly zigzagging while negotiating between the gridded assemblage of vehicles that he has forgotten he owns. Happy's gait has become less stoic and more human. He seems to be in no hurry. Yet his effort is dually dogged.

Happy hesitates for a moment as his right hand clenches the brittle tan canvas cover of the largest vehicle in the complex. It slightly tears as he pulls on it with more force. "Has it been that long, it is so dry-rotted?"

"It's been awhile, huh?" comments Burkowski, as he is now standing next to Happy. Happy nods. Burkowski then makes his way to the rear of the vehicle. They pull the cover off together. It drops to the floor into a noxious cloud of dust and dander that stings their nostrils. Happy sneezes.

"God bless you," responds Burkowski awkwardly as his voice trails off.

The paint on the dark navy-blue cube van has not faded much during its dormancy. Happy affectionately places the palm of his left hand on its facade and slowly moves his hand across it, seemingly reminiscing with each pass of his fingers over a bullet hole. Memories of grandeur, chaos, and heroic spectacle sends shivers down his spine, and emboldens his conscious state. Happy turns his head toward Burkowski and says with a prideful inflection, "This is where it all began, Sam."

Burkowski has exhausted every fathomable angle to try and convince Happy that they should push the cube van into *The Great Lake*, and let it sink into the deep abyss of its forgetful bosom. However, Happy will not spend a single ounce of effort entertaining that notion. The cube van is the only damning relic left from his past that can completely destroy *The Harvest Union's* operations. Happy is always a master of deception and so careful when it comes to keeping their operations a mystery. Burkowski subconsciously despises Happy for this careless oversight. He has always considered it dangerous to have tangible connections to the damning parts of one's past.

Above, Below, and Within

October 12, 1:57 a.m.

Gonzo's fingers close Sonny's eyes for the final time as he crouches beside him; his boots resting in the blood that has pooled and is seeping in between the cracks of the dock's boards. He pulls his brother's mask back to expose his face and cover the damage to his skull. The others watch as he whispers in the dead man's ear. They will never know what he says to Sonny. Perhaps some things are better left unknown. The moment is brief but solemn. Jerry lifts his own mask up momentarily. He kisses his brother's cheek before quickly pulling the mask back down.

Jeremiah and Luke carry Sonny's lifeless body to the *Power Wagon*. Gonzo slowly makes his way to the edge of a nearby low-lying dock. He sits and hangs his legs off the edge. His feet barely touch the water, yet it is enough to wash the coagulated blood from his boots. Meanwhile, Billingsly drags a couple of dead henchmen to the edge of the dock and pokes them with the barrel of his shotgun. He manages to find some rope and ties their legs together to make them less buoyant. Their bodies jerk as he kicks them off the edge with his foot. They fall into the watery abyss.

"What a waste," he mumbles to himself. The Wizard then makes his way to Gonzo and sits beside him.

Billingsly takes a deep breath before he speaks. "Those men back there, they belong to the fish now." Billingsly points to the bodies sinking into the water. His tone angers. "This is their funeral. Do you see a weeping widow? Do you hear any dirges? No. Their graves will be unmarked and forgotten. We will bury Sonny, and Happy will pay for it all."

Jerry does not want revenge. He wants his brother. Yet he can only have one of the two options. He swishes his feet in the water one last time before making his way to his feet. The Wizard follows. The boards of the dock knock beneath their feet, each thud a seemingly hollowed echo into the empty ether that haunts them from above, below, and within. The Shadow Walker and Pewee the Clown join them.

The Beginning

October 12, 1:57 a.m.

"This is the end," says Melanie abruptly. It is a whisper, but loud enough to catch Heather and Redd's ear.

"What do you mean?" asks Heather.

"Tonight is where it ends," responds Melanie as she smirks. The timbre of her voice seems hapless.

There is a brief moment of silence. Heather looks down at Redd, then places her hand on her belly. She now has two heartbeats. She becomes overwhelmed with best parts of God's love, then becomes angry. She grabs Melanie's arm and pulls her aggressively, twisting her around. They are face-to-face yet somehow distant. Heather cannot negotiate with her anger, let alone decipher Melanie's despair.

Heather is still holding onto Melanie's arm as she feels it slowly relax. She pulls her toward her and forces Melanie's palm onto her belly. Heather becomes resolute and focused. Her beautiful frame both rigid and delicate like her heart. Melanie is numb. She wants to feel. She has spent her whole life trying to become the image of what she thought her father wanted her to be. She never knew that she is perfect in his eyes. Yet he was always a monster, and his viewpoint will always be that of a monster. Perhaps she is an anomaly.

Looking into Heather's blue eyes is like looking into the thoughts of God, if they had a color. They are peaceful, steady, fierce, and soft, all within a single breath. Melanie cannot withstand something so reckless and lovely. She cries. Heather softly kisses her on the lips as she gently pushes Melanie's hand further into her belly.

"This is not the end. This is the beginning. Jeremiah will stop all this. And Luke will still be weird."

Melanie looks down as she grins, then back up at Heather. Redd starts laughing. Heather and Melanie follow him without inhibitions.

The City groans; the wind howls, and the Blackguards of Charlatan are somewhere out there creating the end.

The Middle

The engine sputters at first, but succumbs to the physics of air, fuel, and fire. It knocks slightly, like any unkempt engine would, but finally settles into a smooth idle. The fumes of the exhaust reach Happy's nostrils and permeate through him. The noxious aroma is somehow soothing and incites the vigor and romance of a sordid past that he holds dear. He feels vibrant and young as he hobbles to the rear of the cube van. Happy refuses help; he effortlessly climbs into the rear of the vehicle. Burkowski tosses up a Browning Automatic Rifle to him, and places two ammo boxes of .30-06 cartridges on the bed of the cube van. Burkowski will be driving.

Burkowski's hand grasps the pull-down strap of the overhead door. He looks up momentarily before he pulls it closed. Happy's face is vibrant, while the other's seem resolute, yet vacant. Burkowski thinks for a moment that this could all end, if only he drove the cube van off the dock and into *The Great Lake*. He shakes the thought from his head, and is angry with himself for even thinking of it.

Burkowski pulls himself up into the driver's seat. He places his foot on the break, pulls the column shifter into drive, and begins their trek to *The City Square*. Everything seems surreal and in slow motion. The details of the snow-covered road signs, the leaning lamp posts, and the blinking neon lights—they've become vivid and clear. How can such trivial things become so poignant? Perhaps they are the only things that will guide him through this storm; things that are recognizable and calming. We spend so much time mapping out and defining the things in this world that are tangible, yet we cannot understand the things that make us love, laugh, hate, and decide.

A lifetime ago, his father told him, "You can earn money, or it will earn you."

Burkowski's foot subconsciously presses down on the accelerator with more force. He is angry. If he could ever convince his younger self that he shouldn't react to his father's love with protest and revolt, he would. He can't. The last thing that his dad ever told him was "A man must find his own way."

"I wasn't a man. I didn't know a goddamned thing," he says under his breath. His father loved him, even upon the divorce and bitter end of their relationship.

The End

Billingsly is driving. The snow seems as if it's a vacuum drawing itself toward the windshield in an attempt to warn them of the ugly things that exist on the opposite end of its front. It fails.

Jeremiah Revel is sitting shotgun with his tommy gun resting on his lap. Pewee the Clown is sitting in the middle-rear seat with his seat belt fastened. Gonzo is agitated because there is plenty of room for Luke to move over. They have been through this before; Luke will just say, "Studies have shown that the rear middle seat is the safest seat in the vehicle. Sitting in any other seat would be reckless."

"Is that the girls and Redd?" asks Gonzo suddenly. The Wizard, without hesitation, compresses the brake pedal. The *Power Wagon* slides to a halt. Jeremiah opens the door and steps out. There she is. There is Heather. There is his love. He pulls his mask off and lets it fall onto the snow-covered pavement. The fedora follows. Heather runs to him. Jeremiah Revel wraps her up in his arms despite the pain. She wraps her legs around him. Heather cries. Jeremiah holds her for an eternal moment, then lets her slide down so she becomes grounded again.

Jeremiah places his hand on Heather's chin and gently turns her head; she has nowhere else to look other than in his eyes. Even underneath the light of a poorly lit and flickering streetlamp, Heather's eyes seem as if they are a deep and endless abyss, like a reflection of the varied hues of blue that only exist within the runoff pools of some undiscovered arctic melt that only God knows.

Jeremiah is about to speak when Redd suddenly distracts them. "Jesus of Nazareth, get a stable."

Jeremiah and Heather turn suddenly to observe Luke and Melanie engaged in kissing competition; see who can get their tongue farther down the others' throat. They don't seem to notice the other's protest. Jeremiah reaches into his pocket, uses a *Renee's Diner* match—the last one—to light a pack of *Wolfpack Firecrackers*. He throws them at Luke and Melanie's feet. The sound of the popping cracks echo throughout the neighborhood surrounding *Kismet*

Avenue. Melanie screams and laughs; Luke does the same. They dance as if they were walking on hot coals in bare feet. Everyone laughs.

Jeremiah looks down at Heather and asks, "What in the world are you wearing? Polka dots?"

She smirks back up at him briefly and motions with a nod toward Melanie, who is pulling her .357 Magnum from her purse.

"Oh, um, I like the new look," he says as he firmly grabs Heather's rear end with his right hand and pulls her even closer to himself. Jeremiah winces as they kiss.

"I'm sorry, love, my arm is on fire."

Melanie returns the Magnum to her purse. Heather rolls her eyes dramatically at Jeremiah. They both laugh silently together and shake their heads. Melanie suddenly walks up to them and lifts Jeremiah's right arm up to observe the careless bandaging job that was done before.

Melanie reaches into her purse. Jeremiah quickly takes a step back. She pulls out a roll of gauze, medical scissors, *Dr. Kavitee's Antiseptic Cream*, and lipstick. She applies the dark mauve-colored lipstick and says, "A lady must always come prepared."

She pops her lips. Her smile is somehow playful yet angelically sinister at the same time. Jeremiah sits down on the edge of the curb. *Kismet Avenue* is quiet tonight. Melanie gently cuts the bandage off his arm with the medical scissors. It seems as if she has quite a bit of experience redressing a wound. Her father taught her well.

Jeremiah watches Melanie closely. He is perplexed by her simple beauty. She is pretty but in completely different ways than Heather ever could be, and Heather her. This baffles him. Melanie looks up at Jeremiah. He sees hints of her father in her face. Her brown eyes are soft, humble, and fierce. She looks back down, as if embarrassed.

While she wraps the fresh gauze around his arm, she says softly, "You shouldn't look at people like that."

"You shouldn't either," responds Jeremiah immediately. Melanie looks over to the left toward Luke and Heather, who are talking, while Redd is standing by, picking his nose.

Melanie laughs and says, "Hold on."

She scurries over, picks up both the metallic mask and Jeremiah's fedora from the sidewalk. She returns. Jeremiah stands up. He towers over Melanie.

She grabs his pea coat near his chest and pulls him down while rising to her tippy-toes. Melanie kisses him on the cheek, and says, "Thank you, Jeremiah."

For what? He will never know. She gently slides the metallic mask over his head and face. She adjusts it so it sits properly aligned. Melanie then places the fedora on his head and cocks it slightly downward. She looks into Jeremiah's eyes briefly, then raises to her tippy-toes once again, and kisses the metallic mask, leaving a lipstick stain in the shape of her lips.

"Thank you, Mr. Shadow Walker." She exhales, shrugs her shoulders, and says, "This is the end."

Blunderbussted

They drop the girls and Redd off a couple of blocks away. As he watches Heather holding Redd's hand, Jeremiah can't help but reminisce about this same route that he took to *The City Square* when he was a child. But the circumstances are different, and the outcome is within their own resolve.

Jeremiah looks around, and takes a panoramic view of the van. Gonzo is sitting with his elbows outstretched, making sure his left one is jabbing into Luke's ribs with every bump of the vehicle. Luke pays him no attention. He is loading his blunderbuss with 00-sized lead pellets. He is counting out loud as he drops each one in.

"Not too much gunpowder, Luke. You'll explode the barrel." Gonzo interrupts, as he jabs Luke a little harder.

Pewee the Clown turns his gaze toward Speedy and ominously sings, "I would gladly pay you Tuesday for a blunderbuss today." He giggles.

Jeremiah shakes his head with disbelief, then looks at the Wizard. He comes to the realization that Billingsly has not spoken for a while. He has not talked, laughed, or even been angry; he has been completely detached.

"Charles, are you ready for this?" The Wizard's eyes pan from the left to the right, trying to negotiate the path through the blitz-krieg of snow attacking the windshield.

"Is anyone really ever ready to die?"

"No," says Jeremiah raucously, as he slams the fist that is attached to the end of his injured arm into the dashboard above the glove box.

"We must live first so we can die later. This is not a suicide mission."

"What is this then, Mr. Shadow Walker?"

"This is exactly what we thought it would be." Jeremiah hesitates for a moment before continuing. "Michelangelo has the Sistine Chapel. This is our masterpiece." Billingsly smirks. Jeremiah has brought him back.

"Is that them?" asks Billingsly. Jeremiah looks up as the rear door to the cube van in front of them opens. They all duck just before the first bullets pass through the windshield and beyond the rear of the *Power Wagon*. The weight of the large .30-06 rounds seem to bend both time and space as they whisper their promises of death.

"I suppose it's probably them," says Billingsly calmly as the bullets thud into the engine block. Jeremiah raises his tommy gun and rests the barrel on top of the dashboard. The lead flies in the opposite direction of the snow that is attempting to infiltrate the holes in their shattered windshield. Instead of retreating, Billingsly decides to press the throttle. The engine sputters but revs up and engages properly. The Wizard blindly steers the *Power Wagon*, bumping into the rear of the cube van just as they arrive at *The City Square*. The cube van fish-tails for a moment. Luke aims his blunderbuss, fires, and completely devastates all living things on the other end of its barrel.

The End of the Beginning

Give credit where credit is due; men will find clever ways to destroy one another. They craftily engineer destructive devices, refine them, and make them more efficient and easier to administer death. They do so because they must. It is their obligation. They will provide; they will protect; they will evolve. But most of all, they will love endlessly. Men are not the enemy the world, they are the enemy of themselves.

Is this the beginning of the end, the end of the beginning, or the end of the end? Jeremiah does not know. He does not have time to think. Answers will only come upon hopeful reflection. The Shadow Walker was not born of death; he was born of love. He knows this now. Jeremiah knows this now.

The cube van abruptly loses control and flips on its side. Some of its occupants roll across the pavement of *The City Square*. The *Power Wagon* jumps and thuds. Billingsly aggressively turns the steering wheel in an attempt to avoid running into the overturned cube van. The Shadow Walker, Pewee the Clown, and Jack Frost know that they've just ran someone over; this is not a time for sympathy.

The *Power Wagon* momentarily rides on two wheels as the Wizard attempts to keep it under control. The tires screech as it finally comes to a stop. He cuts the engine. The Blackguards of Charlatan exit without hesitation. All is a blur.

The overturned cube van and the *Power Wagon* are a little less than a quarter of a furlong apart. Jeremiah hears the muffled commands of Happy Hal from behind the cube van's cover. He takes his own cover behind a blue postal service mailbox. He can't help but notice the two rusting bullet holes in its facade. His thoughts wander for a moment as he moves his index finger across the uppermost bullet hole. Suddenly, from his periphery, he sees a police cruiser unexpectedly pull up.

The Shadow Walker swings his tommy gun to his rear, steps from his cover, and walks toward the cruiser with august guile. As he approaches the police cruiser, the door opens, and the officer emerges with his service pistol raised toward him. At this moment, the Shadow Walker cannot even hear nor perceive the audible commands of the officer. The officer slowly retreats, gun raised, as the Shadow Walker inches closer.

Suddenly, they both jump for cover behind the cruiser as bullets tear through the ether that surrounds them. Jeremiah intimately knows the sound of that round. He lands on top of Edwards as they fall to the ground. They are both struggling for the gun. The Shadow Walker overpowers him, and suddenly, the barrel of his own service pistol is pressed against Edwards' forehead, while the Shadow Walker's left hand is now wrapped around his throat. Vicious anger consumes Jeremiah. There is nothing left to do or say. He sees the fear in Edwards' eyes. Jeremiah does not want this.

"Officer, we are not your enemy." Jeremiah releases his hand from Edwards' throat, settles his posture, and flips the gun around, handing it back to Edwards with the barrel facing toward himself. Edwards takes it and grasps it with soft intent. He does not know what to think. There is no training for this. Jeremiah swings his tommy gun back from his rear, settles it upon the trunk of the cruiser, and unleashes hell. He pays no attention to Officer Edwards.

Jeremiah throws lead, while Jack Frost, Pewee the Clown, and the Wizard flank and flow. They progress forward toward the coverage of *The Harvest Union*. It seems as if Bandy's relief is not coming. The shell casings melt through the snow and create dark halos in the pavement that surround their brass construct. Luke, Gonzo, and Billingsly fight with fearless resolve. Their courage is resolute. Suddenly, there is silence.

From his vantage point beyond the smoking barrel of his tommy gun, Jeremiah can see Luke, Billingsly, and Jerry pause momentarily. They let down their guard for a moment and ease their posture. Some droning moans and an unfortunate soul screaming, "I don't want to die," can be heard in the distance.

Is this over? Jeremiah asks himself.

The Shadow Walker feels the thud before he hears the echo reverberate into *The City*. The bullet passes through his vest, just below his left ribs, and exits through the rear of him. He drops to one knee. At first it stings, then an immense pain follows. He sits down and leans against the blue postal mailbox. He can hear a barrage of gunfire become background noise. He hurts. The pain is overwhelming, and a dark tunnel begins to close before his eyes. It is so peaceful. And the pain is gone.

There is suddenly a pounding in his chest; it offsets his heartbeat. He doesn't understand why he can feel two. His eyes open, and he sees an angel. The snowflakes catch her eyelashes and melt into her tears. It is the most beautiful thing he has ever seen.

Heather is pounding on his chest with the bottom of her fist. "You cannot leave me, Jeremiah. Our child needs a father, not a ghost."

Jeremiah comes to and sees Melanie and Redd standing behind her. His eyes wander back to Heather. "You're pregnant?"

"Yes."

"I'm going to be a father?"

"Yes."

"Help me up."

Jeremiah stands up on his own will with no help. He gently wraps Heather up into his embattled soul. She cries. "I'm so happy," says Jeremiah as he unslings his tommy gun and hands it to Redd. He pulls out his *Model 1911 Colt 45* and asks the Wizard, Pewee the Clown, and Jack Frost to keep an eye out for trouble.

The Wizard points and says, "Look at that."

The Shadow Walker looks over and observes the seven police cruisers surrounding *The City Square*. It seems as if they are just keeping a perimeter and standing down at the command of Lieutenant Drake Edwards.

Jeremiah slowly begins the trek across *The City Square*. His feelings are beyond repair. His revenge is blurred. His pain is numb. The hand that holds the .45 is steady, yet it no longer wants to administer anymore death. He suddenly feels someone grasp his left hand. Jeremiah turns quickly. It is Melanie. She holds the .357 Magnum in her left hand. She squeezes his left hand hard before releasing it. Jeremiah stops and looks upon her face. He studies the intimate details of her design, and the way the snowflakes get caught in her hair, and how the lights of *The* City are absorbed in her brown eyes. Their destiny will never be more than this shared moment, but

Jeremiah will always love her for this—thick-framed glasses, polka dots, and a Magnum.

They round the blind corner of the cube van and see several dead men, dying men, and Happy Hal lying on the ground. He took a bullet in the upper spine and cannot move anything below the neck. His Browning Automatic Rifle is still in his hand. But he cannot fire it. There is nothing he can do but surrender. Robert James Henry is incapacitated and vulnerable.

Jeremiah keeps his .45 trained on him as he and Melanie approach. Happy starts to laugh mockingly as they tower before him. To Jeremiah's surprise, he sees Melanie in his periphery, pointing her .357 Magnum at her father. Happy coughs up some blood and spits it out. He laughs again mockingly. It is as if he wants death.

Jeremiah cocks the hammer back on his .45 as Happy says, "Go ahead, do it. You are no better than me." He laughs again.

Jeremiah's anger boils inside of him. But he separates himself from it and asks Happy, "Sir, I must ask you. Why does the devil fear God?"

"Why does the devil fear God? This is not a time for riddles, Mr. Shadow Walker. Such nonsense is beyond you." Happy's timbre is noticeably condescending.

"No," says Melanie sternly as she cocks the hammer back on her .357 Magnum. "You will listen to him."

Happy quickly looks at them both and says, "Ever since you were little, I always knew it would be you.

"Enlighten me, Mr. Shadow Walker."

Jeremiah speaks: "The devil fears God because he is capable of a far greater punishment than the devil—the absence of love. Yet God is bound to his promise—the promise of love. We as humans, we do not keep such promises."

The shot echoes through *The City*. Happy is no more. There will be no dirges. There will be no cadence within the tones of an organ reverberating in some church he tried to buy. Happy will be forgotten for any of the good he did. His shrines will decay and his ashes will turn to dust.

The Shadow Walker, Pewee the Clown, and Jack Frost remove their masks. Each of them are happy to see their friends' faces again— those they love. Billingsly stands back and watches with an earnest grin. Jeremiah walks back to Heather. The pain from his wounds are overwhelming. But she looks beautiful standing there in a polka dot dress. She is holding Redd's hand; her blue eyes a vacuum. Neither God nor the devil could ever take his love for her away. It belongs to her and no one else.

ABOUT THE AUTHOR

D. Joseph Ziders is from Buffalo, New York. He graduated from SUNY Cortland in 2007 with a degree in Geographical Information Systems. This is his first endeavor into a full-length novel. He often quips that "I never intended to write one, let alone solicit for its publication." However, the circumstances of his life led to this tale's unexpected invention. He will admit that one of his favorite things to express within his writings is his honesty to the reader. He wants the reader to feel what the characters feel, and to move them in the same way he is moved, as he recklessly pulls you into their world.